"We wer_____ the same _____."

"We were thinking about the last time we were together in a bedroom with a low ceiling. It's still with us, Daphne. The memories are still with us."

"All right," she conceded. "They're still with us. What about it?"

"Imagine a time machine," he said. "If only we could go back, we could undo the bad stuff." Brad paused to let his words sink in, then added, "We *can* do it right this time."

"Do what right?" she asked warily.

"Have our night together."

"What?"

"Make love."

"Now?"

"Not this minute, Daff—but the key is, we *can* go back if we want to. We can relive that moment in time. We've got each other now, and we can relive it the right way."

She allowed herself a full minute to let his suggestion register. "You're nuts!" she blurted out.

ABOUT THE AUTHOR

Judith Arnold has been writing since she was a young child. When no one was available to tell her a bedtime story, she made up her own. At the age of six she put her first story on paper—and has been doing so ever since. After a career as a playwright she turned to her first love, prose fiction, and has been writing romance novels for the past five years, also under the pseudonym Ariel Berk. Along with her husband and two young sons, Judith lives in Connecticut.

Books by Judith Arnold

HARLEQUIN AMERICAN ROMANCE

163–MAN AND WIFE
189–BEST FRIENDS
201–PROMISES*
205–COMMITMENTS*
209–DREAMS*
225–COMFORT AND JOY
240–TWILIGHT

*KEEPING THE FAITH SUBSERIES

HARLEQUIN TEMPTATION

122–ON LOVE'S TRAIL

Going Back

Judith Arnold

Harlequin Books

TORONTO • NEW YORK • LONDON
AMSTERDAM • PARIS • SYDNEY • HAMBURG
STOCKHOLM • ATHENS • TOKYO • MILAN

Published July 1988

First printing May 1988

ISBN 0-373-16255-3

Chapter One

Phyllis had recommended this restaurant as a change of pace. Or, more accurately, a friend of a friend of hers had recommended it, and she had unilaterally decided that she, Andrea and Daphne ought to try it out. The three of them had been meeting for lunch at the same chic midtown Manhattan eatery on the first Wednesday of every month for the past two years and, not surprisingly, they were growing a little bit tired of it. The food there was expensive—Daphne was convinced that the price of each entree was fixed in reverse proportion to the number of calories in the entree. Since she spent at least half of her life on a diet, she usually wound up ordering a flimsy-looking salad, the price of which approached that of a new set of all-weather radials. She'd had no objection to trying someplace new.

This highly touted restaurant, however, left something to be desired. It featured Indonesian fare. Daphne wasn't sure what she was eating, but it tasted weird, spicy in flavor and slimy in texture. She picked at her food and consoled herself with the thought that eating nothing was even less fattening than eating flimsy salads.

The cuisine notwithstanding, these monthly luncheons in the city were something Daphne greatly enjoyed. Phyllis and Andrea had been her closest friends at Cornell, and after their varied wanderings and their respective searches for themselves, all three of them had wound up living in the greater New York metropolitan area, Phyllis and her Significant Other on Long Island, Andrea and her husband in Manhattan, and Daphne in Northern New Jersey.

There were times when, faced with blizzard forecasts or tons of paperwork at the office, Daphne had mixed feelings about dragging herself all the way into the city just to meet her old school chums for lunch. There were other times when she found herself counting the weeks, the days, the minutes until she could reunite with her friends and let down her hair in a way she couldn't with anyone else. And there were times like today, when the trio's monthly luncheon was a pleasant diversion, something Daphne had looked forward to with neither obsession nor dread, but simply with appreciation of her immense good luck in having her friends living a manageable distance from her.

Ever since their meals had been served, Phyllis had been describing her ongoing effort to convince her Significant Other, Jim, to marry her. "I still haven't figured out if the new tax laws help or hurt my case," she complained, prodding her spiced noodles with the tines of her fork. "Jim says we shouldn't bother getting married because they've done away with the Schedule W deduction. I don't know," she concluded with a shrug. "I can't help but think he's handing me a line."

"Line twenty-seven, probably," Daphne quipped. Having never been married herself, she had no idea which line of the 1040 the deduction for married couples used to be entered on. Whenever the subject turned to Jim— as it frequently did at these luncheons—Daphne usually

thought it best to make jokes. If she didn't, she'd probably wind up ranting about what a jerk Jim was. Phyllis
was beautiful, intelligent, professionally successful—and
incredibly dumb when it came to men.

Not that Daphne was an expert on that particular subject. One of the differences between her and Phyllis was
that Daphne would rather be by herself than invest her all
in an unsatisfying relationship. One of the other differences was that, while Daphne was intelligent and professionally successful, she definitely was not beautiful, so
the question of whether or not she'd choose to socialize
with handsome but self-centered men like Jim was largely
academic.

"So what am I supposed to do?" Phyllis rotated her
head so both Daphne and Andrea could view her glum
expression. Phyllis's little-girl pout was familiar to
Daphne. Back in college, Phyllis had seemed to live from
one melodramatic love affair to the next, and she'd had
plenty of opportunities to perfect the pout. Her puck-
ered pink lips and scrunched-up little nose made her look
more adorable than pathetic.

"Do you really want to know what you're supposed to
do?" Andrea asked, gesticulating broadly with her fork.
"You're supposed to say, 'Jim, it's been fun and it's been
swell, but now I'm ready to live like a normal human
being, so please haul your butt out of here.'" Andrea was
a lot blunter than Daphne. She was also a lot messier. As
she waved her fork, a strand of some unidentifiable sliv-
ered vegetable went flying off the end of it and landed on
the floor just inches from Daphne's foot.

Daphne forgave Andrea. At least Andrea had good
taste in men. Her husband was a sweetheart. Eric was
generous, good-looking, and exceedingly tolerant of his
sloppy wife. Not only that, but he earned enough as a tax

consultant so that, combined with Andrea's income as an assistant producer on one of the daytime soap operas taped in the city, they could afford an utterly beautiful, obscenely priced co-op on the Upper West Side. Andrea might not have had as many boyfriends as Phyllis in college, but quality was more important than quantity—and Eric was definitely quality. Daphne wouldn't mind meeting a man like him one of these days.

"I love Jim," Phyllis declared piously. "I'm not going to ditch him just because he happens to believe—with some justification, I think—that marriage is an archaic ritual not necessarily appropriate for everyone."

"Spare us," Andrea snorted. "I'll tell you what Jimbo thinks marriage is: something that's gonna cost him in money and freedom. And the guy's too cheap on both counts to pay the price and make you happy. He's a miser, pure and simple. Am I right, Daff?" she asked, turning her intense brown eyes on Daphne.

Daphne bought time by sipping her ice water. Lowering the glass, she smiled. "Let me put it this way: I wouldn't make a habit of mentioning Jim and Santa Claus in the same breath," she conceded in a halfhearted attempt at tact.

"To tell you the truth, I'm sick of talking about Jim," Andrea announced. "I've got some real interesting news, ladies. Guess who's moving to our little corner of the world?"

"Please," Phyllis groaned, still caught up in the drama of her love life, "don't make us play twenty questions."

"Brad Torrance," Andrea obliged.

"Brad Torrance?" Phyllis exclaimed, her woes abruptly forgotten. "From school?"

"The one and only," Andrea reported. "Eric got a call from him a couple of days ago, saying his company is transferring him to its New York City headquarters. He and Eric were real good friends in school, you know. I'm so happy for Eric."

"The hell with Eric," Phyllis interjected, reflexively running her manicured fingernails through the ash-blond waves of hair framing her pretty heart-shaped face. "*I'm* happy Brad's going to be living nearby. He isn't married, is he?"

Andrea shook her head. "Not unless he's been keeping it a secret from us. When he called with the news that he was being transferred, he used first person singular. 'I'm moving back east,' he said."

"Then there's hope for me," Phyllis deduced, relaxing in her chair and lifting her glass of wine. "If a hunk like Brad Torrance is still single . . . Who knows? Maybe I'll give Jim his walking papers, after all."

"Forget it," Andrea teased, refusing to take Phyllis too seriously. "You and Brad knew each other in college, and the sparks never ignited then. What makes you think they'd ignite now? We're all eight years older and burned-out."

"Speak for yourself, Andrea," Phyllis parried. "I'm not burned-out—I'm just entering my prime. And I bet Brad Torrance is, too. I'd love to put his prime and mine together." She let loose with a mischievous laugh, and Andrea joined her.

Daphne didn't say anything. She sat quietly, twisting her fork aimlessly through the noodles on her plate, listening as her friends continued to babble about Brad Torrance and hoping her face didn't betray her feelings. Andrea reported that Brad had phoned a week ago to tell Eric about his promotion and transfer, that he was more excited about the former than the latter, that he really didn't want to move to the Big Apple but that this was the sort of career boost one didn't refuse. Phyllis talked about how gorgeous Brad had been in college, how his thick, dark hair used to make her think of ranch mink, how she'd always liked guys with small buns and Brad certainly qualified as likable on those grounds. "I hope he hasn't aged," she concluded earnestly. "I hope he's as handsome as he used to be."

He *had* been handsome. Daphne wouldn't argue that. Brad Torrance had been the kind of handsome that reeked of polish and privilege, of abundant self-confidence and grace. His hair had never put Daphne in mind of mink, but then, mink wasn't a substance she gave much thought to. Instead, his thick dark mane had made her think of nighttime, velvet, infinite softness, and his riveting blue eyes had made her think of endless autumn skies, and his smile had made her think of the morning sun, warm with promise, and his body, his tall, slim physique, his well-shaped hands and long legs and broad shoulders and—sure, why not?—his small buns, all made Daphne think even today, so many years later, of the astonishing stupidity she'd been capable of at one time in her life.

Depressed by the thought, she directed her attention back to her friends' dialogue. "So, he's going to be staying with us while he's house hunting," Andrea was saying. "His firm offered to put him up in a hotel, but when Eric invited him to camp out in our apartment, he decided that would be more fun. I'm looking forward to it myself. I'm figuring that he and Eric are going to go out and carouse every night, and I'll be able to watch the prime-time soaps without fighting with Eric over who gets to hold the remote control."

"I wouldn't mind carousing with them," Phyllis volunteered. "But how come Brad's going to stay with you?

Maybe I'm confusing him with someone else from school, but I seem to remember that he had roots in the city."

Andrea nodded. "His parents live somewhere on the East Side. I guess he doesn't want to stay with them." She folded her hand over Daphne's wrist, drawing her back into the conversation. "Now, here's where you come in, Daffy. You can help him find himself a new home."

"No," Daphne said much too quickly. She swallowed and forced a smile, hoping her companions hadn't detected her agitation. "There are a million real-estate brokers Brad could go to," she pointed out. "He can choose whoever he wants."

"He ought to want you. You're an old friend."

"We were never really friends," Daphne argued. She rarely went to such lengths to hide her feelings from Andrea and Phyllis, but this time she felt it necessary. As far as she knew, only two people were aware of what a fool she'd made of herself one ghastly night during her senior year of college: Daphne herself, and Brad Torrance. Just because Brad happened to be planning to transplant himself in New York didn't mean Daphne was obliged to fill her friends in on the embarrassing mistake she'd made so long ago.

"We were all friends," Andrea declared grandly. "We were one big happy family in school. And since nobody else from that family happens to be selling real estate in the New York area these days, I think you ought to get Brad's business."

The last thing Daphne wanted was Brad's business. "I only know about housing in New Jersey," she argued. "I don't know the first thing about what's going on in Manhattan."

"Sure you do. You're a hotshot, Daff," Andrea said, dismissing Daphne's modest claim with a wave of her hand. "You know all the markets around here. But that's irrelevant. Brad told Eric he doesn't want to live in the city. He wants the 'burbs. And there you are, located in lovely, suburban Verona." She smiled, inordinately pleased with herself. "This, ladies, is what they mean by networking. Old college friends become new business clients. Thank me, Daphne, for sending a potential huge commission your way."

"Maybe it'll be a small commission," Daphne countered. "Maybe he won't buy anything I show him. Maybe he'll prefer Westchester." She wondered if her friends could detect in her voice the faint hope that such a possibility might come true.

"How many real-estate brokers does he know in this area? Daff, he's yours, and if he doesn't realize it, I'll whip him into shape."

Don't do me any favors, Daphne muttered under her breath. But she knew the battle was lost. Andrea was perpetually whipping people into shape. If Brad Torrance had the decency to reject her advice that he begin his search for a new home by visiting Daphne's real-estate office, Andrea would harass him, cajole him, torture him—whatever it took to win his compliance.

So Daphne had to expect him to show up at her office. They'd be forced to smile at each other and exchange small talk, and they'd feel clumsy and bashful. Neither of them would risk alluding to that hideous night eight years ago. They'd behave politely, endure an afternoon of house hunting and breathe deep sighs of relief once it was over. Then they'd part ways, go home, and pray that they'd never have to endure such an ordeal again.

Or maybe it wouldn't be an ordeal for Brad. Maybe he didn't even remember his encounter with Daphne. Maybe it had been a mere blip on the radar screen of his life, something that had made absolutely no impression on him. "Do I remember *that* night?" he'd ask if she finally found the nerve to tell him why his presence made her so tense. "And what night might that be, Daffy?"

Maybe what had been the most humiliating experience in her life hadn't even registered in Brad Torrance's memory.

"Well, I don't know about you guys," Phyllis said, motioning toward the waiter, "but some of us have to go back to work." Phyllis was a credit specialist at a midtown bank a few blocks away from the Indonesian restaurant. She had a prestigious, powerful position, one result of which was that she spent vast amounts of her time reading books with titles that all sounded like, "Why Wonderful Women Fall for Deplorable Men."

The waiter delivered the check, and, as usual, an intense debate ensued concerning how to split it. Daphne always favored dividing the total into equal thirds, but Phyllis and Andrea refused to do that. "You never have a drink," Andrea claimed. "It's not fair that you should be paying for our liquor." Daphne had convinced her friends that the only reason she never requested a cocktail or a glass of wine with her meal was that she didn't want to return to her office in a muddled mental state. The few times she got together with her friends in the evening, she generally asked for wine and pretended to enjoy it, discreetly managing to avoid swallowing more than a sip or two. Such a charade was easier than admitting that she no longer drank liquor—and then being badgered to explain why.

Brad Torrance could explain why, she pondered grimly. Brad Torrance could explain, from personal experience, what happened to witless young women who couldn't hold their booze.

Once the bill was settled, the three women left the restaurant together. The early-April afternoon was slightly overcast and the air had a nip to it, but spring was definitely moving into the region. The daffodils and tulips Daphne had planted in the flower bed in front of her house were beginning to sprout, and she hadn't bothered to bring a coat into the city with her.

She and her companions strolled together as far as the bank where Phyllis worked. "Here's an idea," Phyllis proposed before saying goodbye. "Why don't we have a party to welcome Brad to town? You and Eric can host it, Andrea."

"Thanks a heap," Andrea grunted, although she was grinning, clearly able to figure out the motive behind Phyllis's suggestion. "If I had this party, you'd have to bring Jimbo with you, Phyllis. He'd never let you go to a party without him. And if he's there, how are you going to flirt with Brad?"

Phyllis produced her cute pout again. Then she smiled. "All right. If I can't go after him, Daffy can. How about it, Daffy? I'm giving him to you."

Daphne understood that, coming from Phyllis, this was an extremely generous offer. Nonetheless, she had no desire to accept it. "No, thanks, Phyllis," she declined. "Brad Torrance was never really my type."

"Brad Torrance was everybody's type," said Phyllis.

"Daphne's type is *safe*," Andrea pointed out. "Brad was never safe."

"You're right," Daphne swiftly agreed. "So if you're going to have this party, Andrea, do me a favor and invite some safe men. Or else count me out."

"Bo-ring," Phyllis intoned.

"Okay, ladies. I've gotta get back to show biz," Andrea said, taking a northbound turn onto Seventh Avenue. "As soon as Brad gets his bearings, I'm going to send him along to you," she warned Daphne. "And please, Daff, sell him a house or something. I'm looking forward to seeing him, but I don't want his search for a house to turn into the endless summer."

Daphne shaped an overly bright smile. "I'll do my best," she promised, not bothering to finish the sentence: she'd do her best to behave maturely and courteously if and when she had to spend any time with Brad Torrance. She'd do her best to pretend that that horrible Saturday night eight years ago had never occurred.

"No, Mom, it's all right," Brad said into the phone. Good God, he hadn't even unpacked yet. He'd barely had a chance to put down his bags before Penelope Torrance had telephoned Eric's apartment and demanded to speak to her son.

"You keep telling me it's all right," she retorted in an artfully lofty tone, "but I don't see how it can be all right for you to be spending time right here in New York City and not be staying with your own mother."

"Mom," Brad said as calmly as he could. "Eric is my friend. He and Andrea have tons of room here..." He heard Eric snickering behind him when he said that. So they didn't have tons of room. Brad would sleep on their fire escape before he'd consider staying at his mother's apartment.

"Room isn't the issue. The issue is, you have a home in New York, and that's where you belong."

"I don't have a home, yet, but I plan to buy one," Brad said, his voice becoming hoarse with fatigue. After a tiresome flight out of Seattle, with delays during take-off and landing and the worst excuse for food he'd ever been served on an airplane, he didn't have the stamina to deal with his mother right now. His composure slipping, he tugged off the corduroy blazer he was wearing over his shirt and jeans and draped it across the back of a chair. Andrea picked it up, and Brad watched her carry it toward the coat closet. Distracted by a magazine she glimpsed along the way, she dropped the jacket onto an end table, lifted the magazine and wandered in the direction of the kitchen, reading as she went.

Living with Eric and Andrea wasn't going to be as easy as staying in a hotel would have been. But it would be much more fun than living with his mother—and it wouldn't be for long. As soon as he found a new house, he could return to Seattle and settle his affairs there.

"It's because of your father, isn't it," his mother charged. "You're going to move in with him."

"No, Mom, I'm not," Brad said wearily. He felt a tap on his shoulder and turned to find Eric presenting him with a cold bottle of beer. Brad took it and nodded his thanks. "I'm not staying with either of you, Mom," he said back into the phone. "I'm staying with Eric and Andrea for a week or so, and then—"

"Do you know what housing is like around here?" his mother interrupted. "You aren't going to find a place so fast."

"I'm not going to live in New York," he explained, certain that he'd had an identical conversation with his mother less than a week ago, when he'd called her from

Seattle to inform her of what day he'd be arriving to begin his search for a residence. "I don't want to live in the city. I'm sick of city living. I'm going to find a place outside the city limits, and—"

"Do you know what housing is like in the suburbs?" his mother again cut him off.

"I'm willing to learn. Mom, I've got to go. When things calm down a little, I promise I'll call you and we'll get together. I love you, Mom. Goodbye." He hung up before she could speak.

"Welcome to New York," Eric said, grinning and lifting his own bottle of beer in a mocking toast.

Brad trudged across the living room and collapsed onto the couch. He used the toe of his left foot to pry off his right shoe, then reversed the process. Once both shoes were off, he propped his feet up on the coffee table and took a long draught of beer. "How did my mother get your phone number?" he asked.

Eric sat on the Eames-style leather chair across the room from Brad. "I hate to break the news to you, Brad, but we're listed in the phone book."

Brad cursed. "That means my father can look up your number, too," he groaned before indulging in a laugh. "I really appreciate your putting me up, Eric. It's bad enough having to talk to my mother for five minutes on the phone. If I had to live with her . . ."

"Your mother isn't any worse than most mothers," Eric argued. "I met her at our graduation, and she seemed okay to me."

"She *is* okay," Brad conceded. "She's better than okay. She's a lovely lady, and I really like her—most of the time."

"She's a looker, too, if I remember correctly," Eric remarked.

Brad grimaced. Until recently, he had been quite proud of the fact that he had a great-looking mother. He used to love it when, in grammar school, he'd bring his classmates home to play and they'd comment on how little like an actual mother Penelope Torrance looked. "She's better looking than Beaver Cleaver's mom," one of his childhood friends had once observed.

His mother's appearance hadn't been a concern of Brad's until recently, when it occurred to him that men other than his father might find her attractive, and might choose to act on it. If another man entered the picture—if another man hadn't already entered the picture—his parents' marriage might be beyond salvation. "The thing is—" he sighed "—at the moment . . . they're kind of split."

"Your parents are divorced?" Eric looked properly concerned. "Hey, man, that's too bad. When did it happen? Why didn't you tell me?"

"No, Eric, they aren't divorced," Brad corrected his friend. He laughed again, amused by Eric's comically confused expression. "They're split, separated, going through some sort of weirdness at the moment. They live in two apartments these days, but they get together every few days, either to bicker or to fool around in bed. Then they go their separate ways again and complain about each other to me. If I stayed with my mother while I was in the city, she'd spend the whole time telling me how awful my father is. If I stayed with him, he'd hand me the same lines about her."

"So they're living apart."

Brad nodded. "If you ask me, the whole thing is incredibly extravagant. I know what housing costs are like in Manhattan. It seems like such a waste to be spending their money paying for two apartments."

"They can afford it," Eric reminded him. "They're rich."

"That they are," Brad concurred with a nod before taking another sip of beer.

Brad's parents weren't just rich; they were rich in the way only certain New Yorkers could be. They weren't high society, they weren't glitterati, but they lived extremely comfortably in a city where only the well-to-do could live the least bit comfortably. Both of them had descended from affluent families, and Brad's father had supplemented what they'd inherited by buying his own seat on the stock exchange. His mother didn't deck herself out in jewels, and his father didn't collect Ferraris, but money was a given in the Torrance household. It had always been assumed that Brad would attend private schools, that he would dress in clothing from the better stores, and that he would grow up knowing that he was entitled to certain things simply by virtue of his being a Torrance.

It was also assumed that if Penelope and Roger Torrance were in the midst of a marital squabble, they would live in separate apartments. Expense was not an issue. The only issue, as far as Brad could tell, was to which parent Brad would extend his allegiance. So far he'd managed to maintain his neutrality, but now, with this promotion and transfer to New York, his parents were both actively campaigning for his loyalty.

"So, when are you supposed to start your new job?" Eric asked him.

Brad rolled his head backward until it was resting against the top of the sofa's bolster cushion. He was exhausted. He'd spent the past few weeks overseeing the sale of his condominium, arguing with representatives of various moving companies and helping to break in the fellow who'd been promoted to replace him at the Seattle office of the corporate head-hunting company he worked for. Logically, Brad knew that in a few months the move would be behind him; he'd look forward to taking on the responsibilities of his new position. But at the moment, he didn't even want to think about it.

"They said I can start whenever I'm ready," he told Eric. "But I can't shake the suspicion that if I'm not ready within a month or two, I'll wind up at the bottom of everybody's list."

"It sounds like a great job," Eric reminded him, evidently sensing that Brad's enthusiasm was at a low ebb. "Vice-President of Something, isn't it?"

"Assistant Vice President for Marketing Services." It was a pompous title, but Brad liked the sound of it. More than that, he liked the prestige and power it encompassed. He was shrewd and talented, and he made it a point to excel at just about everything he considered important: at one time schoolwork, and now his career, his squash game, his investments. Being a Torrance might mean taking certain things for granted, but it also meant putting forth a superior effort to achieve what one wanted.

Andrea materialized in the arched doorway leading to the dining room, minus her magazine. Her hair was a dark shag of curls and her Mickey Mouse sweatshirt had a mysterious pink stain on one sleeve. In all the years Brad had known Andrea, she'd never quite figured out how to put herself together. She was an attractive, intelligent woman, and he could understand how Eric would have fallen in love with her. But she also had a tendency to look like a bag lady much of the time.

"How's your mom?" she asked Brad.

"You don't want to know," Eric answered for him. "It's one of those stories that makes you realize we're a lot squarer than our elders."

"Yeah, I tell you, we've got to keep an eye on our parents' generation," Andrea said, reaching over the back of Eric's easy chair and filching his beer bottle. "They're a pretty wild group." She took a sip, handed the bottle back to her husband, and then crossed to the couch and plopped herself down next to Brad. "So, Brad, not that I want you to feel unwelcome or anything, but when do you plan to start house hunting?"

"The sooner, the better." Andrea's question didn't make him feel unwelcome. He knew she approached all issues directly, and he admired her lack of coyness. "It's really nice of you guys to put me up. But if I start stinking like a fish after three days, I can always hit the firm up for a hotel room."

"You don't have to move out in three days!" Eric protested.

"Of course he doesn't," Andrea agreed before turning back to Brad. "But if you're interested in finding a house, the person you should get in touch with is Daphne Stoltz. Did you know she's a real-estate broker? She's got an office in Verona, New Jersey, and—"

"Daphne Stoltz?" Stunned, Brad uttered her name in a taut, raspy voice.

Andrea stared at Brad, apparently bewildered by his reaction. "Daphne Stoltz. From school. You remember her, don't you? She was taller than me, with kind of frizzy light blond hair, eyeglasses—"

"I remember her," Brad said, anxious to silence Andrea. He took a deep, desperate swig of beer and turned to stare through the window at the purple night sky.

Daphne Stoltz. Daffy, everybody used to call her, with her cascade of kinky yellow hair, her pale skin, her green eyes hidden behind a pair of thick-lensed wire-rimmed glasses. She was a little too tall, a little too heavy, a little too undefined. She'd been a close friend of Andrea's, along with that stacked chick who used to frost her hair, Phyllis Something-or-other. But whenever their entire crowd of friends got together—Andrea and her girl friends from her dormitory, Eric and his buddies from the fraternity—Daffy had always been on the periphery, hanging back, smiling mysteriously and keeping her secrets to herself. It wasn't that she was ugly or stupid, but... She hadn't been like the other girls. She hadn't been loud or wild or aggressive. She hadn't talked nonstop about herself. She hadn't dressed particularly stylishly or funkily. All in all, she'd done nothing to make herself noticeable.

Except for one night, when she'd approached Brad. Out of the blue, just like that. They had never exchanged more than stereotypical greetings and superficial remarks about their classes before that night; they scarcely knew each other. But suddenly there she was, presenting him with something no normal twenty-one-year-old male would ever turn down.

Brad had been a normal twenty-one-year-old male. And afterward, he'd hated himself. Eventually, the hate had softened to disgust, and then to a lingering guilt. In time, he had succeeded in convincing himself that he hadn't really done anything so terribly unforgivable, that Daphne had probably been almost as much to blame for what had happened as he was, and that it was time to put the incident behind him, to forget about it and move on.

That was years ago. It had been simple enough to shove the entire incident out of his mind when he'd presumed he would never see Daphne Stoltz again.

"Daphne Stoltz," he murmured, half to himself. Hearing his voice shape her name jarred him from his meditation. He scanned his surroundings—a high-ceilinged living room in an ornate pre-War building on Riverside Drive in Manhattan, with the man who was arguably Brad's best friend seated across the room from him, and his best friend's wife on the couch beside Brad—and absorbed the fact that his best friend's wife had some insane idea that he should get in touch with Daphne Stoltz. "Why am I supposed to see her?" he asked, scrambling to remember what it was that Andrea had been telling him.

She scowled. "It must be jet lag," she diagnosed his inattentiveness before explaining, "The reason you're supposed to see her is that she's a realtor. She manages the Verona office of a small real-estate firm. They've got, oh, maybe half a dozen offices scattered around northern New Jersey, and I know she'd love to show you some properties. Are you at all interested in living in northern New Jersey?"

Brad wasn't going to lie just to avoid having to see Daphne. He was interested in living anywhere that would offer him an uncomplicated commute to Manhattan.

Besides, even if he swore that he didn't want to look for a house in New Jersey, he'd probably have to see Daphne anyway. She was Andrea's friend, and he was Andrea's house guest. One way or another, he was going to have to face Daphne Stoltz.

"Verona," he mumbled. He hoped his discomfort wasn't evident to Andrea, since she was pushy enough to question him about it if she noticed. "Where's that?"

"Northwest of Newark, maybe a half hour out of the city," Andrea told him. "It's got good bus service into the city—and there's a train station not far away, in Montclair, I think. Of course, you could commute by car, but nobody in his right mind would drive into Manhattan every day."

Nobody in his right mind would do business with a woman he'd once treated so shabbily, Brad thought. At least nobody who had a heart would. Brad wanted to think that whatever sins he might have committed in the past, he wasn't heartless.

"Sure," he said. Maybe he had a heart, but he also had enough sense not to let Andrea comprehend how very much he'd like to avoid Daphne. Spending a day with her might be an uncomfortable experience, but it was far preferable to letting Andrea know that one night during his careless, thoughtless youth, he'd been a first-class bastard—and that Andrea's dear friend Daphne had been the one to suffer for it.

Chapter Two

The Verona branch of the Horizon Realty Corporation was located on the town's main thoroughfare, a winding avenue lined with shops and offices. Few had familiar names; there weren't many chain-store franchises or national outlets in Verona's shopping district. Most of the stores seemed to be modest mom-and-pop establishments: a hardware store, an ice-cream parlor, a five-and-ten, a bakery, a children's clothing boutique.

Brad liked Verona. He'd made up his mind that he didn't want to live in New York City, but he hadn't really been eager to become a surburbanite, certainly not if all the suburbs had to offer were tract houses and massive shopping malls. No doubt some suburbs fit that description, but Verona seemed more like a self-contained village, homey and welcoming. Brad could picture himself living in a place like this.

He didn't want to like Verona. He didn't want to like anything at all today. He had driven west from Manhattan in the Ford Escort the company had rented for him, figuring he'd kill a day looking at houses with Daphne Stoltz and get the damned thing over with. Then he could return to Eric's apartment with a clear conscience. He could swear to Andrea that he'd taken her advice and allowed Daphne to show him every house she knew of for sale in northern New Jersey, that he'd loathed each and every one of them, and that he wanted to try his luck with a new broker in a different part of the tri-state area. And then Andrea would have to get off his back.

The only problem was, Verona appealed to him. The photographs of houses displayed in the front window of the realty office might have unconscionably high prices printed underneath them, but the houses did look attractive and comfortable. Brad wasn't going to reject a promising swath of the New York City suburbs merely because he didn't want to have to go house hunting with Daphne Stoltz.

She was expecting him. Andrea had called her last night and told her Brad wanted her to show him some houses—Brad had considered this a gross misrepresentation of what he wanted, but he'd kept his mouth shut—and Daphne had told Andrea to have Brad come to the office the following day. She hadn't balked, so he couldn't balk, either. If Daphne was going to be stoical about this compulsory reunion, so would he.

Inhaling deeply, he straightened his blazer with a shrug of his shoulders, raked his fingers through his tousled black hair and entered the office.

The interior was bright. Ceiling lights reflected off the white walls to give the room an almost offensive cheerfulness. Huge bulletin boards displaying more photographs of houses hung on opposite sides of the room. A couple of flourishing plants stood in clay pots near the front window, drinking in the morning sunlight through the glass. Four desks were arranged symmetrically, two on either side of the door. Each contained a prism-shaped brass name plate, but none of them bore Daphne's name.

A man in a suit and tie sat at one of the desks, talking on the telephone with the receiver tucked between his ear and his shoulder so he could jot notes on a pad. The only other person in the room was a woman, also conservatively dressed, using a photocopy machine at the rear of the room. Since she had her back to Brad, he was able to study her for a moment, unobserved. She appeared to be middle-aged, with a matronly figure and dark brown hair arranged in a moderately bouffant style. Brad couldn't believe that Daphne had changed—or aged—so drastically.

The woman pulled a few sheets of paper from the tray on the side of the machine, then turned around and revealed to Brad that she definitely wasn't Daphne. She presented him with a polite smile. "Good morning," she said, tapping the paper into a neat stack. "Can I help you?"

"I'm here to see Daphne Stoltz," he answered, then felt compelled to add, "I've got an appointment," as if to emphasize that this was a business call, not a personal one.

"She's in her office," the woman informed him, beckoning him toward the rear of the room. Brad was brought up short by the news that Daphne had her own office instead of working at one of the desks in front.

The dark-haired woman ushered him to a short hallway leading to the rear of the building. The first door they came to was open, and the woman indicated it with a wave of her hand. "That's Daphne's office."

Brad approached the door quietly. It wasn't that he wished to sneak up on Daphne, but he did want a chance to see her before she saw him. He was hoping that catching a preliminary glimpse of her might somehow prepare him for this meeting, give him an idea of what to say or a clue as to how she felt about spending a day with him.

He waited until the middle-aged woman had returned to her desk in the front room before peering inside Daphne's private chamber. Like the front office, this back room was brightly lit. In addition to photographs of houses, the large bulletin board occupying the far wall contained a big calendar with notes and schedules scribbled inside each date's square. Another wall held a few framed documents, one identifying Daphne as a licensed real-estate broker, another claiming that she was a state-certified assessor. A cloth-upholstered love seat rested against a third wall, and two matching chairs faced the broad oak desk where Daphne sat talking on the phone.

She looked good, Brad thought with inexplicable relief. The telephone receiver blocked part of her face from his view, but he could see enough to know that the past eight years hadn't been unkind to Daphne. Her hair was the same flaxen shade he remembered, but the frizz had relaxed somewhat, shaping small, bubbly curls that tumbled loosely to her shoulders. She still wore eyeglasses, but the frames she had on, a honey-colored brown with lenses the shape of old-fashioned television screens, flattered her more than did the circular wire-rims she'd worn in college. Her nose was too small for her face, but it managed to hold her eyeglasses in place.

Brad's gaze shifted downward to the shapeless linen blazer she had on over a simple silk blouse of bright turquoise. A narrow gold wristwatch adorned her slender left wrist. She looked a bit thinner than he had remembered. The sweep of flesh under her jaw was smooth and taut, and her cheeks were hollow beneath her angular cheekbones. Her nails were polished. As she spoke into the phone, her voice was soft but solid.

It occurred to Brad that Daphne Stoltz was no longer the clumsy, gawky college girl he remembered. She was clearly a woman on her way, poised and accomplished. He directed a silent curse at Andrea for having failed to warn him.

"Well, it's only my opinion," Daphne said into the phone, "but if you're planning to move in a couple of years you're better off with the variable. The rates are going up, but the variables are still a couple of points lower. Either way, you've got to get the application process started right away, Ms. Cleary. If there's a good chance the interest rates are going up, the bank is going to sit on your application.... Fine, Ms. Cleary. Just get the paperwork started, and let me know if you have any problems. Take care." She hung up and swiveled to face the doorway.

"Hello, Daffy."

As soon as the words hit the air, Brad regretted them. He ought to have called her Daphne; it would have been more respectful. It was just that when Andrea talked about her she usually referred to her as "Daffy." Brad had called her "Daffy" in college, but there didn't seem to be anything particularly daffy about her right now.

She stared up at him as he hovered in the doorway, awaiting an invitation to enter. The lenses of her eyeglasses made her eyes appear flat, a pale green. She had on lipstick, he noticed, also a pale hue. Her coloring seemed strangely washed out, but Brad acknowledged that a darker lipstick would have made her look like a clown.

She wasn't pretty. She hadn't been eight years ago, and she wasn't now. But there was a directness about her looks, an unpretentiousness that Brad admired.

"Hello, Brad," she said, her voice as quiet and cool as it had been during the telephone conversation Brad had eavesdropped on. He inferred from her impassive tone that she intended to treat him the same way she'd treated Ms. Cleary over the phone: as a client. "Won't you come in?"

"Thanks." He entered the office, surveying it one more time before he sat in one of the chairs across the desk from her. His vision took in the calendar, the African violet residing on one corner of her desk, the tidy oak bookcase behind her. The leather upholstery of her chair. The plush area rug. "What are you, the boss here or something?" he asked.

She favored him with a tentative smile. "I'm in charge of this office, if that's what you mean," she replied. She folded her hands above her blotter, and Brad focused for a moment on the tapered shape of her fingers, the enameled pink ovals adorning each fingertip, the amethyst ring on her right ring finger. No wedding band, he noted. If Daphne had been married and Andrea hadn't informed Brad, he would have throttled Andrea the minute he returned to New York.

Not that he cared one way or another about Daphne's marital status. He just wanted to be prepared, that was all.

"So," he said, wondering if he was coming across as awkward as he felt. "How have you been?"

"Fine," she said.

A heavy silence descended over the office. Brad shifted in his chair, balancing one leg across the other knee. He inspected the brown leather deck shoe on his foot, the length of beige corduroy covering his leg, the brass buckle of his belt, the faint wrinkles webbing his cotton oxford shirt beneath his tweed jacket. Daphne's outfit would be appropriate for the C.E.O. of a multinational corporation, and here he was, dressed like a prep school sophomore.

"How did you wind up in real estate?" he asked, anxious to break the silence. "That wasn't your abiding goal in life when we were in school, was it?"

Once again, Brad wished he could have retracted the words. He didn't want to reminisce about when they were in school. He didn't want to dredge up old memories about what a louse he'd been back then. In his entire life, there had been perhaps only two occasions when Brad had done something he'd subsequently been enormously ashamed of. One of those occasions had occurred when, at the age of five, he'd made fun of the way a neighbor with cerebral palsy spoke. The other had occurred with Daphne, and he certainly didn't want to spoil the day for both of them by reminding her of it.

Evidently his comment didn't disturb her—unless the flicker of a shadow across her eyes was a reflection of her emotions rather than the overhead light on the lenses of her glasses. Her lips curved into another tentative half smile, and she said, "No, Brad. It wasn't my abiding goal in life."

Damn. Was he imagining that her tone was accusing, or was it really? Was she actually trying to tell him that he'd had a hell of a nerve sleeping with her when he hadn't even known her well enough to be aware of her career plans?

Or was it just his conscience speaking, that rattling old vestige of guilt that he ought to have overcome by now?

"I more or less stumbled into real estate," she elaborated. Brad was grateful to her for reviving the conversation when he'd all but let it die. "I held a couple of merchandising jobs after college, and I took classes in different things. Somewhere along the way, I decided on a whim to take a course in real estate, never guessing I'd have an aptitude for it."

"Well, you obviously do have an aptitude for it," he concluded, gazing around her office one more time. *Merchandising,* he pondered, trying to remember what Daphne had majored in. How could he remember something he'd never known in the first place? Daphne Stoltz had been as much a stranger to him then as she was now.

He supposed he could always ask Andrea about what Daphne had studied in college. But if he did that, Andrea would ask him why he wanted to know—and he didn't have an easy answer to that question.

"I understand you've been transferred to a New York-based job," Daphne remarked.

"That's right."

"What's your field?" she asked.

Brad might have been consoled by the fact that Daphne knew as little about him as he knew about her. But he wasn't. "Head-hunting," he answered.

"You mean job placement counseling, that sort of thing?"

He attempted some levity. "I sure don't mean the other kind of head-hunting—you know, the jungle kind, with all that blood and gore."

She digested this item with another impassive smile, refusing to laugh outright at his joke. "Well, Brad," she said, pulling a lined legal pad toward her and plucking a pen from the top drawer of her desk, "why don't you tell me a little about what you're looking for in a home?"

Daphne was no fool. She wanted to get down to business so neither she nor Brad would have to strain themselves any longer, pretending that they were enjoying this banter. He thanked her for her briskness with a tacit nod and said, "Most importantly, I'd like someplace no more than an hour outside Manhattan. The quicker the commute, the better."

She lifted her eyes to him. He wondered whether they were really as wide set as they seemed, or whether it was an illusion caused by her eyeglasses. He also wondered why she hadn't worn her hair at its present length when she'd been in college. The soft, face-framing shape of it was much more becoming than the wild waist-length mop of hair had been then.

"Are you aware of what housing costs are like in any community that offers a quick commute to New York?" she asked.

"I know the prices are way up there."

"They're higher than that," Daphne corrected him. "They're way, *way* up there."

"I know, Daff," Brad assured her. "My parents live in New York. I know what property values are like in this part of the country."

"We're talking two hundred thousand dollars, minimum," she said. "For a small but nice condo, or a slightly larger fixer-upper."

"Yes, I know," he insisted—he hoped for the final time. Daphne didn't have to lecture him. He wasn't an ignoramus.

"Well," she said, "I don't want to waste your time or mine, Brad. So let's make sure we're on the same wavelength, okay?" She opened her pen with an ominous click. "How much will you be earning in your new job?"

None of your damned business, he almost retorted. Personal finances were a subject Brad had been raised to believe sacred, not open to idle discussion. But he checked the reflexive indignation that filled him and forced himself to relax in his chair. "Enough," he answered evasively.

Daphne's expression was unreadable. "I have to ask," she asserted. "I have to know whether you're going to be able to afford—"

"I'll be able to afford it," he said curtly.

She continued to stare at him, her large eyes glowing enigmatically, her lips twisted into that wry smile of hers. Damn her, but she was going to win the stare-down, he realized, a fraction of a second before he spat out, "Sixty thousand plus a year-end bonus."

She made no indication that she was impressed by his above-average earnings—or that she was afraid his earnings wouldn't be enough to pay for housing in the area. "How much do you have available for a down payment?" she asked emotionlessly, scribbling a note to herself on the pad.

Again he had to check the impulse to protest that he was under no obligation to describe his liquidity situation to her. "Assuming the sale goes through, I'm going to make a nice profit on my condo in Seattle," he said tensely. "Really, Daff, if you show me something I can't afford, I'll let you know. You can trust me."

A shadow flickered in her eyes again, and this time Brad was convinced that it had nothing to do with the overhead light. What she was thinking, he guessed, was that she *couldn't* trust him, and that he had some nerve asserting that she could.

She could trust him now, though. Except for that one brief lapse, he had always been remarkably trustworthy around women. Besides, his presence in Daphne's office this morning had nothing to do with his behavior, good, bad or otherwise, toward women. It had to do with the business of purchasing a house. Daphne didn't want to waste her time or his in showing him houses he couldn't afford. Fine. He didn't want to waste their time, either.

His resentment of her nosy questions dissipated, replaced by an undefined sense of frustration. He wanted her trust. He *needed* it. It would be proof that she forgave him, that he no longer had to feel guilty about whatever transgressions he'd committed so many years ago. It was over, done with, and if only Daphne would trust him now, he could put the past to rest.

She seemed to be scrutinizing him, sizing him up, trying to determine whether he was worthy of her trust. "Believe me," he muttered, surprised by the vehemence in his tone, "I can afford whatever you want to show me."

Daphne chuckled. "In that case . . . I don't suppose I want to show you the cute little cottage in Upper Saddle River that I've got a listing on. The asking price on it is one-point-five million."

Brad conceded to himself that he couldn't afford that. But he wasn't going to admit it to her. There was something irritatingly patronizing about her attitude. Maybe this was her way of knocking him down a peg.

"Here," she said, pulling a thick paper-bound book from the bookcase behind her and handing it to him. "It's the most recent Multiple Listing Service catalog. I have a few places in mind I'd like to show you, but I've got to make a phone call first. Why don't you thumb through the book and see if anything catches your eye."

She rotated in her chair, reached for the telephone and spun the cards in her Rolodex. Brad understood that he'd been dismissed.

He opened the catalog to the first page and studied the miniature photos of houses listed for sale and the accompanying tiny descriptions enumerating each house's features. He was unable to translate a few of the abbreviations, but he couldn't ask Daphne to interpret them for him; she was busy talking to another broker on the phone, setting up an appointment to view a house that afternoon.

Even if Daphne weren't on the phone, Brad probably wouldn't ask her to clarify the book's jargon to him. She had already gotten the upper hand enough this morning. Brad saw no need to parade his ignorance before her.

Had she really gotten the upper hand, though? Lowering the Multiple Listing book to his lap, he contemplated the woman seated across the desk from him, chatting congenially with her colleague on the phone and absently twirling her index finger through a curling lock of hair below her ear. She certainly seemed harmless enough when he viewed her objectively.

Maybe she had no desire whatsoever to knock him down a peg. Maybe he was being unjustifiably defensive.

Of course, that was all it was. He was being defensive because Daphne was no longer the inept, ungainly coed she used to be. He was being defensive because she had improved with age much more than he had, and because she seemed to have risen above the past much more effectively.

"See anything you like?" she asked, breaking into his ruminations.

He jerked his head toward her. Daphne was smiling pleasantly, and Brad did his best to adopt her brisk cordiality. Returning her smile, he set the book down on her desk and shrugged. "I'd rather look at what you'd like to show me," he told her.

"All right," she said, pulling her briefcase from the well beneath her desk and shoving back her chair. As soon as she stood, Brad leaped to his feet. He knew his manners, and he wanted to impress upon Daphne that he did.

Just a bit more defensiveness on his part, he muttered inwardly, wondering why the hell he felt such a strong desire to win her forgiveness.

HE WAS BETTER LOOKING than she'd remembered.

Not that she had ever considered him bad looking, Daphne meditated as she steered her car through the late-morning traffic toward the scenic park that was one of Verona's most charming assets. Since Brad seemed relatively unfamiliar with the area, she planned to take him on a brief tour of Verona, the Caldwells, Cedar Grove— the towns her office of Horizon Realty served—to give him a feel for this part of New Jersey. While she drove, she pointed out interesting landmarks and provided useful information: "That road will eventually lead you to Bloomingdale's, if you're into high-class shopping," or "Here's the entrance to Caldwell College," or "This is one of the better golf courses around here." It was her standard speech, altered to suit the individual client. She wasn't sure whether or not Brad played golf, but she doubted he would want to hear about the school system in each town.

As she spoke, she glanced frequently at him. Each time she did, she was struck by how handsome he was. His hair was still thick and black, cut in a casual style that was just barely short enough to be acceptable in the business world. His eyebrows were thick and dark, too, and his complexion had a robust golden glow. His burnished coloring created a startling contrast with his eyes, which were an unexpectedly clear light blue. He had a strong chin, a straight nose and teeth as white and even as an orthodontist could dream of. But it was those piercing blue eyes that Daphne kept returning to, eyes much too beautiful to belong to a man.

He had always been handsome. But back in school, Daphne had never really considered him her type. He'd been good-looking the way Paul Newman or Tom Selleck were: the kind of good-looking for which, as Phyllis used to say, "You wouldn't kick him out for eating crackers in bed." Brad Torrance was someone whose appearance Daphne had admired from a distance, someone whose attention she'd never bothered trying to attract. He was Eric's friend and she was Andrea's, so their paths were bound to cross every once in a while. But when it came to getting crushes, Daphne preferred to keep her fantasies well within the realm of the possible.

He must have been surprised the night she'd approached him. In the year and a half they'd been acquainted, the most intimate conversation they'd ever had involved an analysis of the pretzels being served at a party they'd both attended. Brad had argued that they were stale, and Daphne had maintained that they were still edible. From such dialogues great love affairs rarely blossomed.

What they'd had wasn't a great love affair. It was one night, one truncated, vaguely sordid night, the kind of night that left you with a hangover not just in your head but in your soul.

It all began with the call Daphne had gotten that afternoon. Her parents had phoned her with the splendid
news that Helen was engaged to be married. Daphne
wasn't the type of woman to begrudge her sister such
happiness, even if Helen was two years younger than
Daphne. She was in no hurry to get married; if Helen
wanted to tie the knot before she turned twenty-one, that
was all right with Daphne.

What demolished her was that Helen's fiancé was
Dennis Marlow. Dennis, the boy next door, the boy—and
then the man—with whom Daphne had been madly in
love ever since the day his family had moved into the
house next to hers when she was twelve. She and Dennis
had done everything as a twosome: walked, and later
driven, to school together, collaborated on science proj-
ects, swapped comic books and perused copies of *Play-
boy* purloined from Dennis's father's night table. They'd
taped each other's rock-and-roll albums, helped each
other with their homework, provided alibis for each other
when one of them was in trouble.

As they got older, they had discovered the facts of life
together. They'd kissed, they'd touched, they'd experi-
mented. They'd been such good friends, such inseparable
ble pals that it had seemed perfectly natural for them to
learn about their bodies together.

But for Daphne, it had been more than simply youth-
ful experimentation. She had loved Dennis. He'd loved
her, too, she supposed, but as far as he was concerned, it
hadn't really been a romantic love. Daphne had been his
buddy, his fellow explorer. The incestuous implications
notwithstanding, he'd ultimately come to think of her as
a sister.

Or, more precisely, a sister-in-law. After all they'd been
through, Dennis decided that the woman he truly de-

sired wasn't Daphne but her kid sister. Daphne, he would later explain to her, was the greatest, terrific, one-in-a-million, the best friend a guy could have. What he didn't need to explain was that she wasn't petite and pretty, aspiring to devote her life totally to a man and ask only for his affection in return. Daphne wasn't Helen.

The news of Helen's engagement agonized Daphne. She shut herself up inside her dormitory room, refusing to speak to anyone until Andrea and Phyllis picked the lock and forced their way inside. When she told them what had happened, they supplied her with tissues and compassion. They hugged her, they commiserated, they fed her M & M peanuts. They took turns inventing gruesome ends for Dennis—to which Daphne would object, "But then Helen'll wind up a widow!" or "But then she'll have to go without sex for the rest of her married life!"

"Forget about Helen," Andrea exhorted Daphne. "Forget about them both. Eric's frat is on tap tonight. Come on, get smashed and forget about the whole thing."

"Men aren't worth it," Phyllis added knowingly. "Look how many times I've had my heart broken—and how many times I've recovered. I know whereof I speak, Daffy—men stink, and they aren't worth crying over. Come to the party with us. It'll do you some good to get out and shop around. A few beers, and you'll be saying, 'Dennis who?'"

Daphne let them talk her into it. After dinner that night, she accompanied Phyllis and Andrea across the hilly, frozen campus to the fraternity house where Eric and his friends lived. In the rec room in the house's finished basement, the jukebox was blasting lively dance music and kegs of beer were being emptied at a rapid clip.

Daphne rarely refused a glass of beer during her college days, and every now and then she'd indulge in a second or even a third glass.

That night, she didn't bother to count how many glasses she indulged in.

The air in the frat house basement was thick with cigarette smoke, and the lighting was kept to a minimum. Bodies gyrated on the dance floor at the center of the room, where all the furniture had been cleared away. The volume of the jukebox was cranked way up, causing the chairs and benches shoved up against the walls to tremble slightly whenever a bass riff was played.

Thinking back on it, Daphne would remember little else about the party itself. What she would remember most vividly was that the basement was hot and stuffy and noisy, that the only two solutions to these problems she could come up with were to drink more beer and to leave the party, and that when the first solution began to pall she turned to the second.

She staggered out the door and down a short hallway to the stairs. Brad Torrance was seated on the bottom step, rolling up the sleeves of his shirt. "Hey, Daffy," he had greeted her amiably, craning his neck up to view her. He didn't bother to stand in her presence.

"How come you're out here?" she asked, pleasantly surprised that she wasn't slurring her words.

"It's too hot in there," he said. He lifted a sweater from the step beside him. "Can you believe I was wearing this? I came out here to cool off."

"It's much more comfortable out here," Daphne agreed.

"Yeah." Belatedly, Brad rose to his feet. Daphne noticed that he'd opened the top two buttons of his shirt. He had a nice neck, she reflected, strong but not too thick, rising elegantly from the horizontal ridge of his shoulders. All in all, he was a knockout, she concluded. A bit too good-looking for her, but she definitely wouldn't kick him out for eating crackers.

It dawned on Daphne, as she contemplated Brad's wonderfully proportioned physique and dimpled smile, that Dennis Marlow wasn't the only man in the world. In her besotted condition, this thought struck her as a profound revelation.

"Well, I've got to take this up to my room before somebody rips it off," Brad declared, shaking the wrinkles out of the sweater.

"I'll come with you," Daphne invited herself. Sober, she would never have suggested such a thing. But that night, she was drunk, and she didn't care. All she wanted was to forget about Dennis, forget that she'd ever loved him, forget that her sister was more desirable than she was. All she wanted was for Brad to prove to her that, despite Dennis's rejection of her, she was still a woman worthy of a man's attention.

It was a hell of a lot to want, but at the time Daphne didn't think she was asking for too much.

Brad weighed her offer for a minute, then shrugged. "Sure. Come on up if you'd like," he said, stepping aside so she could join him on the stairs.

His room was on the top floor of the fraternity house, in a converted attic room beneath the eaves. He'd gone to some effort to decorate it. A framed Modigliani nude gazed across the room from the wall above the bed, a rug had been thrown over the linoleum floor and matching curtains framed the dormer windows. The room was tidy, books and papers stacked neatly on the desk and toiletries lined up in a row on top of the bureau. The bed was made. In retrospect, it would occur to Daphne that Brad might have straightened up his room and made his bed because he'd been planning to pick up a woman at the party and bring her upstairs. He'd been planning to score.

In retrospect, lots of things would occur to her. But not then. She wanted to be beyond thinking that night.

Brad folded his sweater and placed it in a bureau drawer. Then he crossed to his desk and opened another drawer. "Would you like a drink?" he asked, switching on the fluorescent lamp above the blotter.

"Okay," Daphne said stupidly.

Brad pulled an already-open bottle of wine from the desk drawer and tugged out the cork. Then he turned off the overhead light, leaving most of the room in shadow. He led Daphne to the bed and they sat together on it, side by side. He filled two ceramic mugs with wine and handed one to her.

They didn't talk. They sipped their wine, sitting so close on the mattress that their thighs nearly touched. Daphne stared at the small pool of bluish light the fluorescent lamp spilled onto the surface of the desk. She wondered why she couldn't taste the wine she was drinking, why she couldn't feel Brad next to her. She wondered why she felt so cold.

Eventually, Brad set his mug down on the floor beside the bottle. When he removed Daphne's mug from her hand, to put it on the floor with his, she didn't protest. He slid his arms around her, kissed her, and eased her backward on the bed until she was lying underneath him.

She wanted to enjoy it—or else to block the whole thing out, to put her mind on hold and pretend none of it was occurring. But she failed on both counts. She remained painfully conscious of Brad's weight on her, of his hands peeling off her clothing and his, of his warm,

damp breath tickling the skin of her shoulder in a tor-
turous way.

Daphne suffered more torture than just the constant,
almost abrasive tickle of his exhalations. There was the
scratchiness of his unshaven chin as he nuzzled her neck.
The pain of his knees digging into the soft flesh of her
thigh. The pressure of his hard, slightly hairy chest
smashing down onto her breasts. The stinging pinch at
her scalp when his fingers got tangled up in the snarled
curls of her hair. His aimless kisses, landing here and
there, without purpose or effect.

Yet she remained where she was, doing her inebriated
best to return his kisses and to shift out of the way of his
bony knees. She remained in the hope that things would
improve, that gradually everything would start to feel
better. She stayed because Brad had such beautiful eyes
and she hoped that somehow, perhaps, they'd trans-
form the experience into something equally beautiful.

They didn't, of course. It wasn't beautiful. It was embarrassingly quick and bad, and when it was over,
Daphne felt more sober than she'd ever felt in her life.

"I'm sorry," she mumbled, practically shoving him
away from her and sitting.

"Hey," he said hoarsely, extending his arm. "You
don't have to go."

"Yes, I do," she insisted, too chagrined to look at him.
At that moment, she hated them both for having done
what they did—and for having done it so poorly. She was
unable to escape from herself, but could escape from
Brad, and her only aim at that point was to flee from him
before he found out how much she hated him.

His hand alighted on her leg, but he couldn't prevent
her from leaving. She swung off the bed, resenting her
sudden sobriety because it forced her to acknowledge the

most peculiar details of his room, imbedding them in her memory so she'd never be able to forget. The wine they'd been drinking was a Mosel; the mugs had the college logo imprinted on them; the book on the top of the pile on Brad's desk was Volume One of Kierkegaard's *Either/ Or*. Brad's blanket was the same heavenly blue color as his eyes.

Another thing she would never forget was that Brad didn't beg her to stay. He didn't even *ask* her to stay. All he said was, "You don't have to go," as if the choice were totally hers.

If it was, she was willing to make it. She left the fraternity house, went back to her dorm, took a long, scalding shower and then got into bed, burrowing deep beneath the blankets, and wept.

It had happened in late February, which meant Daphne had to spend only three more months on the same campus with Brad before they both graduated and went their separate ways. When they saw each other during those three final months, Brad did a better job than Daphne of acting as though nothing of any significance had ever transpired between them—which led Daphne to believe that to Brad, the incident had had no significance at all. But even when he was pretending friendliness toward her, he never looked directly into her eyes. He always steered his gaze to just above hers, as though he were fascinated with her forehead. And after he asked her one or two banal "How's it going?" questions, he always shifted his attention away, as if he couldn't bear to hear her answers.

She recovered. Daphne imagined that most people had done some horrendous, mortifying, utterly moronic thing at least once in their lives, and those people with a sane approach to life ultimately put the memory of whatever they'd done into deep storage and went on. If it were possible to go back and correct one's mistakes, Daphne would gladly do it. She'd go back to that night, refuse every glass of beer she was offered, talk for a few minutes with Brad about how stuffy the basement room was, and then, when he said he wanted to take his sweater upstairs, she would respond, "Okay, Brad. See you later," and march back into the stuffy basement room in search of someone to dance with.

But it wasn't possible to go back, so Daphne did what she could: she went forward.

"When are you going to show me a house?" Brad asked.

Daphne shot him a quick glance. He didn't appear bored as he lounged in the passenger seat next to her, but he was obviously eager to see some residences. "Right now," she said, turning back onto Bloomfield Avenue and scanning her wristwatch. A few minutes past eleven o'clock. They'd have time before lunch to look at a six-year-old ranch house she'd recently listed. At $210,000, it was absurdly overpriced, but then everything in this part of New Jersey was.

Maybe Brad would like it. Maybe after looking at it and a few other houses Daphne intended to show him, he'd think of her as a woman who was much too sensible to drink a lot of beer and jump into bed with a man.

Not that Daphne gave a damn about what Brad thought of her, of course. Not that she cared the least bit.

Chapter Three

As it turned out, they managed to look at two houses before lunch. They spent less than fifteen minutes at the ranch house; Brad stalked through the six small rooms, poked his head into the narrow bathroom, and stormed out the front door, grumbling that anyone who'd pay in excess of two hundred thousand dollars for such a tiny house had to have a screw loose somewhere.

"I warned you," Daphne admonished him. "The housing prices are really inflated around here."

"It's not that I'm unwilling to pay two hundred thousand dollars," Brad defended himself. "But I'd like to get something more than a one-toilet shack for the money."

His comment didn't bode well. Around these parts, a second bathroom could add upward of thirty thousand dollars to a house's price.

Hoping to put him in a more receptive mood before they took a break for lunch, Daphne drove him to a town house she had among her listings in one of the elite condominium complexes. For a price comparable to that of the ranch house, he could get two full bathrooms there. The master bathroom even had a sunken marble tub.

"Two-twenty, and you don't get a private yard?" he griped.

"That's the concept behind a condominium," she reminded him, her patience beginning to flag. "No private yard means you don't have to mow your lawn or weed your flower beds."

"What the hell do I need a marble tub for?" he muttered, marching out of the building and heading down the winding front walk toward Daphne's car. "I never take baths. I'm a shower person."

In an effort to mollify him, she brought him to one of the more expensive restaurants in Verona for lunch. They didn't have to wait long to be seated, and as soon as a waitress neared their table, Brad requested a Scotch on the rocks.

"Iced tea," Daphne said when the waitress asked if she wanted a drink. The waitress left them with menus and departed.

"You're going to make me drink alone," Brad deduced, his tone laced with suspicion.

Given that Daphne no longer partook of liquor, her companions invariably had to drink alone. "I don't drink when I'm working," she explained. It wasn't the whole truth, but it wasn't a lie, either.

Brad leaned back in his chair and regarded her across the linen-covered table. "Is that your strategy? You get your client smashed, and he'll agree to buy anything for any price."

Daphne smiled demurely. "I have the feeling, Brad, that no matter how smashed you got, you'd still put up a fuss about a house you considered overpriced."

"In other words, any house around here."

She held on to her smile, refusing to let him rile her. She knew that, given the comfortable income he'd be earning in his new position, he could afford any of the houses she planned to show him today. And he couldn't be as shocked about the prices as he pretended to be—he'd insisted that he was aware of the inflated housing costs in the area. All of which meant that what was bugging him was something essentially unrelated to the house and the condo Daphne had shown him.

What was bugging him, she surmised, was the identity of the realtor showing him the houses.

The waitress arrived with their drinks and asked if Daphne and Brad were ready to order their meals. Daphne lifted her menu, skimmed it and asked for a bowl of gazpacho and a garden salad. Brad cast her an unreadable glance, then took her menu from her, handed it along with his to the waitress and requested a hamburger. "Are you on a diet?" he asked Daphne once they were alone again.

Daphne scrutinized him carefully. She studied the smooth fall of his glossy black hair across his high brow, the square shape of his jaw, the thin line of his lips, the brilliant blue radiance of his eyes, and finally his neck. It was still one of the nicest necks she'd ever seen on a man. It was the sort of neck that tempted a woman to graze it with her lips—if she was sober and responsible, and if he was more than passively receptive.

"What makes you think I'm on a diet?" she countered. She had hoped her voice would emerge sounding amiably detached, but it didn't. She came across as petulant, as if she were eager to rise to Brad's unspoken challenge and wear as big a chip on her shoulder as he was wearing on his.

"You've lost weight since college," he said.

"I'm surprised that someone like you would even notice," she shot back, then bit her lip and cursed her temper. How could she have uttered such a snide remark in front of him? How could she have allowed herself to appear so touchy?

Her caustic comment had an unexpected effect on him. Rather than rallying with an equally insulting comeback, he softened. His lips curved in a hesitant smile and his eyes remained on her as he reached for his Scotch glass. He ran his index finger around the rim and shrugged. "You *have* lost weight, Daff. The fact of the matter is, you're looking great."

She accepted his compliment in the spirit in which it was given—a simple observation, devoid of ulterior meaning. "I was too fat in college," she reminded him. "I was still carrying around the 'freshman twenty' when I graduated."

"The 'freshman twenty'? What's that?"

"The twenty pounds lots of girls gain their freshman year of college."

"Why do they do that?" Brad asked, apparently fascinated.

Daphne laughed. "I don't know," she admitted. "Maybe it has to do with leaving home for the first time. All of a sudden, you don't have your mother on your back, nagging you that if you aren't pretty you won't get a date for the prom and your life will be ruined."

"Did your mother do that?" Brad inquired.

Daphne tried to interpret the gentle undercurrent in his voice. He sounded a touch indignant, a touch amused that mothers would put such pressure on their daughters. "Yes, she did," Daphne answered honestly. "And I did go to my senior prom. I can't say whether or not it's saved my life from ruination, but I did get a prom date."

"Whoever he was, he was lucky," Brad said.

Why was Brad suffering from this sudden compulsion to flatter her? she wondered. Evidently he felt the need to make amends for his earlier surliness. "Whoever he was," she responded before taking a sip of iced tea through the straw, "he's now my brother-in-law."

"Oh," Brad said, then lifted his glass and drank. His gaze lingered on Daphne as he swallowed and lowered the glass back to the table. As her statement registered on him, his expression sharpened and his smile faded. "*Oh,*" he repeated, apparently struck by the notion that something in the situation she had just described wasn't quite kosher. "He's your brother-in-law?"

"He married my younger sister," Daphne explained. "Even though he and I went to the prom together, we were never that serious." There were times for candor, but this clearly wasn't one of them. Daphne hadn't intended to discuss anything personal with Brad. Just because she had accidentally exposed a piece of her past, she didn't have to compound her error by letting him know how badly her erstwhile prom date had wounded her. If she did, she might slip even further and inform Brad of precisely what she'd done in her mindless effort to console herself—and that particular subject was definitely and permanently off-limits, as far as she was concerned.

"I didn't know you had a sister," Brad commented. Then he rolled his eyes heavenward and swore softly. "It's ridiculous, Daff—the last two years of school you and I traveled in the same circles, and yet we know so little about each other."

They'd done a hell of a lot more than travel in the same circles, but she couldn't deny his assertion that they knew shamefully little about each other. She had no idea whether Brad had any siblings, either. If Phyllis and Andrea hadn't discussed it the previous Wednesday, Daphne wouldn't have known that Brad was a native New Yorker.

"Why don't you want to live in the city?" she asked.

The question obviously took him by surprise, but the waitress's timely arrival with their lunches gave him a chance to recover. He spent a long time pouring ketchup onto his hamburger, then closed the seeded bun around it and lifted it to his mouth. Instead of biting into it, he raised his eyes to Daphne's. "My parents live there," he said.

She didn't consider that an adequate answer, but she thoughtfully allowed him to swallow before inquiring further. "You don't want to live too close to your parents, is that it?"

"Of course that isn't it," he refuted her. He took another bite of his hamburger, set it on his plate, chewed and reached for his Scotch. When the glass was halfway to his lips he changed his mind and put it back down on the table. "I love my parents," he confessed. "I love them both very much. They're a wonderful couple. They're also borderline lunatics, and . . . yeah, I'd rather not be living too close to them at the moment." He savored a drink of Scotch, then met Daphne's gaze again. "New Jersey isn't Seattle," he allowed. "There's no way I can work in Manhattan and *not* live near them. But I'm tired of city living. I've spent too much of my life surrounded by the hustle and bustle. I want peace and quiet. God, I sound like an old fogy, don't I?" He gave in to a self-deprecating laugh.

Daphne joined his laughter, although she didn't think he sounded like an old fogy at all. After college, she'd lived first in Chicago and then in Atlanta. The excitement of those cities had enthralled her for a while, but eventually she'd had enough. Her mother kept carping about how she'd never meet a marriage-minded bachelor if she kept herself buried in the suburbs, but Daphne hadn't met any suitable representatives of that particular species in Chicago or Atlanta, either.

Besides, she'd learned a long time ago that it was fruitless to live your life waiting for Mr. Right.

"The suburbs offer a lot that the city doesn't," Daphne noted. "A little less congestion, a little less noise—a lot less taxes. Not far from here there's an excellent professional theater company, and between Brendan Byrne Arena and the Garden State Arts Center you'll find plenty of pop music concerts—"

"Skip the spiel," Brad cut her off with a good-natured grin. "You don't have to sell me on New Jersey. I'm here looking, aren't I?"

"You're here today. Tomorrow you might turn your back on New Jersey and take your business to Westchester."

"And you'd be out a whopping commission."

"That's not what's important."

"Oh?" Brad's eyebrows rose and his smile gave way to a look of bemusement. "What's important, Daphne?"

She drew a blank. *Something* was important about Brad's search for a house in New Jersey, something beyond the fact that for the first time since he'd walked into her office that morning, he had called her "Daphne" instead of "Daffy" or "Daff." Something was much more important than her interest in earning a commission.

She wanted to do business with Brad because she wanted to accomplish something positive with him. She wanted to make something work, to wind up with something beneficial from her association with him. She couldn't go back and rewrite their history, but counterbalancing that history with something worthwhile and meaningful would be almost as good.

She couldn't possibly explain her feelings to him. Dipping her spoon into her soup, she tossed around various discreet replies to his question. He was waiting for her to say something; she had to come up with a response of some sort.

"Let's just say I want to do it for old-time's sake," she said finally, grateful for the shield her eyeglasses provided and annoyed with herself for desiring a shield at all. "I want you to wind up with a nice home, and I want to be the one to find it for you, just for old-time's sake."

He could have pounced on her; he could have demanded that she explain why it mattered that she and no one else found a nice home for him. He could have recoiled from her, arguing that he was in the market for a house, not a psychological adventure, and that he had no intention of letting her work out her demons on him. He would have been completely justified in claiming that the best thing either of them could do for old-time's sake was stay away from each other.

But he didn't react negatively to her statement. He didn't even press the issue. He only took another hefty bite of his hamburger and grinned. "It's no wonder you're successful, Daphne," he conceded. "You know how to make a client feel special."

Daphne didn't always succeed in making her clients feel special. But, no matter how hard she endeavored to treat Brad as she would any other client, she couldn't alter the fact that he *was* special. Whether that was good or bad was irrelevant. Brad Torrance was special to Daphne; there was no way around it.

"NEW JERSEY," Roger Torrance sniffed. "You may as well look for a house in Outer Mongolia."

Brad clamped his lips shut. He honestly didn't want to argue with his father. That Roger and his estranged wife tended to be exceedingly provincial about their beloved New York was a given. Brad would just have to ride out their contempt.

He and his father were seated at a relatively secluded table at his father's club. Roger was a club man, and he'd made no effort to hide his enduring hope that, once Brad took up residence in New York City—there was no doubt in his mind that was where Brad would take up residence, of course—Brad would become a member of the club, too.

At one time, Brad might have considered that a fine idea. He'd eaten at the club with his father many times, ever since he was a child. He used to adore the dining room's ripe ambience, the brocade wallpaper and Oriental rugs, the massive fieldstone fireplace occupying one wall, the musty photographs of club officers dating back to 1836. Brad had been no older than nine or ten the first time his father had brought him here for lunch, and he'd been dwarfed by the plush upholstered chair he'd been given to sit on. The waiters had considered it hilarious beyond belief that he'd ordered a Cheez-Whiz sandwich on raisin bread for lunch.

Tonight, he had ordered prime rib. The portion was huge, the meat pink and juicy. Brad ought to have wolfed it down, but instead he kept thinking about what Daphne had told him about the "freshman twenty." He also thought of her current figure, slim and lithe. In her case, twenty pounds made a world of difference.

Not that she'd turned miraculously into Miss America. She would never be classically pretty. But there was

something intriguing about her appearance now, something that made her much harder to ignore.

"How many houses has this *broker* shown you?"
Roger asked, pronouncing the word "broker" as if he
considered it a euphemism for Satan.

"Four," Brad told him. "And one condo. I'm going
back tomorrow so she can show me a couple of other
properties. And probably to take a second look at one of
the houses she showed me yesterday. It's got possibili-
ties."

Roger speared a chunk of his filet mignon with his fork
and studied it as if it were the most significant object in
the universe. Brad's father often examined trivial objects while he sorted his thoughts. It gave him an appearance of indifference—and it drove Brad's mother up
the wall. "How much?" he finally asked.

"Two sixty."

"Two hundred sixty thousand dollars?" Roger's eyes
widened slightly. They were as striking a blue as his son's;
whenever Brad looked at his father, he felt as if he were
gazing into a time-travel mirror. Thirty years ago, Roger
Torrance had looked almost exactly like Brad; thirty
years from now, Brad thought it safe to assume that he
would look exactly like his father. "For that much
money, you could buy yourself a cozy little co-op in
town."

"I don't want a cozy little co-op in town," Brad retorted. "I want a reasonably spacious house surrounded
by grass and trees. I want to live somewhere where I don't
have to see the air I'm breathing."

"You disappoint me, Brad," Roger said before pop-
ping the cube of beef into his mouth. As he chewed, he
shook his head and his eyes took on a canny glow. "It's
your mother's doing, isn't it?" he guessed.

"What's my mother's doing?"

"She's buying you a house outside the city to keep you from moving in with me."

Brad rolled his eyes. "Number one, she isn't buying me a house. *I'm* buying me a house. Number two, she doesn't want me moving to New Jersey any more than you do. She wants me to live with her. And number three—" he accelerated, aware that his father was about to interrupt "—I'm thirty years old, and I'm not going to live with either of my parents ever again. Unless, of course, you or Mom become incapacitated in your old age and need someone to look after you full-time."

"I have no intention of becoming incapacitated," Roger said sanctimoniously. "I can't speak for your mother on that score." He nibbled on his potatoes au gratin, deep in thought. "This—this *broker*," he remarked, once again uttering the word with great distaste, "you say she's a woman?"

"Wake up, Dad," Brad muttered. "Lots of women work in real estate these days."

"That's not my point," Roger countered. "You've never been as practical as I am; you tend to romanticize certain things. Anyone who could possibly want to live in New Jersey is obviously lacking in sensibility. My question, Brad, is: does this broker of yours have some sort of hold on you?"

"A hold on me?" Brad snorted. "Of course not."

"She hasn't clouded your sense of reason with her beauty, has she?"

"No, Dad." Brad almost added that Daphne Stoltz wasn't beautiful, but he refrained. He felt oddly protective toward her, as if he had to defend her against his father's totally unjustified disapproval. "She's competent, she's knowledgeable, and she's very successful at what she does.''

Roger wavered. Success—even a woman's success—was something he held in high esteem. But, much as he might admire Daphne's success, he clearly didn't want it to extend to his own son. He sipped from his wine goblet, then sighed. ''Well, if she's all that competent, I suppose she can't be too beautiful,'' he concluded. ''I have yet to encounter a woman who boasts both beauty and competence.''

Brad suppressed a shudder. Now was hardly an appropriate time to battle his father over the old man's archaically sexist view of the world—especially since Brad had been trying and failing for years to convert his father to a more feminist philosophy. Nor did Brad feel like explaining that the older he got, the more he recognized that competence in a woman was more valuable than beauty.

That was why Daphne Stoltz looked so good these days, Brad acknowledged with a jolt of amazement—not because she'd lost the ''freshman twenty,'' not because she'd styled her hair more attractively and bought new eyeglasses, but because she was competent, successful, ambitious, because she was no longer a mousy student with no discernible concept of herself. Quite the contrary, she was a disciplined, self-directed woman who knew what she was doing and where she was going.

If in college she'd been as well put together as she was now, Brad would never have taken advantage of her intoxicated state and brought her to his room. He probably would have been her friend, a genuine friend, and if she came to him drunk and vulnerable, he would have walked her back through the wintry night to her dorm and made sure someone there got her safely into her bed, where she could sleep it off alone. If Daphne Stoltz had been the woman she was now, Brad would never have had sex with her.

The peculiarity of that notion startled him. Now that Daphne had proven herself smart and interesting, he ought to be more willing, not less, to think of her in sexual terms. Yet he wasn't. He wanted her friendship, but not her body, not her love. She didn't turn him on.

He cursed beneath his breath. Damn it, but he'd inherited more than his father's thick hair and blue eyes. He'd inherited the man's close-mindedness. Daphne wasn't pretty, and no matter how intriguing Brad found her intellectually, he couldn't bring himself to think of her as a potential lover. And that seemed wrong to him, because her intellect was, indeed, quite intriguing. He really did want her to be his friend.

Over his father's protests, Brad skipped dessert. He didn't want to spend another hour sitting at the club with his father, discussing the rebellion inherent in his decision to take up residence outside the city limits. Nor did he wish to listen to his father's version of the ongoing war between his parents. "It's late, Dad," he excused himself. "I've really got to go. I've got a busy day planned for tomorrow."

"Yes," Roger said with obvious disdain. "You have to cross the river to the wilderness to look at more houses. Suit yourself, Brad. Live in the boondocks if you will. But if in my dotage I do become incapacitated, I'll thank you to put me in a nursing home here in town rather than transport me to that barren wasteland west of the Hudson."

Brad allowed himself a weary smile. He wasn't going to persuade his father of New Jersey's virtues tonight— and, in all honesty, he didn't really care what his father thought about the state. Whether or not Roger Torrance approved of his son's choices didn't matter to Brad.

What mattered was that he himself had to approve of his choices. He approved of his choice regarding a place to live. But the other choice, the choice he'd made about Daphne, didn't sit well with him. It troubled him that he'd pigeonholed her as he had. It troubled him that he couldn't bring himself to think of her in an amorous context. She had so much going for her, and yet...nothing clicked between them. He could gaze into her round green eyes and feel nothing but respect for who she was today and remorse for what he'd done to her long ago.

He ought to feel more, but he didn't. And it bothered the hell out of him.

"HAVE YOU HEARD from Andrea about the party?" Phyllis asked.

Daphne wedged the telephone more snugly against her ear, as if she could keep Brad from listening in on the conversation. He already knew about the party Andrea and Eric were hosting in his honor Saturday night; he'd mentioned it that morning when he'd arrived at Daphne's office. But she held the receiver tight and averted her eyes, just as she always did when she received a personal telephone call at work. It was an old habit dating back to her first job after she'd graduated from college, as an assistant buyer at a department store in Chicago. Her boss had been a tyrant, demanding that employees refuse all phone calls not related to business. Of course the staff had disobeyed, but they'd learned to be secretive.

"Are you going to be there?" Phyllis asked.

"Probably. Are you?"

"I wouldn't miss it for the world," Phyllis declared. "What's Brad like these days, anyway? Andrea tells me you've spent a couple of days taking him around to look at houses."

"He's fine," Daphne reported. Brad couldn't help hearing, and he glanced up curiously, apparently conscious of the fact that she was talking about him. She smiled whimsically, then slowly and deliberately inspected him as he watched her, lifting her eyeglasses up to her forehead and squinting at him. "He hasn't aged too badly, Phyllis," she reported, lowering her glasses back into place. "No gray hair, no double chin, no signs of an incipient potbelly."

Me? Brad mouthed, jabbing his thumb into his chest as he stared at Daphne.

She covered the mouthpiece with her hand and whispered, "It's Phyllis Dunn, from school. She's going to be at the party Saturday, and she wanted to know how you looked."

Brad nodded; evidently, Phyllis's name rang a bell. Then he grinned. "No potbelly, huh," he whispered back. "Has she got a potbelly?"

"You'll find out Saturday night," Daphne answered before turning her attention back to her caller. Phyllis was chattering about something, and Daphne had missed half of it. "What?"

"I said, the good news is that Steve and Melanie Persky are coming down from Armonk for the party," Phyllis reported, naming a couple of other friends who dated back to Daphne's college days. "The bad news is that Andrea invited a bunch of her soap-opera cronies, so the party's going to be overrun with weird theater types."

Daphne laughed. Unlike Phyllis, she found Andrea's professional colleagues colorful and entertaining. "How about Jim? Are you bringing him along with you?"

"I can't see a way out of it," Phyllis lamented. "Are you coming alone?"

"I was thinking I'd bring Paul Costello," said Daphne.

"Bo-ring," Phyllis chanted.

"How can you say that? You've never even met him," Daphne complained.

"I figure, if you're dating him, he must be safe," Phyllis rationalized.

When Daphne had started dating Paul, about a year after she'd moved to Verona, he hadn't been especially safe. An English teacher at one of the local high schools, he was sharp, passably handsome, and possessed of a quirky sense of humor. He and Daphne had given the romance their best shot, but after about six months they were forced to admit that the chemistry wasn't right. "I can't help it, Daphne," Paul had confessed, "but I think of you as a sister. I'm really sorry."

Daphne had been sorry, too, at the time. Now, many months later, she was beginning to sense that it was her lot in life to be thought of as a sister by every interesting man she met, and she was doing her best to accept it. Despite the fact that their relationship never caught fire, Daphne and Paul enjoyed each other's company, and they frequently saw each other when they were both free. That Daphne was free more often than Paul made her only the slightest bit jealous.

"Sometimes he's safe and sometimes he isn't," Daphne allowed, refusing to submit to Phyllis's condemnation of Daphne's social life. "You can judge for yourself Saturday night. I've got to go, Phyllis. The guest of honor is drooling all over my M.L.S. book." She said the last part loudly for Brad's benefit. He glanced up from the Multiple Listing catalog, grinned and stuck out his tongue, pretending to pant.

"He's there now?" Phyllis exclaimed. "Give him a kiss for me, Daffy. I'll see you in a couple of days."

Daphne said goodbye and hung up the phone. "Phyllis asked me to give you a kiss," Daphne related.

Brad's grin widened. "On her account, or your own?"

Daphne considered an assortment of answers before opting for honesty. "Hers," she replied. "But I'll let you wait until Saturday. Kisses should never be delivered by middlemen."

"Spoilsport," Brad teased before turning his focus back to the catalog open on his lap. "I'm almost at the end of the West Caldwell listings," he told her. "Let me just skim these last two pages."

"Have you found anything you want to look at?" she asked.

He shook his head. "What I've found is that you've already shown me the best bets. But this is informative. Give me one more minute, okay?"

She'd already set up a few appointments before he arrived at her office a half hour ago. But she encouraged most of her clients to peruse the listings in the catalog, just in case she overlooked a property they might wish to see. Before he'd begun reading, Brad had asked her to educate him on the lingo in the book. She had explained to him that "a cozy little charmer" meant the house wasn't much bigger than a toolshed, that "very special" meant the floors were uneven and a mismatched wing had been added off the garage, and that "this one won't last" meant the house had been on the market for over a year. Thus armed, Brad had tackled the listing book.

Daphne wasn't sure what had happened between yesterday and today, what had changed between them to make her feel more comfortable in Brad's company. Perhaps it was simply that he seemed more comfortable around her.

Shortly after he'd arrived at the office, Brad told her about the dinner he'd had with his father the night before, during which his father had referred to New Jersey as a wasteland. He told her that he was rather taken by the expanded cape she'd shown him the previous day, the one priced at $260,000, and that he'd like to see it again if they had time that afternoon. He told her he'd stopped by his new office that morning to shake a few hands, and his associates there had sworn that, while they didn't want to pressure him, they sure hoped he'd settle in soon because they could really use him at his desk. He'd also mentioned the party Andrea and Eric were going to hold in his honor.

Brad was undoubtedly used to being needed and feted, Daphne mused as he turned to the last page of West Caldwell listings and resumed reading. He hadn't sounded boastful when he'd mentioned the party or the avid reception he'd received at the office. Instead, he'd sounded at home, as if he were confiding in an old friend.

Daphne was hardly Brad's old friend. Yet she greatly preferred his mood today to his gruff demeanor yesterday. While she usually didn't like to mix business with pleasure, she saw no reason to reject Brad's friendship, whatever it entailed.

"Nothing," he said, shutting the book and placing it on her desk.

"All right. We'll look at what I've already set up."

Daphne knew the first house they visited would be a bust the minute they stepped inside. The selling broker, an overbearing woman named Midge, was waiting for them in the living room, and she immediately wrapped a plump arm around Brad's shoulders and swept him away, babbling about what a fabulous family home this would make. "There's a wonderful playroom for the children," she enthused. "Do you have children, Mr. Torrance? No? Well, don't give up. My husband and I tried for seven years before we hit the jackpot. What? No wife? Well, a nice young man like you ought to be able to find someone sooner or later. Come along, let me show you this absolutely adorable nursery upstairs...."

The second house Daphne took him to was the sort which, in the M.L.S. book, was usually described with the phrase "has great potential." The place was falling to pieces. Several windows were cracked, some roof shingles lay on the ground near the front door, the electrical wiring was inadequate and the linoleum in the bathroom had been stripped off to reveal the warped floorboards underneath. "It's under two hundred thousand," Daphne pointed out cheerfully as Brad dusted the cobwebs from his hands and strode out of the house, smoothly sidestepping the fallen shingles.

"What a bargain," he grunted, climbing into the car and staring straight ahead, as if he couldn't wait for her to transport him from the dilapidated building. "Can you honestly picture me rewiring a house?"

"You could hire a contractor."

"Daphne, look at me." He extended his hands beneath her nose. "Not a single callus. I'm helpless when it comes to repairing things."

"I'm sure you aren't."

"I am. Whenever anything breaks, my instincts tell me to run for cover."

"Everyone's instincts tell them that," Daphne granted, starting the car and pulling away from the curb. "But when the option isn't available, most people roll up their sleeves and tackle the problem as best they can."

"Do you think I'm like most people?" Brad asked, gazing at her profile as she concentrated on the road.

"I don't know," she answered, sensing that he was hinting at something far removed from house repairs, but not at all sure what it was.

"There have been times, Daff..." His voice drifted off, and his gaze left her to focus on the dashboard. "Times when I was so lazy, I just threw away whatever was broken and...yeah. I ran for cover. I'm rotten when it comes to fixing things."

Daphne considered his words. He was obviously no longer talking about "handyman's specials" or even broken objects. He was talking about friendships, relationships, broken feelings and messy affairs. One messy affair in particular, perhaps.

Her recollection of that affair was that she, not Brad, had been the one to run for cover. And if there had been anything to repair, it would have been as much her responsibility as his to fix it.

They'd both failed—but neither of them was noticeably broken anymore. Houses couldn't mend their own roofs, but human beings had an awesome talent for regenerating themselves.

"I wouldn't worry about it," Daphne said, keeping her tone as light as possible. "We'll stay away from fixer-uppers from now on."

He turned back to her, and she could feel the glittering blue light of his eyes bathing her. She risked a swift glance at him and absorbed his wistful smile. "That's probably a wise policy."

Avoiding fixer-uppers meant taking the chance of missing a property that, with just a bit of tender loving care, could be made perfect. On the other hand, the odds of finding such a rare house were slim, and she and Brad had already agreed that they didn't want to waste time.

So she drove him to the next house on her schedule. The roof was tight, the floors were covered with plush carpets and no-wax tiles, the walls had been papered recently and every window frame sported a double-layer thermopane. The appliances were new, the lighting fixtures attractive, the yard recently mowed and the shrubs pruned. The house boasted a price tag approaching $300,000—a staggering amount, but worth it for a dwelling that was clean and safe, with no surprises and no additional work necessary. This was a house that demanded nothing from its owner other than a fat wallet and an appreciation of its pretty practicality.

Daphne wasn't terribly shocked when Brad told her he loved it.

Chapter Four

"It's not that I hate driving in the city," Paul insisted as Daphne's car emerged from the Lincoln Tunnel into Manhattan. "It's that I hate *parking* in the city."

"No explanation necessary," Daphne assured him, navigating her car deftly through the traffic-congested midtown streets. "I don't mind driving."

"The last time I parked my car on a New York City street," he went on, evidently disagreeing with her about the necessity of an explanation, "my radio antenna got ripped off—literally. And you know as well as I do that in this city, parking in a garage costs an arm and a leg."

"There aren't any garages on Andrea's block, so don't worry about sacrificing your arms and legs," Daphne told him. "My car has one of those power antennas. It automatically retracts as soon as I turn off the radio. It can't get ripped off."

"Your radio can," Paul said ominously.

Daphne chuckled, and the sound of her quiet laughter helped to calm her nerves.

She had mixed feelings about attending this party. She always enjoyed seeing Andrea and Eric and Phyllis—although she could happily do without Phyllis's Significant Other—and she was especially pleased that the

Perskys would be at the party, too. Seeing Brad was what made her edgy.

More specifically, what made her edgy was seeing Brad in the context of a party. The two of them had gotten along well during their forays into the New Jersey housing market. They had both proven that they were mature and civilized, able to function in each other's company on a professional basis, able even to loosen up and joke with each other on a certain level. But house hunting was business. At a party, there would be booze and music and cigarette smoke and hordes of people—all in all, an atmosphere painfully reminiscent of a night in Daphne's past that she'd prefer to forget.

At least she had Paul with her. Although she hadn't explicitly mentioned it to him, her primary reason for bringing him along was for protection. His company would keep her from dwelling on the last party she'd been to where Brad was also in attendance. At least she hoped it would.

Apparently persuaded that Daphne honestly didn't mind driving, Paul relaxed in his seat as best he could, given his lanky build. He had the sort of broom-handle physique that baggy pleated trousers were designed for, and he tended to dress with enough panache to be considered a far-out dude by his students. Despite the evening gloom, his hair seemed to glow. Given its coppery color and its short, curly tufts, Paul's mane often reminded Daphne of a shredded carrot salad.

In his stylish trousers, two-tone shirt and narrow knitted tie, he appeared more fashionable than Daphne. When she'd picked him up at his apartment half an hour ago, he had assured her that she looked terrific. Being a realist, she didn't aspire that high; she'd be content to look reasonably good. Attired in a swirling skirt with a colorful floral pattern and a violet scoop-necked sweater, with her hair falling in golden ripples around her lightly made-up face, she had more or less attained that modest goal.

When she'd chosen her outfit that evening, she had tried to convince herself that Paul was the person for whom she was fixing herself up. But the closer her car got to Andrea's Upper West Side address, the more strongly Daphne suspected that she'd dressed with Brad in mind. Not that she wished for him to find her alluring—not that she believed such a thing was even possible—but she did want him to know that she was a survivor. She wanted him to recognize that eight years after her debacle, she knew how to dress up and snag an escort and enjoy herself at a party.

Assuming, of course, that she did manage to enjoy herself tonight.

She found a parking space only four blocks from Andrea's building, which she considered a good omen. Hooking her hand through the bend in Paul's arm, she strolled with him down the sidewalk to the elegant apartment building overlooking Riverside Park. In the mild spring evening, the park exuded the aromas of re-awakening plant life, grass beginning to sprout and shrubs beginning to bud. By the time she and Paul reached the building, Daphne was feeling at ease and self-confident.

They had to identify themselves to the doorman's satisfaction before being permitted to pass through the lobby to the elevator. As they rode upstairs, Paul asked, "Am I going to know anyone at this shindig besides Andrea and Eric?"

"I don't think so," Daphne replied. "Not unless you watch any daytime soaps. Rumor has it Andrea invited a bunch of her actor friends."

"Really?" Paul's eyes grew round and bright. "Certified celebrities? Can I ask them for their autographs?"

Daphne knew from his tone of voice that he was kidding. "I don't see why not," she played along. "A certified celebrity ought to be able to sign an autograph for a certified maniac. All in the certifiable family, Paul."

They stepped off the elevator and walked down the hallway to Andrea's apartment. Through the closed door Daphne could hear a babble of voices, indicating that the party was already in full swing. She had to ring the doorbell several times before it was answered—by someone she'd never seen before. "Come on in," the unfamiliar woman greeted them, waving them into the entry foyer. "Drinks are in the kitchen, snacks are in the living room, and Andrea's in the bathroom, as it were." From her welcome, Daphne suspected that the woman was one of Andrea's more bizarre actress friends.

"I'm going to get a drink," Paul whispered as he ushered Daphne into the living room. "Can I get you something?

"A glass of ginger ale," she requested.

"Bless your sober little heart. I love it when you drive," Paul murmured, giving her arm an affectionate squeeze before he vanished into the dining room en route to the kitchen.

Daphne rotated to find herself face-to-face with Phyllis, who looked breathtaking in a black silk cocktail dress with a blinding rhinestone brooch pinned to one shoulder. Not bothering to say hello, Phyllis bore down on her with an accusing scowl. "Why didn't you tell me he was gorgeous?" she demanded to know.

It took Daphne only a couple of seconds to figure out whom Phyllis was referring to; there weren't too many gorgeous men having a party held in their honor at Andrea's and Eric's apartment that night. She grinned at Phyllis's transparent behavior. "You already knew Brad was gorgeous," she pointed out.

"I knew he *was*," Phyllis clarified. "I didn't know he still *is*. Listen, Daffy, how much would it be worth to you to take Jim for a walk around the block so I can spend a little time with Brad?"

Daphne erupted in laughter. "First of all, Phyllis, we would make it all the way around the block and back here in under ten minutes. I have the feeling that what you've got in mind might take a bit longer than that."

"Not necessarily—"

"And second of all," Daphne continued, cutting off Phyllis's protest, "I'm not going to entertain your date when I came with my own."

"Oh, right. Where is this guy, anyway? I'd like to check him out."

"He's getting us some drinks," Daphne told her. "And there's no need to check him out. We're just friends."

"Boring," Phyllis mumbled. "If you're just friends, then maybe I wouldn't be doing anybody any harm if I did meet him, would I?"

Phyllis was welcome to try her luck with Paul, but Daphne had no intention of spending the party keeping Phyllis's lover distracted while Phyllis prowled around. "Forget it, Phyllis," Daphne warned her. "I'm not going to take Jim for a walk, no matter how much you think it might be worth to me. I have much better sources of income, thank you."

Phyllis pursed her lips, pretending to be irritated by Daphne's teasing. Her irritation became genuine when, a few seconds later, Jim sidled up next to her. Daphne considered Jim a fine hunk of manhood, arguably better looking than Brad. Jim was more muscular, with thicker shoulders and a brawnier build. He had a boyishly handsome face, although he frequently appeared slightly lecherous to Daphne, as if he were sizing up every woman he encountered as a potential conquest. Phyllis invariably fell for men who might have sprung physically from the pages of *G.Q.* and emotionally from *Penthouse Forum.* Jim was no exception.

"Hey, Daphne," Jim hailed her as he wrapped a possessive arm around Phyllis. "Howzit going?"

"Fine, Jim. How are you?"

"Can't complain."

"How's business?"

"Well, you know what they say," he quipped with a wink. "No matter whether the economy's going up or down, people always gotta take a leak." Jim ran a plumbing supplies company. He spoke in a lazy New York drawl, but his slangy speech didn't fool Daphne. She knew he was extremely shrewd and professionally successful.

"There you are," Andrea bellowed, elbowing her way through her milling guests to reach Daphne. She had on a pair of harem pants and a gauzy blouse with beads embroidered onto it. Daphne wished she looked as attractive as Andrea did in such exotic outfits. Then again, Daphne wished she looked as attractive as Phyllis did, period. "I found Paul in the kitchen, attacking the ice bucket," Andrea reported once she reached Daphne's side. "He told me that I'd find you in the living room. It wasn't easy, I'll tell you."

"You've got quite a mob scene here," Daphne observed. "How many people did you invite?"

Andrea shrugged and grinned. "We owed a ton of invitations. I've got my people from work, Eric's got his. No sense wasting a party."

"What about Brad?" Daphne asked. As soon as she spoke his name, she felt an undefined stab of panic. She shouldn't really care about how he fit into the party. She shouldn't be thinking about him at all. She should just pretend that this was a typical gathering at Andrea's apartment, not a replay of any other party in her past.

"Oh, he's around here someplace," Andrea remarked vaguely. "So," she said, turning her dark eyes on Jim, "when are you going to do the honorable thing with Phyllis, already?"

"What honorable thing?" Jim asked with feigned innocence.

"Marry her, you dolt."

Jim laughed and tightened his hold on Phyllis. "Well, Andrea, you know what they say: Why buy the milk, when you can get the cow for free?"

"That doesn't sound right to me," Andrea muttered, eyeing Daphne in search of confirmation.

In a perverse way, it did sound right to Daphne. But to say so might insult Phyllis, so she only smiled. "I think I'd better give Paul a hand with the ice bucket," she said, easing away from Phyllis, Jim and Andrea and weaving among the small knots of people clogging the room. She barely missed getting singed by a haphazardly wielded cigarette; she almost tripped over a wiry young man demonstrating a yoga position on the floor; near the entry to the dining room, she was waylaid by the Perskys, and she chatted with them for a while. Then Eric caught her eye and waved her over, asking her to mediate a dispute he was having with some of his accountant colleagues over the deductibility of property taxes.

By the time she reached the kitchen, nearly a half hour had passed. She wasn't surprised to find Paul leaning against the counter, surrounded by two men and a woman, all of whom were engrossed in Paul's description of contemporary teenage lingo. A glass of ginger ale stood on the counter near where he rested his hips.

"Now, the word 'like' is perhaps the most versatile word in the typical teenager's speech," he explained. "Not only does 'like' function as a conjunction, but it has also evolved into an ellipsis of sorts—oh," he said, smiling as his eye caught Daphne's. "Where have you been, Daphne? Your ginger ale is going flat."

"No kidding," Daphne responded with a grin. She acknowledged Paul's audience with a polite nod, took a sip of the ginger ale and grimaced. Worse than flat, it was tepid. "I thought you were supposed to come and deliver this to me in the living room."

"I probably was," Paul conceded, smiling sheepishly. He introduced Daphne to the three people and then reverted to his grammatical analysis of the word *like* in the contemporary adolescent's vocabulary.

Daphne listened for a couple of minutes, then excused herself and departed from the kitchen. She'd heard Paul speak many times about his students and their idiosyncrasies, and while she usually found his comments entertaining, she wasn't in the mood to be entertained tonight—at least not until she saw Brad and proved to herself that he could no longer spoil a party for her.

Where was he, anyway? This party had been thrown to celebrate his impending move to New York—yet he didn't seem to be present. Puzzled, Daphne meandered through the crowd in the dining room, tossing quick smiles of recognition at some of the guests as she worked her way toward the living room. She traversed it as best she could, this time more alert to the fellow doing yoga on the floor and the cigarette smokers. She checked the sofa, the Eames chair, the upholstered window seats. No Brad.

Her curiosity increasing, she left the living room for the hallway. The bathroom was empty. The door of the guest bedroom was open, and when Daphne peeked inside she spotted one of the male stars of Andrea's soap opera in a passionate clinch with one of Eric's associates at the accounting firm—both of whom, Daphne recalled, happened to be married to other people. She closed the door with a discreet click and continued down the hall to the master bedroom. The door was shut, and she wondered whether her entrance might interrupt a couple in an even more compromising position.

She tapped lightly on the door, then inched it open. The lamps on both night tables were turned on, filling the room with an amber light and encouraging Daphne to push the door all the way open.

Brad was seated on the edge of the double bed, his back to the door. His knees were spread apart and his elbows were balanced on them. He propped his head in his cupped hands and stared out the window at the darkening night sky. He seemed oblivious to Daphne—and to the party raging in his honor just down the hall.

Daphne was startled. Not that she thought of Brad as a party animal, but she couldn't imagine why he was sitting there, all alone, instead of participating in the festivities.

She allowed herself a moment to study him. The cotton of his shirt stretched smoothly across his shoulders and upper back, revealing the sleek lines of it. Daphne decided that she preferred his slim build to Jim's hulking one. Brad's forearms were slim, too—he'd rolled up the sleeves of his shirt, and she could see the bronze skin he'd exposed, the dark webbing of hair, the lean muscles tapering down to his bony wrists. She recalled the afternoon, a couple of days ago, when he'd shoved his hands beneath her nose and pointed out the absence of calluses on his fingers and palms.

Daphne would bet her entire savings account that Jim had calluses all over his hands. Maybe Jim was the more typically handsome hunk of the two, but Daphne found Brad's refined appearance much more to her liking.

Whatever Brad's reason for isolating himself from the rowdy party down the hall, Daphne wasn't going to disturb him. She reached for the doorknob, intending to close the door and leave him in peace.

He turned suddenly. As soon as he saw her, his lips curved into a broad grin and his blue eyes widened with delight. "Hey, Daff," he called to her.

She was too tactful to ask him why he'd holed himself up in solitude in the master bedroom. "I was looking for a place to fix my hair," she fibbed with an apologetic smile. "I can use the mirror in the bathroom, though, if you want to be alone."

"No, come on in," he said, waving her inside.

She didn't want him to think she'd been lying, so she walked directly to the dresser and examined her reflection in the mirror above it. Her hair looked fine to her, but she patted and prodded it a few times with her fingertips.

"How's the party?" Brad asked.

Daphne turned from the mirror and appraised him. He certainly didn't look like a man desperate to avoid a social gathering. Faint dimples marked his cheeks, and his eyes continued to glow, their brilliant color set off by his thick, dark lashes. "Hot and crowded," she answered, assuming that Brad must have left the party for the bedroom because he needed a moment's respite from the crush of people and the stuffy air.

Just like the last time, Daphne recollected, unable to ignore the obvious connection. Here was Brad, cooling off outside the party, and here was Daphne, finding him...

Perhaps he was able to read her mind. Or perhaps his smile faded for some reason totally unrelated to his memory of that fraternity party eight years ago. Either way, his solemn expression informed Daphne that he didn't want her company. "Well," she said with forced brightness, "I guess I'll be getting back—"

"Stay a minute," Brad cut her off, gesturing for her to join him.

Daphne's innards tensed up. She didn't want to sit beside him on a bed and think about the last time she'd found herself in such a location with him.

Of course, she might be reading much too much into his invitation, his enigmatic gaze, his decision to escape a noisy party by shutting himself up in a bedroom. Thoughts of that last time might be the furthest thing from Brad's mind. To bolt at his friendly invitation would be cowardly and rude.

Drawing in a deep breath, she crossed to the bed and lowered herself gingerly onto it, as far from Brad as she could be without tumbling off the end of the mattress. She arranged the flowery fabric of her skirt primly across her knees and folded her hands in her lap. Then she waited for him to say something.

Brad's face relaxed into a grin again, and he hoisted himself higher on the bed, leaning his shoulders against the headboard and swinging his legs up so that his feet brushed Daphne's thigh. He crossed his ankles and sighed. "It's great seeing the Perskys again," he re-

marked, his tone light and cheerful. "The last time I saw
them was at our fifth-year reunion. Did you go to that?"
he asked, frowning slightly as he tried to remember.

Daphne shook her head. "I was living in Atlanta at the
time," she explained. "It would have cost too much
money to fly to Ithaca just for the weekend."

Brad had probably been living in Seattle then, and he'd
been able to afford the trip. Even without his big salary,
she realized, he was rich. Rich and gorgeous. It didn't
seem fair.

"Well, it's good seeing them," he remarked. "Steve
told me Melanie's pregnant, only nobody's supposed to
know about it yet."

"If nobody's supposed to know about it, why are you
telling me?" Daphne said, feeling her stomach start to
unclench. She was beginning to accept that this was going
to be a safe little chat and nothing more, nothing she
couldn't handle.

Brad laughed. "If nobody's supposed to know about
it, why did Steve tell me? I assume it's not what we call a
well-kept secret." He flicked a bit of lint from his trousers, then settled back against the headboard again. "It's
good seeing Phyllis Dunn, too," he said. "She looks
fantastic."

"She always did," Daphne pointed out, not at all en-
vious. After having grown up with a pretty sister, and
having befriended pretty classmates in college, Daphne
was used to being surrounded by women who were better looking than she.

"Who's the big lug she's got with her?"

"Jim," said Daphne. "They're living together at the
moment—but don't let that stop you."

"Don't let it stop me from what?" Brad asked innocently.

"Phyllis thinks you look fantastic, too," she said slowly, wondering whether his ingenuousness was just an act. Or was he truly unaware of Phyllis's interest in him?

He snorted in disbelief. "In that case, Phyllis needs those eyeglasses even more than you do."

Daphne detected nothing false in his tone. She laughed, amazed. "You *do* look fantastic, Brad," she told him. "You're a handsome man. I should think you'd be aware of that by now."

He contemplated Daphne thoughtfully. "I've had better days," he confessed somberly. "Today was a rough one, and I don't feel fantastic, so it's hard for me to imagine that I look anything other than wiped out."

Daphne smiled sympathetically. "Are you coming down with something?"

He shook his head. "I had lunch with my mother today."

A deceptively simple explanation. Daphne understood that something about his mother was troubling him, and she sensed that he wanted to talk about it. She wasn't certain why he wanted to talk about it with her, of all people, but he certainly seemed to be looking for a willing listener. "Did your mother give you a hard time?" she asked.

"Other than the fact that she wants me to live with her instead of moving to New Jersey, no. She gave my father a hard time—in absentia. They're having some problems."

"Marital problems?"

He nodded. "I really don't know why, Daff. They're so great together. They're both attractive, accomplished people. They have the same taste in everything. They're even good in bed, from what I gather. But...they've gotten it into their heads that they don't belong together anymore."

"They're adults," Daphne gently reminded him. "They must know their own feelings."

"I'm not so sure," Brad argued. "They're a perfect couple, Daffy. They've been married for thirty-three years. I love them both, Daff—and I'm convinced that they love each other, too."

"Sometimes love isn't enough," Daphne pointed out. She was speaking hypothetically, having had too little experience with love to offer a knowledgeable perspective on the subject.

"Love and marriage both?" he posed. "Call me old-fashioned, Daff, but I believe in marriage. I believe it's there to hold two people together until they can figure out how to make their love stronger. I guess it doesn't necessarily work out that way." He sighed dismally. "I don't know what it is that's tearing them apart. Worse than that, *they* don't seem to know what the hell it is."

Despite his pensive smile, Brad was obviously anguished about his parents' difficulties. For some reason, Daphne was astonished by his attitude. So many people got divorced these days. She imagined it must be hard to take when one's own parents were splitting up, but it wasn't as if Brad were a little boy caught in a custody battle.

If her parents were considering a divorce, she'd be anguished about it, of course. But Brad...

He'd never revealed his vulnerability to her before. That was why she was so surprised by his sensitivity concerning his parents' dilemma. She'd always thought of him as rich and gorgeous, but never human enough to suffer. He always seemed so confident, so positive of his strength and good fortune, so secure of his place in the world. She simply couldn't imagine Brad Torrance as the victim of an emotional upheaval.

Except that here he was, in front of her very eyes, obviously depressed. "Maybe they'll work it out and get back together," she suggested. She had no grounds for such an optimistic prediction, but he seemed to be in dire need of cheering up.

He offered Daphne a small grin. "I hope so," he said. "They really do belong together. I'm just hoping they realize that before they do something they'll regret."

Daphne returned his bittersweet smile. How strange, she thought, that the last time she'd found herself sharing a bed with Brad they'd engaged in the most intimate of acts, and yet she felt closer to him now than she had then. "Buck up, Brad," she said. "Put it out of your mind for now. There's a party out there just waiting for you to make the scene."

He nodded and pushed away from the headboard. "You're right, Daff," he said. "I guess I'd better go face my fans." He smiled again, a heartfelt, radiant smile that penetrated Daphne with its wonderful warmth. He leaned toward her and kissed her cheek. "Thanks," he whispered, standing and then extending his hand to help her to her feet.

His kiss meant nothing, she reassured herself. It was the sort of kiss friends gave friends, the sort of kiss that punctuated a moment of sentimental gratitude. It meant nothing at all—and it meant so much that Daphne reflexively tightened her fingers around his as she rose from the bed.

They left the bedroom together. Brad released her hand as soon as they entered the hallway, allowing her to walk ahead of him. Two of Andrea's actor friends were staging a mock fist fight before a spellbound crowd in the arched entry to the living room. To avoid interfering with their vigorous performance, Daphne and Brad detoured into the dining room. It occurred to Daphne that she still hadn't managed to have a drink, and she continued on into the kitchen, planning to get a glass of cold soda.

She wasn't terribly surprised to discover that Paul was exactly where she'd left him the last time she'd seen him. He had loosened the knot of his tie, and his audience had changed, but he was still leaning casually against the counter and discoursing on the peculiar characteristics of his students.

"What they consider rock and roll is really nothing more than the product of a few technicians and a few big businesses," he pontificated. "Today's so-called rock music has little of the down-home grittiness of the old Stones or even the Beatles."

"Where's your On-Off button?" Daphne interjected, poking him in the ribs. She turned to his audience and grinned. "Pick a subject, any subject. Paul will talk about it ad nauseam."

"What he was saying was interesting!" argued an overly made-up woman with two earrings in each ear.

Paul laughed good-naturedly. "Not to worry, folks— Daphne is the love of my life. Therefore, she's allowed to insult me whenever her little heart desires." He wrapped his arms around her, planted a noisy kiss on her forehead, and then let go of her. "Let me guess, love of my life—you want some of that ginger ale I promised you an hour ago."

"Better late than never," she said, scouring the counter in search of a clean plastic cup. She found one, handed it to Paul and caught a glimpse of Brad hovering in the doorway, watching her.

"Is he the love of your life?" he asked quietly, a curious smile teasing his lips as he directed his gaze toward the energetic red-haired man dropping ice cubes into the cup for Daphne.

"No," she clarified. "*I'm* the love of *his* life. Paul, this is Brad Torrance. Brad, Paul Costello."

Paul twisted around, noticed Brad's outstretched right hand and hastily set the bottle of ginger ale on the counter so he could return the handshake. "So, you're the man of the hour," he said grandly. "One of that old Cornell gang of Daphne's. Shall we burst into a chorus of 'High Above Cayuga's Waters'?"

"Spare us," Daphne cut him off with a laugh.

"So," Paul said, his eyes shuttling between Brad and Daphne, "why aren't you two watching the rumpus in the living room? Those two actors teach a course in how to choreograph stage fights. I caught part of their performance, and they're really convincing."

"We'd rather listen to you drone on and on about sixties rock and roll," Daphne joked, taking the cup from Paul and sipping some of the icy beverage.

Brad had drifted to the refrigerator, where he helped himself to a bottle of beer. He twisted off the cap and took a long drink. Then he smiled. "I'm not into fights, either as a spectator or as a participant," he said, then added, "Daphne and I were talking." Daphne briefly wondered whether he'd taken seriously Paul's claim about her being the love of his life, and whether he felt obliged to reassure Paul about what he and Daphne had been up to.

"Talking, huh," Paul repeated, mixing himself a gin and tonic. "Let me tell you something about this old schoolmate of yours, Brad—she generously volunteered to do all the driving tonight, so I can get plastered. Tell me, am I wrong to be madly in love with her?''

"Even if she didn't let you get plastered, you wouldn't be wrong," Brad answered, shooting Daphne an amused look.

It took Daphne a moment to remember that one of the reasons she'd brought Paul with her was to prove to Brad that she hadn't been permanently scarred by the events of the frat party she'd left with him eight years ago. Her strategy seemed to be working; Brad evidently believed that Paul was Daphne's boyfriend.

Now she was unexpectedly overcome by the urge to correct the impression Paul had created. She didn't want Brad thinking erroneously that anything more than a friendship existed between her and Paul. Not ten minutes ago Brad had bared his soul to her when he'd described to her his worries about his parents. He had trusted her enough to share his deepest concerns with her. She couldn't deliberately mislead him.

But before she could say anything, Paul was talking again. "You're right, Brad, you're absolutely right. Plastered or stone-cold sober, I adore this lady." He slipped his arm around her narrow waist and pulled her to him. "Dorothy Parker had it wrong—men *do* make passes at girls who wear glasses."

"I'm a woman, not a girl," Daphne pointed out sternly.

"Don't complain, sweetheart. I got the gender right, didn't I?" He tasted his drink, grimaced, then leaned across the table to get the green plastic lime-juice container. He added a few drops to his drink, tasted it again, and nodded in satisfaction. "So, Brad, Daphne tells me you're in the market for a new house."

"She ought to know," Brad confirmed. "She's my realtor."

"She's the best," Paul swore.

Whatever her strategy might have been, she couldn't help thinking that Paul was laying on the compliments a little thick. She could tell by his tone that his exaggerated flattery was a result partly of his zany sense of humor and partly of the number of gin and tonics he'd consumed, but Brad couldn't know that. "Paul and I are just good friends," she informed him, realizing at once what a cliché that was.

"No truth to the rumor," Paul chimed in, embellishing the cliché. "We're just friends." He leaned forward confidentially and whispered, "More's the pity, Brad, given that she's dynamite in bed."

Daphne almost dropped her drink in embarrassment. Paul couldn't have realized that Brad was in a better position than anyone else to know how untrue Paul's flippant remark was. But if anyone knew how dreadful Daphne could be in bed, it was Brad.

Too many times after that ghastly night, Daphne had berated herself for her lack of skill and seductiveness. If only she'd been more experienced, more talented, more romantic, the incident wouldn't have been so horrible. It had been bad because *she'd* been bad. She hadn't been dynamite in bed—she'd been a dud.

Paul could have made such a silly, meaningless remark in front of anyone else and Daphne could have brushed it off with a laugh. But not in front of Brad. Not in front of the one man who knew from experience the extent of Daphne's wretchedness as a sex partner.

"Excuse me," she muttered, spinning on her heel and storming out of the kitchen. She hated herself for overreacting to Paul's teasing, but she couldn't bear to be in the same room as Brad. She couldn't bear the possibility that her eyes might accidentally meet his, and she'd see cruel laughter in his gaze, remembrance and mockery. She couldn't bear it.

So, once again, she ran away.

Chapter Five

Guilt, Brad concluded, was a peculiar affliction. Just when you were beginning to believe that it could be in full and permanent remission, it reared up again in a more virulent form.

Right now, he was feeling doubly guilty: guilty for what he'd done to Daphne eight years ago, and guilty for having thought that he no longer had any reason to feel guilty. Just because they had managed to spend a few more or less amicable days in each other's company while they looked at houses didn't mean Daphne had recovered from their disastrous interlude in his fraternity house bedroom. Just because he had felt extraordinarily comfortable with Daphne when she'd sought him out at the party last night—just because talking to her about his parents had boosted his spirits so much—didn't mean she had granted him absolution for his past actions.

He steered off the interstate at the Verona exit and braked to a stop at the end of the ramp. According to the directions Andrea had given him, Daphne's house was only a few minutes' drive from the exit. A few minutes wasn't nearly enough time for Brad to figure out what he'd say to Daphne when he saw her—assuming he did see her. Given the unseasonably balmy weather that afternoon, she could be out for the day, frolicking in the park she had driven past the first time he'd visited her office. Or she could be working; realtors sometimes met with clients or hosted "open houses" on Sundays. Or she could be out on a date with that boyfriend of hers.

That idiot boyfriend of hers, Brad amended, indignant on Daphne's behalf. The guy had the audacity to take her to a party, assert in front of witnesses that he was madly in love with her, and then make a crack about her performance in bed! Admittedly, what he'd said had been complimentary, but it had obviously embarrassed the hell out of Daphne. Such crass teasing might be excusable coming from a friend, but not from a lover.

Brad recognized that Daphne had been more than just embarrassed by her boyfriend's joke. The instant her gaze had intersected with Brad's across the kitchen, her cheeks had turned crimson and she'd fled from the room.

It was all Brad's fault, entirely his fault for having once made her feel inadequate in bed. *He'd* been the one who'd been inadequate, and she shouldn't ever, ever be embarrassed about her part in what had happened—or hadn't happened. That was what he'd come to Verona to tell her—if only he could figure out a way to put it into words without embarrassing them both even further.

A driver in a car behind him on the exit ramp honked his horn, jolting Brad's attention back to the road. He glanced at the sheet of paper on which Andrea had written the directions, turned right, and headed north toward Bloomfield Avenue.

Daphne's house sat on a small lot at the end of a winding side street. An ancient maple tree stood squarely on the front lawn, casting a massive shadow over the sloping roof of the house. In another era, the L-shaped brick-and-redwood ranch house, with its broad picture window and its attached two-car garage, might have been considered a modest middle-class dwelling. But nowadays, in this neighborhood, Brad estimated its worth at a quarter of a million dollars. Despite all the house hunting he'd done in the past week, he still found laughable the notion that he and his school friends could be living in houses with such astronomical price tags.

Daphne was kneeling in the grass beside the flower bed underneath the picture window, yanking weeds out of the dark, loamy soil. She had on an oversize shirt, blue jeans and sneakers; her hair was held back in a bandanna and her hands were protected by work gloves. Next to her on the grass was a small straw basket and a hand spade. She used a garden claw to loosen the weeds from the soil.

Brad coasted to a halt at the curb. Engrossed in her labor, Daphne didn't look up. He permitted himself a moment to admire the bright yellow daffodils and red tulips she'd cultivated before focusing fully on her.

The shirt she was wearing wasn't just large, he acknowledged—it was a man's dress shirt, with tails that fell to her knees and shoulder seams that drooped down her arms. She had rolled the sleeves up to her elbows and left the collar and the second button undone. The shirt made her look thinner than she was, a tiny, fragile creature all but lost within the voluminous garment.

He didn't want to think of Daphne as tiny and fragile. He wanted to think of her as strong, indomitable, the sort of woman likely to leave dozens of men with sentimental smiles spread across their faces as they reminisced about how dynamite she was in bed.

But he knew that wasn't the case. And, while he hated the idea, he suspected that his inept actions eight years ago were at least partly to blame.

He shoved open the car door, and the squeak of the hinge prompted Daphne to glance over her shoulder. Seeing Brad, she scowled, tossed the garden claw onto the grass, and stood, dusting the dirt from the knees of her jeans.

Praying for courage, he took a deep breath and started toward the front walk. "Hello, Daphne," he said quietly.

She continued to stare at him. The color in her cheeks was as high as it had been last night at the party, and although Brad wanted to believe that was a result of her physical exertions in her garden or the warm spring sunshine, he couldn't shake the comprehension that his presence was what was causing her to blush.

The sun glared on the lenses of her eyeglasses, making her eyes invisible to him. He wished she would move her head so he'd be able to see her eyes again, and perhaps to find in them a hint as to how she felt about his unexpected invasion of her private turf. If he was to be denied a view of her eyes, then he wished she would speak, giving him an opening so he'd know how to proceed.

But she did neither. She remained motionless, her hands encased in those huge work gloves, her lips pursed, her hair frizzing beneath the bandanna in the afternoon heat.

"We need to talk," he announced. He realized that he'd stated his request too bluntly, but her silence wasn't making this easy for him.

"Now?"

"Yes."

She turned and bent to study her flowers. Then she exhaled, tugged off her gloves, and dropped them into the basket. After gathering her tools and lifting the basket, she straightened up and shrugged.

Without a word, she headed around the side of the house. Brad followed. The back yard was spacious, blessed with several adult fruit trees and rimmed by dense evergreen hedges. An enclosed porch extended from the rear of the house. Brad trailed Daphne up the concrete steps to the porch and through the screen door.

While she placed her gardening equipment on a shelf in one corner, he stood idle, his patience beginning to unravel as he waited for her to say something. When Daphne moved toward the door leading into the house, he checked himself before chasing her inside. He had enough sense to recognize that she wouldn't want him in her home, and she confirmed his guess by waving toward one of the wrought-iron porch chairs which were placed around a matching glass-topped table. "Would you like something to drink?" she asked, reaching for the doorknob.

Brad supposed the situation might be more palatable if he were crocked. "What have you got?"

"Apple juice, o.j., ginger ale, iced tea..."

So much for getting crocked. "Iced tea sounds good."

She vanished into the house.

Brad settled himself on the chair and took a deep breath. The air here smelled much better than what he'd been inhaling in Manhattan. It was clean, fresh, fragrant with the scent of grass and flowers. At Eric's apartment, whenever you opened a window you were nearly knocked off your feet by the stench of automobile exhaust.

Maybe air pollution was what had driven Daphne to leave the party early last night, Brad thought hopefully.

He discarded that idea with an unvoiced curse. Daphne had left early for one reason only: because her nitwit boyfriend made a joke about her skill as a lover—in front of Brad.

She'd been drinking ginger ale at the party last night, he recollected. All sorts of booze had been available, but she'd imbibed ginger ale straight. She had avoided liquor the day she'd taken Brad out for lunch when he was house hunting, too. Maybe she was a teetotaler.

If she was...perhaps he was being paranoid, but it didn't seem unreasonable to assume that he was to blame for that, too. She'd been drinking the night of their encounter at the frat house. Everyone had been drinking, but Daphne had clearly been under the influence. Now she didn't touch alcohol—at least not when Brad was around. Maybe she wasn't actually a teetotaler, but simply was afraid to drink in Brad's presence.

Definitely paranoid. Brad sighed grimly.

Daphne returned to the porch with two tumblers of iced tea. She had taken off the bandanna and washed her face, and she didn't appear so flushed anymore. She set a glass down in front of Brad at the table, then moved to the opposite side of the table with her own glass. Brad eyed the two other chairs she might have chosen to sit in; obviously she wanted to sit as far as possible from him.

"Maybe I'm paranoid," he said aloud, deciding to share his self-diagnosis with her.

She arched her eyebrows slightly, then took a sip of her drink. "What makes you think that?"

"Well..." No, he wasn't going to waste his breath grilling her about why she'd chosen to sit on one particular chair instead of the others. He hadn't driven all this way on a beautiful Sunday afternoon to be evasive and cowardly. "You left the party awfully early last night," he noted.

Again, he wondered if he was being too blunt. If he was, Daphne seemed willing to accept his tone. She didn't even question his seeming non sequitur. "Did I miss anything exciting?" she asked.

He shrugged. "As far as I was concerned, the highlight of the party was the time I spent in the bedroom with you." He could tell by her startled expression that he'd expressed himself poorly, and he hastened to come up with a more tactful phrasing. "I mean talking with you, Daphne. It really felt good to talk to you about my mother."

She nodded again. "Paul and I would have stayed later, but he had an early day planned for today, and he wanted to get home before midnight."

She was lying. Even if Brad hadn't been able to tell by her shifting eyes and her fidgeting fingers, he would have known she was lying. He knew why she'd left early—and she knew he knew.

"We're going to have to talk about it," he resolved.

"Talk about what?" she asked, batting her eyes.

"You know damned well what." He was angry that she was forcing him to spell it out, but now that he'd gotten started, he wasn't going to back down. "The time we slept together."

Daphne pressed her lips into a straight, tense line and dropped her gaze to her glass. If she'd blushed before, now she appeared pale to him, clearly distraught. She took a bracing gulp of iced tea, then eyed Brad over the rim of her glass. "We didn't actually *sleep* together," she reminded him.

All right. She had acknowledged the subject. It existed for both of them; they wouldn't be able to retreat from it any longer. They were going to talk about it, talk it out, talk it through. They were going to clear the air and, if they both survived, establish a lasting truce.

"You're right," he conceded. "We didn't sleep together. That was a big part of the problem."

"Was it?" She laughed uneasily. "There were so many problems, Brad—I hardly think it matters whether or not we actually fell asleep."

"It did matter, Daphne," he argued. "It *does* matter. Can we talk about this?" he belatedly thought to ask.

Daphne laughed again, a little less nervously this time. "If you think it'll make a difference."

"God, I hope it will," he groaned. Then his gaze met Daphne's and he reluctantly joined her laughter. Last night, when he'd been keyed up about his parents, Daphne had gotten him to relax. Today, when he was twice as keyed up, she was getting him to relax again. He wondered if she was aware of how much he appreciated her knack for cheering him and calming him. "Daphne," he said, reaching across the table to take her hand, then thinking better of it and drumming his fingers against the glass surface. "Daphne, I still feel pretty lousy about that night. I know it's been a long time, and I'd always assumed—or at least hoped—that you'd forgotten all about it. But last night, when your boyfriend made that comment and you bolted—"

"He's not my boyfriend," Daphne corrected him.

Brad frowned. He had been sure the two were a couple. Brad's first impression of the guy had been less than positive, but he'd certainly seemed awfully affectionate toward Daphne. "What's wrong with him?" he asked, seeking an explanation for why a man who claimed to adore Daphne wasn't her lover. "Is he gay or something?"

"No." Daphne took a frustratingly long time to sip her iced tea. She lowered the glass, propped her feet up on an adjacent chair and folded her arms across her knees. "We tried dating for a while, but it fizzled out," she informed him. "We really are just good friends, and we've never been much more than that."

"Then why was he saying all those things, about how much he loves you?"

"That's his sense of humor, augmented by a few drinks," she explained, then reconsidered and added, "I guess he loves me as a pal. He was only kidding around last night. He couldn't have known you were the wrong audience to kid around in front of."

"He doesn't know about us?"

"*Us?*" Daphne scoffed. "One night notwithstanding, Brad, I'd hardly consider you and me an 'us.'"

"You know what I mean," Brad countered. It was suddenly vitally important to him to know who, besides himself and Daphne, might be aware of what a selfish creep he'd been with her back in college.

She allayed his fear. "I never told anyone," she said. "Did you?"

"Not a soul."

"Not even Eric?" At Brad's solemn shake of the head, she asked, "Why not?"

His laughter this time was derisive. "Do you think I want the word spreading around that I'm inadequate in bed? Do you think I'd want anyone—even my best friend—to know I botched it so badly a lady stormed out of my room teetering on the brink of tears? No, Daphne, that's not the sort of news I'd like publicized, thank you."

Daphne's eyes grew round, as if Brad's assessment of what had occurred was unfathomable to her. "*I'm* the one who botched it, Brad. *I'm* the one who was inadequate in bed.''

"No," Brad said firmly. "It was my fault, Daphne, and even if I'm about eight years overdue, I want to apologize. It was my fault. I did a terrible thing, taking advantage of you—"

"Taking advantage—!" Far from accepting his apology, she seemed ready to hurl her glass at his head. He'd never seen her so infuriated. She swung her feet down to the floor, shoved herself out of her chair, and marched to the end of the porch and back. When she reached the table, she planted her hands on its surface and bore down on him fiercely. "Let me tell you something, Brad: *I* was the one who engineered that little bit of stupidity. *I* was the one who went up to your room. You didn't gag me and tie me up and haul me over your shoulder. I went, voluntarily. I knew what we were going to do upstairs, and I went. So don't hand me that garbage about how you took advantage of me.''

Brad was dumbfounded. When he had tried to predict Daphne's reaction to his apology, he had anticipated that she might deny he was as big a louse as he claimed to be: "Oh, don't feel so bad, Brad, it's over and done with." Or she might agree totally with him: "You're right, what you did stank and you *should* be sorry." What he hadn't expected was that she'd fight with him over who deserved the bulk of the credit for the fiasco.

"Daphne," he said placatingly, wishing she would sit back down so they could talk reasonably. "Daphne, you were drunk at the time."

"So were you."

"Not as drunk as you were."

"Oh, yeah?"

He tried hard to maintain his equanimity under this latest assault of hers. "Daphne, given my body weight...given my higher tolerance for alcohol..." The hell with it. Why quibble? He hadn't been completely sober that night. If he had been, he would have done a better job of making love to her—or he wouldn't have made love to her at all.

She folded her arms across her chest, her expression oddly triumphant.

"Sit down," he ordered her. He couldn't organize his thoughts when she was so close to him, glowering down at him with those big green eyes of hers. "Sit down and let's straighten this thing out."

She glared at him for a moment longer, then begrudgingly complied, resuming her seat across the table from him. He scrutinized her, taking in the tangled blond mop of hair framing her face, the tautness around her lips, the two vertical lines pinched into her forehead above the bridge of her nose. There was something perversely funny about Daphne's inability to see that night for what it had really been, but he didn't dare to smile.

"Daphne," he said in his most ameliorating voice, "what I sense here is that you're letting some misplaced feminist sentiments cloud your memory."

"Who said anything about feminist sentiments?" she asked loftily. "You're the one making absurd claims about the ability of men to tolerate alcohol."

"Forget about the alcohol," he snapped. "What I'm talking about, Daphne, is taking responsibility for what happened. It was a college party. I brought you to my room. I plied you with wine—"

"I accepted the wine," she cut him off. "I could have refused it, but I accepted it and I drank it." She shook her head in amazement. "I can't believe you're saying this,

Brad. I approached you, remember? I invited myself up-stairs. It was my doing, my fault, and, yes, I take full re-sponsibility for it. I can't believe you think you did anything wrong."

"I can think of at least one thing I did horrendously," he muttered, cringing at his memory of the cold, bitter look she'd given him as his body had slid away from hers.

"That was my fault, too," she said softly, her rage spent. "Contrary to popular rumor, I'm *not* dynamite in bed."

"That's beside the point," he debated, although he was fast losing track of what the point was. "I should have satisfied you, and I failed."

"I failed, too," Daphne remarked. "I know, you're a man, so you must have been satisfied on a certain level, but—"

"It doesn't work that way, really," he said gently. He was overwhelmed by the sudden, desperate need to hold her, to make her see things the way they truly were. This time when he extended his arm across the table he com-pleted the gesture and clasped her hand with his. She didn't pull back, so he closed his fingers around hers and smiled pensively. "For a man, there's relief and there's ecstasy. Maybe what I felt at the time was relief—but that's not what satisfaction is all about. The ecstasy comes only if your partner is right there with you. If I'd done a better job of it, we both would have been satis-fied. As it turned out, neither of us was."

The corners of Daphne's lips twitched upward. "So, it was a *job*, was it?"

If she hadn't been wearing that mysterious smile, if she hadn't woven her fingers comfortingly through his, he would have thought she was being sarcastic. She wasn't, though. She was being ironic, which Brad considered a perfectly appropriate attitude under the circumstances. "Why did you approach me that night?" he asked, genuinely curious. It was one of the questions that had haunted him long after she'd stalked out of his room. "We hardly knew each other, Daff. Why me?"

"Oh, Brad..." She sighed, but her lips remained curved in that tenuous smile. "It's a long story."

"I'm all ears."

She sighed again. "Well, to start with...I was in a pretty bad mood that day," she told him. "I had just found out that the person I considered the love of my life was going to marry my sister."

"Your prom date?" The bastard! Brad erupted inwardly. One thing about Daphne—she sure knew how to pick losers. Her prom date left her for her own sister, her date at Eric's party made tasteless jokes at inopportune times...and Brad himself was probably the biggest loser of the bunch.

"Dennis was more than just a prom date, Brad. We'd known each other for years, and we'd..." She issued a shaky breath and abandoned the thought. "Anyway, when I found out he was going to marry Helen, I—I went a little crazy. That's not to imply that I didn't know what I was doing with you," she added quickly. "I did. I just—maybe I just stepped a little bit out of character."

"And you had too much to drink."

"I had too much to drink. But—"

"Why *me*?" he repeated. "The party was loaded with guys. Why did you pick me?"

"Because you were there?" she half asked, then shook her head. "I knew you, Brad. I knew who you were." That was hardly a sufficient reason, and as soon as Daphne saw his disgruntled look she acquiesced with another shake of her head. "I honestly don't know, Brad.

Maybe I sensed on some subliminal level that you were the sort of guy who wouldn't make my life hell afterward. You wouldn't be indiscreet. You wouldn't . . . you wouldn't laugh at me.''

He was moved by her statement. He'd been afraid that Daphne would justify her having selected him by saying something like, "You were cute," or "I thought you'd perform well." She hadn't, though. He didn't believe he was as decent as she seemed to think he was, but he wanted to believe it. Hearing her describe him in such kind terms filled him with a tender warmth.

Her eyes met his. "When I went to your room..." she murmured, then glanced away, as if she couldn't bear to look directly at him. "When I went to your room, Brad, it was only because I wanted to forget about Dennis. And that's about as rotten as you can get. I was the one taking advantage of you. So please don't tell me it was your fault.''

Daphne Stoltz taking advantage of him? No, it hadn't been like that at all. Brad had never viewed it that way, and he wasn't about to view it that way now. "Why don't you drink liquor anymore?" he inquired in an almost accusatory tone.

"Because I don't want to do anything that awful, ever again," she answered simply. "The liquor doesn't explain what I did, Brad, but I'm not going to run the risk of getting drunk and doing something so awful again. I just don't think it's worth taking that kind of chance.''

Brad tightened his grip on her. He felt the slender bones in her fingers, the tapering of her wrist. "It seems kind of ridiculous that I've spent all these years thinking I was to blame for the whole damned thing, and you've been busy thinking you were to blame.''

"Maybe we were both to blame," Daphne granted. "I'll tell you this, Brad—if I ever get my hands on a time machine, one thing I'm going to do is turn it back eight years and live that one night over again. I'd live it very differently, naturally."

"Amen," Brad agreed. Then he loosened his hold on her and grinned. "You'd refuse to go upstairs with me?"

Daphne appeared bemused. "Can you think of another way to make that night right?"

"Assuming you *did* come upstairs... I'd make love to you, instead of whatever the hell it was we did. I'd romance you, Daff. I'd make it as good as I could for you, so if you did make the mistake of coming to my room, you wouldn't regret it for years afterward."

She chuckled, aware that his words were underlined with humor. "Such altruism," she teased. "If you made it that good for me, it would be that much better for you."

"That's the way these things work," he confirmed, mirroring her grin. "Of course, I'd expect you to pitch in and do your part, too."

"Of course."

His smile faded as he regarded her. "Do you know what else I'd do if we were able to get hold of a time machine?" he continued, no longer joking. "I'd take it back to our senior year of school and spend more time talking to you. You're wonderful to talk to, Daff."

"Thank you."

"I mean it. Last night, when I started ranting and raving about my parents—"

"If that's your idea of ranting and raving, Brad, you're too suppressed. I thought we were having a pleasant chat."

"Okay. I'm a pleasant ranter," he allowed. "I didn't even tell Eric about the lunch I'd had with my mother. I wasn't going to tell anyone. But then you found me, and it seemed so easy to unburden myself to you.... I wasn't kidding when I told you that was the highlight of the party for me."

"I think it was the highlight for me, too," Daphne said. "I like talking to you, too, Brad."

He lifted his half-consumed glass of iced tea in a toast to Daphne, then drained it. He was feeling a lot better now than he'd felt when he left the city an hour ago. The fact was, he was feeling a lot better now than he'd felt in years. "When Andrea advised me to use you as my realtor," he confessed, "I wanted to run the other way. I thought it was going to be so awkward."

"It was," Daphne reminded him.

"At first," he granted. "But now I'm glad she pushed me into it." It elated him to realize that Daphne could be his friend—that she already *was* his friend.

He supposed that it was sometimes possible for a lover to evolve into a friend, but such a transition had never happened in his own life. He tended to choose his lovers for romance, not for friendship. He picked women who were beautiful and witty, who supplied one half of an ideal couple for which he was the other half. He selected women who had the potential to be for him what his mother was for his father—at least, what she had been for his father before their marriage began to falter: someone whose talents complemented his, whose background matched his, whose taste paralleled his.

He tended to choose friends, on the other hand, by his ability to talk comfortably with them. By that standard, Daphne Stoltz was without a doubt a fine friend.

Perhaps it wasn't so terribly surprising that she would be. He couldn't really consider her a former lover, at least not by any legitimate definition of the term. What had occurred between them so long ago had nothing to do with love.

What was occurring between them right now had everything to do with friendship. And Brad would gladly drink many, many iced-tea toasts to that.

I BET HE THINKS OF ME as a sister, Daphne contemplated as she pulled on an attractive short-sleeved sweater. When her head popped through the neck hole her curls burst out around her head like little yellow springs. She shook them loose, then tucked the hem of the sweater into the waistband of her slacks and fastened the fly. Fully clothed at last, she peeked out of her bedroom window, which overlooked the back yard.

Brad was standing next to the apple tree, shielding his eyes from the sun as he gazed up at the pinkish-white blossoms dotting the branches. Daphne followed his gaze. Perhaps if she were more diligent about spraying insecticide on her trees, she might be able to harvest a bumper crop of fruit in late September. While she wasn't a fanatical partisan when it came to insects, she had enough concern about the environment to avoid chemical warfare and instead share her tree's fruit with some of Mother Nature's lesser creatures.

She didn't want to think about insects, though. She wanted to think about the tall, dark man with the spring-sky blue eyes who had felt compelled to drive all the way to Verona to tell her he understood why she'd taken a powder last night. She wanted to think about how honest he'd been, how noble in claiming responsibility for something that wasn't his fault, how attuned he'd been to her feelings then and how sensitive he still was now.

She wanted to think about how much she enjoyed his company. Obviously, he enjoyed her company, too. He wouldn't have insisted that she change her clothes and spend the rest of the afternoon with him if he didn't want to be with her. He could have slapped himself on the back for having done his good deed, and then returned to the haven of Andrea's and Eric's apartment until his next house-hunting trip, which was scheduled for Wednesday afternoon.

But he'd been firm about her abandoning her perennials for the day: "Your garden looks great, Daff, so don't waste the rest of the afternoon on it. Go put on some clean clothes, and we'll check out that park downtown."

It wasn't a date or a come-on. Brad had absolutely no interest in Daphne as anything other than a pal. One more desirable man treating her like a sister, she thought with a sigh.

In truth, she wasn't bothered by the thought of having a brother-sister relationship with Brad, because she'd never been in love with him. She had loved Dennis, and she had come dangerously close to falling in love with Paul Costello, but she'd never even considered Brad someone she could love. He was *too* desirable: too good-looking, too wealthy, too polished. Too decent. Who else but an immeasurably decent man would have done what Brad had done today?

Turning from the window, she ran her brush through her hair a few times, grabbed her purse and left the bedroom. Brad was waiting for her by the back door. She locked up, then spun her key ring in search of her car key.

"I'll drive," he said.

"You don't know your way around here," she argued. "You'll get lost."

"You can keep me on course," he suggested. "If I'm
going to be moving here, I wouldn't mind getting a feel
for the community."

"Suit yourself," she said, accompanying him around
the house to the rented car parked at the curb.

Once they were both settled in the car, she gave him
perfunctory directions to the park. He pulled away from
the curb, shifted gears and tapped his fingers against the
steering wheel. "Whose shirt were you wearing?" he
asked.

Startled, Daphne glanced down at her sweater. "I'm
pretty sure it's mine," she said, bewildered.

He glanced toward the becoming peach-colored
sweater, then grinned and returned his gaze to the road.
"I mean before, when you were gardening. That man's
shirt."

He seemed to be fishing for personal information.
Given the deeply personal nature of their conversation on
her back porch, and the fact that he wouldn't learn anything particularly scintillating from the line of question-
ing he'd taken, she didn't object. "It was my father's,"
she answered. "He passes his shirts along to me once they
start fraying at the cuffs. I spend a lot of time doing
house repairs and gardening, and the shirts come in
handy."

Brad digested her answer, deep in thought. She hoped
he wasn't viewing her as her father did whenever he presented her with his old shirts: as a pitiful single lady who
didn't have a husband to grout the bathtub for her, or
prune the shrubs or change the screens in the storm
doors.

"Is it strange, living in a big house all by yourself?" Brad asked, hinting that perhaps he *had* been viewing her as a pitiful single lady.

"First of all, it's not such a big house," she answered, keeping her voice level. "Second, you've lived all by yourself, too. You should know just how strange it is."

"I've been living in an attached town house condominium," he corrected her. "That's different from a whole house, with your own four walls and your own grass to mow." He shot another quick glimpse at her, then grinned. "Frankly, whenever I think about moving into that house you showed me, it strikes me as weird. Me, all alone, with three different toilets to choose from."

"I admit that house is bigger than you need," she agreed. "But a larger house is usually a better investment than a smaller one—better resale value."

"Besides, those two and a half bathrooms will come in handy when I do business entertaining."

"Good point," Daphne agreed. "And maybe someday you'll get married and put a diaper pail in one of them."

Brad guffawed.

"Why did you ask me about the shirt?" Daphne asked, figuring that if he could be nosy, so could she.

His grin vanished, taking his dimples with it. "The truth?" he asked. "I was wondering whether you'd inherited the shirt from a boyfriend."

Brad's comment should have surprised her. That it didn't was itself surprising. "Why?" she asked, wondering why he was so interested in learning about the possible existence of a man in her life.

He mulled over his reply. "Andrea and Eric are married, Melanie and Steve Persky are married, Phyllis has that he-man plumber she's living with . . . and you go to parties with a guy who's just a friend of yours. Is it that you're just between lovers, Daff?''

Sure, she was between lovers. So what if the gap between one lover and the next spread across years? She wished she could come up with a sassy, lighthearted response to Brad's probing, but she couldn't. Not after she and he had been so honest with each other at her house. "I don't date much," she said blandly.

"Why not?"

"Why not you?" she challenged. "How come you're still single?"

Brad accepted her nosiness as she had accepted his—without complaint. "I came mighty close to getting married in Seattle."

"Oh? How close?"

"Close enough for me to ask her what size ring she wore." He lapsed into thought for a moment, then smiled wistfully. "Nancy and I were together for a long time, and we talked about marriage pretty frequently. She was a terrific lady—beautiful, cultured, well-educated . . ."

"And . . . ?"

"And it just didn't work out."

Daphne gazed across the seat at him. He was remarkably handsome in profile, his nose creating a sharp angle that balanced the rugged line of his jaw. She couldn't imagine why a woman wouldn't want to marry Brad.

"We fought all the time," he elaborated without prompting. Reflecting on what he'd said, he laughed. "Constantly. About everything. But . . . she was one terrific lady."

Daphne remembered what Midge, her fellow real-estate agent, had told Brad when he and Daphne had visited one of the houses Midge had a listing on. "In the inimitable words of my colleague, Midge, a nice young man like you ought to be able to find someone sooner or later."

"Ah, yes, I remember," he said with a nod. His dimples took hold again, and he eyed Daphne playfully. "Bless the woman's heart. I feel so much better about my prospects now. Isn't that the park up ahead?"

"Uh-huh. There's an empty space between the station wagon and the Samurai. Grab it before someone beats you to it. On a day as gorgeous as this, parking around here can be a real hassle."

Brad swerved into the empty spot, yanked the parking brake, and switched off the engine. "Come on, Daffy," he said as he climbed out. "This place is teeming with healthy-looking young people. Let's see if we can find ourselves some suitable spouses before sooner turns into later."

Daphne returned Brad's grin and opened her door. Watching his loose-limbed stride as he circled the car to help her out, she couldn't help thinking that, unlike her, he wouldn't have any difficulty finding himself one of those suitable spouses—sooner rather than later.

Chapter Six

It was unanimously decided that, while Indonesian food made for an interesting epicurean adventure, adventure wasn't really what Phyllis, Andrea and Daphne were looking for in their monthly luncheons. On the first Wednesday in May, they decided to congregate at a new café Andrea had heard about which was supposed to have tame cuisine and reasonable prices.

In Daphne's opinion, no salad costing twelve dollars, not even one featuring imported Belgian endive, fresh capers and Dijon mustard dressing, was reasonably priced. But she didn't care. She could worry about money in the future—and she undoubtedly would, once the euphoria wore off. Today, she was determined to be carefree about the practicalities.

During the train ride into Manhattan, she had considered sharing her good news with Andrea and Phyllis. But so far, she hadn't mentioned it. For one thing, it was still too new to her; she herself had only just received word that morning, when Bob Battinger had called her from the Montclair office. She wanted a chance to accustom herself to the situation before she started talking about it to others.

For another, Phyllis was jabbering nonstop on the subject of her relationship with Jim. Her diatribe had begun the moment the three women were seated in the restaurant. She had paused only long enough to order cocktails for herself and Andrea, and again, briefly, when their entrees were delivered to the table. But she was going great guns now, and Daphne wouldn't dare to interrupt her.

"Jealous! Can you believe it?" Phyllis huffed. "He says he's jealous because of the way I looked at Brad at the party. *Looked* mind you—that was all I did. So I said, 'God gave me two good eyes, and I have every intention of using them.' To which he said, 'God gave you a brain, and I don't see you using that very often.'"

"Leave him," Andrea advised. "Hand the jerk his walking papers and kiss him goodbye."

"It's not so simple," Phyllis argued, indulging in a melancholy sigh. "I do love him, you know. But just because I love him doesn't mean I can't look at Brad, does it? You're happily married, Andrea, and I bet you look at Brad all the time."

Andrea laughed. "To tell you the truth, I'm getting a little sick of looking at him. Next Monday is going to be the two-week anniversary of his arrival on our doorstep, and if he hasn't settled on a house by then, he's going to cash in his return ticket to Seattle. Why don't you sell him a house already, Daffy?"

"We're getting close," Daphne told her friends. "He's half the distance to making an offer on an expanded cape I showed him. As a matter of fact, I'm supposed to meet him at his office after lunch today, and we're going to drive back to New Jersey and check it out one more time. I'm doing my best, Andrea."

Andrea laughed again to reassure Daphne that she was only kidding. "I'm not all that sick of him, yet. He offered to move to a hotel after last weekend, but Eric and I said absolutely not. As house guests go, he's been terrific. Our apartment's neater than it's been in months, thanks to Brad. He's always picking the wet towels off the bathroom floor, he washes any dirty dishes he finds in the kitchen sink—"

"And he's something to look at," Phyllis broke in. She turned to Daphne. "I know Brad isn't your type, Daff, but don't you think he's something to look at?"

Daphne grinned and twirled her straw through her glass of club soda on the rocks. "Sure, he's something to look at. So is urban blight."

Phyllis scowled. "It's easy for you two to talk. You've both gotten to spend so much time with him since he came to New York. You've gotten to gaze into those bedroom eyes of his, and ogle his luscious body..."

"Especially his cute little buns," Andrea snorted. "Phyllis, if you want to make a move, make one. Dump Jim and go after Brad. What's stopping you?"

"I don't know." Phyllis sighed again and eyed Daphne dolefully. "I don't even know if I'd like Brad, if I ever got to know him. But he does seem to have a lot going for him. What do you think, Daff?"

Daphne meditated. Ever since Brad had visited her at her house Sunday afternoon, she'd been thinking about how very much he had going for him: the gallantry, however misguided, to have accepted full responsibility for her foolishness in college, the courage to force her and himself to confront their past, the sensitivity to believe that a man's satisfaction came primarily from satisfying his woman. That he picked up the bath towels and washed the dishes at Andrea's apartment was nice; that he had bedroom eyes and a good build was also nice. But when Daphne thought about Brad's most winning attributes, she thought about integrity. Decency. Honesty. The kinds of characteristics she looked for in a friend.

"I think," she said, remembering to answer Phyllis, "he's very sweet."

"Sweet!" Phyllis shuddered. "If he's sweet, I probably wouldn't like him at all."

An hour later, after a typical squabble over how to divvy up the restaurant bill, Daphne said goodbye to her friends and strolled east to Madison Avenue, where the New York office of Brad's firm was located. He had mentioned to her that he felt obliged to make more regular appearances at his new office; the people he would be working with there seemed to expect it, and he considered it good politics to show up every now and then. When Daphne had informed him about her plan to meet Phyllis and Andrea in the city on Wednesday, he had suggested that she meet him in his office afterward so they could drive back out to New Jersey together. It saved Daphne a return trip on the train, and she was looking forward to having Brad's company for the ride.

She was also looking forward to selling him a house. She had a gut feeling that he'd make his final decision on a house very soon, possibly that evening. Buying a house could be nerve-racking, but it was also exciting. Daphne was pleased to think that today might be the big day for Brad—and even more pleased to think that she'd play a part in it. She wanted him to buy himself a house, not so she could reap her commission, not so she could settle old scores or remedy old insecurities, but simply because she cared for him.

The afternoon was slightly overcast but warm. Tucking her purse securely between her elbow and her ribs, she dug her hands into the deep pockets of her loose-fitting blazer and strolled along the crowded sidewalk, whistling. Whistling wasn't something she ordinarily did, but today she felt as if her only options were to whistle or to fly—and flying, without benefit of an airplane, wasn't possible.

So she whistled: the theme from *Bridge on the River Kwai*, "Heigh-Ho, Heigh-Ho" from *Snow White and the Seven Dwarfs*, all the great classics of whistling she could think of. She was happy about more than just her imminent meeting with Brad, more than just the likelihood of selling him a house. She was whistling because she hadn't yet shared her good news with anyone. It was all hers, her own secret, and she reveled in it with a smugness bordering on greed.

Brad's office was located in a foreboding modern skyscraper with exposed steel girders and gray-tinted windows. She entered the gloomy lobby, scanned the directory until she found the name of his firm, and rode upstairs in the elevator.

She didn't know much about corporate head-hunting, but judging from the company's lavishly appointed reception area, she deduced that wowing potential clients was a significant part of the business strategy. The forest-green carpet was thick and plush, the walls were covered in wallpaper which, if not authentic raw silk, closely resembled the stuff, and the wall behind the receptionist's semicircular desk—which appeared to have been carved out of a solid block of ebony—held an enormous Jackson Pollack canvas. The receptionist appeared to be a refugee from a modeling agency; she was young, thin, impeccably made up and sporting an unspeakably modern hairdo that featured spikes pointing every which way.

Such a glamorous woman would look absurd working in the staid suburban offices of Horizon Realty, Daphne thought with a chuckle.

She crossed the reception area to the desk, her mid-heeled pumps sinking into the carpet with every step. "My name is Daphne Stoltz," she identified herself. "I'm supposed to meet Brad Torrance here." The receptionist offered her a practiced smile and signaled Brad on her intercom.

He entered the reception area several minutes later, slinging on his blazer as he marched toward Daphne in long, energetic strides. "You're not a minute too soon," he welcomed her, grabbing her arm and steering her briskly to the door. "Let's get out of here."

"What's going on?" she asked in bewilderment as they waited for an elevator.

Brad groaned. "I told those clowns that if they wanted, while I was in the office today, I could meet a few candidates for a new secretarial position. I mean, I was flattered that they were giving me a chance to voice my opinion. Next thing I know, they're parading fifteen Katie Gibbs graduates through my office and expecting me to do all the interviews. I thought they were going to screen the first round and narrow it down to a few finalists before they dragged me into it."

"Ah, the responsibilities of management," Daphne said with spurious sympathy. By the time she and Brad had reached the building's ground-floor lobby, she'd begun to whistle "I Whistle a Happy Tune" from *The King and I*.

Brad smoothed the collar of his hastily donned jacket, then eyed her suspiciously. "What are you doing?"

"Whistling," she answered. More than whistling, she was practically bouncing as she walked beside him down the block to the parking garage where he'd left his car.

Brad stared at her. A slow smile crept across his face as he fell victim to her contagious exuberance. When his curiosity finally got the better of him, he curled his fingers around her elbow and tugged her to a stop. "Okay, I'll bite. Why are you whistling?"

"Why shouldn't I be whistling?"

"Why shouldn't *you* be whistling?" he echoed, considering his answer. "Children are starving in Africa. We're destroying the ozone layer. Even as we speak, Daffy, Soviet submarines are patrolling the waters of the North Pole. Three good reasons, right off the top of my head."

Daphne laughed. "All right, I'll stop."

"Don't stop," Brad retorted, simultaneously amused and irritated by her unexplained good humor. "Just tell me why you're whistling."

"Oh, I don't know." Daphne approached the garage's cashier booth with Brad and waited as he slid his wallet from his hip pocket and presented the cashier with his ticket. "Now that you've got me thinking about the ozone layer, I'm all depressed."

Brad surrendered to a reluctant grin. "It's a silver Ford Escort," he told the cashier as he counted his change. Then he turned back to Daphne. "Come on, Daff, tell me. Did you sell that million-dollar estate in Saddle River?"

"Upper Saddle River," she informed him. "And I haven't sold it yet, although on Monday I got two requests for the video tape we filmed about it. But if you really want to know..." She deliberately dragged out the telling, partly to see how long Brad's patience would last and partly to come to terms with the fact that he was the very first person she was going to tell. "I've been offered a partnership in Horizon Realty."

"A partnership?"

"A full partnership in the company. One of the partners is retiring, and the other two invited me to buy out his share of the corporation."

Brad's blue eyes sparkled with delight. "Hey, that's great, Daphne," he said. "That's terrific!" Impulsively, he wrapped his arms around her and kissed her cheek.

Daphne returned his hug, then returned his kiss. It suddenly seemed marvelous to her that Brad was with her for this special occasion. Andrea and Phyllis were much closer friends, and yet they often seemed less than totally involved in the ups and downs of Daphne's life. *Oh, that's Daffy,* seemed to be their attitude. *Of course she's scored a professional coup. What do you expect? That's Daff for you, stable and safe and making her way through this world without any major crises.*

They would have been excited for her, of course. They would have cheered, raised their cocktails in a toast to her, congratulated her... and then resumed quarreling about what Phyllis ought to do with Jim.

But Brad's focus was solely on Daphne, his only apparent desire to share her joy. Andrea and Phyllis wouldn't have hugged Daphne, but Brad did—and it felt wonderful. His arms were strong, his embrace powered by the sheer delight he took in her good fortune. She felt flooded with warm emotion for him, an emotion much more intense than what she'd felt the night he had taken her to bed.

Shocked by that realization—shocked that in the middle of an effusively friendly embrace she could think about Brad in sexual terms—she relaxed her hold on him.

As her hands fell from his shoulders she comprehended how acutely conscious she was of their awesome sturdiness, and as she took a discreet step back from him she acknowledged how delicious his lean male body had felt against hers. As he released her, she suffered an inexplicable stab of loss.

One couldn't lose what one had never had in the first place, she reminded herself, trying to expunge her memory of his light kiss. Thinking of Brad as a man wasn't safe; weren't Phyllis and Andrea always saying that Daphne preferred safety?

"There's your car," she mumbled as one of the attendants cruised up the ramp in the silver Ford.

If Brad noticed the alteration in Daphne's mood, he didn't comment on it. He opened the passenger door for her, then climbed in behind the wheel and merged with the traffic on the street. "Now tell me more about this partnership offer," he urged her, using a stop at a red light to remove his jacket and toss it into the back seat. He managed to loosen his tie and unbutton the cuffs of his shirtsleeves before the light turned green again. "When did you find out?"

"This morning. Mr. Battinger called—I mean, Bob—" Daphne laughed faintly. "I guess I can stop thinking of him as Mr. Battinger now, if I'm going to be his equal in the firm." Talking about the partnership offer was certainly much less perilous than thinking about how good Brad's arms had felt around her. She hoped she and Brad could talk about business until they reached the house he was considering buying, and then they could talk about that, and by the time they'd run that topic into the ground, Daphne wouldn't have to worry anymore about reliving the sensation of Brad's lips brushing her cheek.

"There are three partners, you said?"

Daphne nodded. "Three male partners, the youngest of whom is in his late fifties. I'm going to fit right in," she concluded with a dry laugh.

"Obviously they think you will," Brad pointed out. "Partnership decisions aren't made frivolously, Daff. I'd give my eye teeth to be offered a partnership at my company."

"It'll happen to you, too, someday," Daphne assured him. "Maybe even before you start losing your teeth." She took some small pleasure in the thought that even though Brad had fantastic looks, affluence and beautiful women like Phyllis fawning all over him, he didn't have a partnership offer—and Daphne did.

Brad accepted her mild teasing without complaint. "Okay. I want to hear all the details. What did the guy say when he called you?"

Daphne smiled. She couldn't imagine Phyllis and Andrea grilling her about the minutiae of her conversation with Bob. Yet Brad's interest in her success didn't seem forced. Once more she contemplated how right it was for her to have shared her news with him first, rather than anyone else. "Bob asked me to drive over to the Montclair office to discuss some important business. I went over, and there were all three partners. Mr. Hayes—Gerald—had a heart attack a few months ago, and all the office managers had been informed that he was thinking about retiring. Well, the three of them told me they'd talked it over and decided that they wanted me to take his place. I'm still kind of stunned."

"How are the finances going to work out?" Brad asked.

Daphne resisted the temptation to chide him for raising that particular question. That the company was successful was what made the partnership something worth having—but it was also what made buying in so expensive. Daphne had resolved that she wouldn't even think about how she was going to pay for Hayes's partnership share until tomorrow. Today, all she wanted to do was savor the idea of it, to wrap herself up in the flattering pleasure of it.

"They'll work out somehow," she said vaguely. "I haven't gone to work on it with my calculator, yet, but I'll figure out a way to pay for it, somehow."

"I'm so happy for you, Daff," Brad murmured, weaving from lane to lane as he approached the entrance to the Lincoln Tunnel. "What have you got planned for tonight? How are you going to celebrate?"

The car entered the cavelike darkness of the tunnel. Daphne squinted until her eyes adjusted to the murky yellow lights lining the tunnel. They illuminated Brad's face in a flickering amber pulse. Somehow, in this dark, echoing world, she found herself thinking again of the swift, reflexive hug he'd given her, and the graze of his lips across her cheek. It wasn't love she was thinking about, but something else, something akin to celebration.

When Brad had kissed her eight years ago, the occasion had called for whatever was the exact opposite of celebration. Mourning? she wondered. Misery? She ought to associate erotic thoughts of Brad with that dismal incident.

She ought to avoid having any erotic thoughts of Brad altogether. Surely he hadn't had any erotic thoughts of her when he'd hugged her. Just because the strobelike yellow lights kept throwing his handsome face into stark relief didn't mean Daphne had to respond to his extraordinary good looks.

"I haven't given much thought to celebrating," she allowed, realizing that he was waiting for an answer. "I guess when I get home from work, I'll break open a bottle of apple juice and live it up. Maybe I'll even whistle some more."

Brad issued an exaggerated yawn. "You're really aiming to break a few laws, Daff, aren't you," he droned. The car emerged into the glaring daylight on the New Jersey side of the Hudson, and Daphne squinted again. "I've got a better idea," he suggested, cruising around the ramp to the highway.

"Better than apple juice and whistling?"

"I'll take you out to dinner."

"You don't have to do that," Daphne said quickly.

"If I *had* to, I wouldn't want to. How about it, Daff? We'll check out the house one last time, and then stuff our faces." He shot her a swift glance, then turned back to the road and grinned. "Let's go someplace fattening. Do you like Italian food?"

Daphne loved it. She also shunned it whenever possible. "If I merely mouth the word spaghetti I gain three pounds. Oh, no!" she moaned, pressing her hands against her abdomen. "I said it! I can already feel the pounds swelling up inside me."

"That settles it," Brad said decisively. "Spaghetti, garlic bread, and zabaglione for dessert. You could use a couple of pounds, Daffy."

"A couple, maybe. Three, no."

Brad shot her another brief look, then laughed confidently. Daphne could tell, by reading his resolute expression, that her waistline was doomed.

A half hour later, they arrived at the house. It was deserted; the owner had been transferred to Boston, and he'd had to move before he could sell the place. Between

Daphne and a next-door neighbor, however, the property was well tended. Daphne had hired a lawn care company to keep the yard in pristine order, and she'd placed a few lamps on timers inside the house so it wouldn't look dark and abandoned at night.

Brad waited for her to unlock the front door, and they entered together. She lingered in the entry, allowing him to wander through the first-floor rooms by himself.

The owner had left the carpet in the living and dining rooms, but once Brad entered the kitchen Daphne was able to hear his footsteps clearly. Unable to see him, she pictured his long legs carrying him to the sink, to the stove, to the back door and out to the porch. Even though her eyes were aimed at the recently painted newel post at the bottom of the stairs, her mind focused on a picture of the tailored slacks Brad had on, the cotton shirt with the rolled-up sleeves, the dangling necktie. The strong arms that had nearly lifted her off her feet in his enthusiasm. The dimpled smile, the even white teeth. The striking blue eyes gazing out from that darkly tanned face.

She had always known that he was attractive. But why, when she and Brad had finally made their peace with that ghastly interlude in their past, did Daphne suddenly discover herself dwelling on how desirable he was, and how exciting it would be for such a desirable man to think of her as something other than a sister?

Maybe she ought to start whistling again.

She was halfway through the "Star-Spangled Banner," and well beyond the paltry one-octave range of her whistle, when Brad returned to the entry. "That's it for down here," he said. "Let's go upstairs."

She would have let him go upstairs himself, but it was obvious that he wanted her with him. She led him up the stairway to the second floor.

"What's the asking price?" Brad questioned her as they ascended, even though he knew very well what it was.

"Two hundred fifty-nine nine," she quoted.

Brad followed her into the master bedroom. Like the two smaller bedrooms, it was built under the eaves, with the ceiling sloping on either side of the full-shed dormer. Only at the edges of the room did Brad have to bend to prevent himself from bumping his head. "How much play is there in that price?" he inquired.

Daphne knew this routine well. It came with almost every purchase of a house, and she enjoyed the give-and-take of the final negotiations. She viewed such negotiations as a cross between chess and poker—mostly skill, but with a varying amount of luck and bluff involved. "What are you thinking of offering?" she asked.

Brad peered out the side window. "Two thirty?" he suggested.

"Try a lower starting offer," Daphne counseled him. "I think you could get it for under two forty. Offer two twenty."

"I've got to get back to Seattle," Brad pointed out, spinning around. "I'm supposed to be back there next week. I haven't got time to play games with the seller. I want to settle this thing fast."

"I'll negotiate on your behalf," said Daphne. "I'm your broker, Brad. If you're sure in your mind that this is the house you want, I'll get it for you at the lowest price I can."

"But you're *his* broker, too," Brad noted. "Whose interests are you going to be representing in the negotiation, his or mine?"

"Both," Daphne assured him, not at all disturbed by his mildly suspicious attitude. "He's got a valuable property here, but he's paying two mortgages and he's anxious to get rid of one of them. He'll get a fair price, and so will you. Trust me."

Brad leaned his hips against the windowsill and scrutinized her. His smile spread slowly across his face again, lazy and dimpled, and he folded his arms over his chest. "Do you really think I should trust you, Daff? You're a hotshot wheeler-dealer. A bunch of middle-aged male partners don't invite just any thirty-year-old female upstart to become a partner. They invite the sharpest, shrewdest person they can get their hands on. Maybe I shouldn't trust you for a minute."

Daphne knew Brad was teasing her, but she was reassured by the humor in his tone. "You've got to trust me," she reminded him, grinning. "We're friends."

Brad weighed her assertion, then nodded in acceptance. "I suppose if you can't trust your friends, you're in pretty bad shape." He shoved away from the sill and slammed his head into the angled ceiling. "Ow!"

Daphne tried unsuccessfully to stifle a laugh as she hurried across the room to his aid. "If you really want to live here, Brad, you're going to have to watch your step."

He grunted and rubbed the crown of his head. "Tell me about it," he muttered.

She pushed his hand away, wove her fingertips through the soft dark strands of his hair and felt carefully along his skull in search of a lump. "Are you seeing stars?" she asked solicitously. "Double vision?"

"If you're asking me whether I've given myself a concussion, I think the answer is no," Brad assured her, tilting his head to accommodate her gently probing hand. "But if you want to pretend I'm seriously injured so you can pamper me, be my guest. I'll start with a stiff drink, and then maybe a hot bath..."

"If I found a bump, I'd bring you an ice pack," Daphne said brusquely, pulling away her hand. "That's about the limit of my nursing talent. I'm not very good at pampering people."

He smiled. "You definitely don't seem like the pampering type," he agreed, shaking off the last of his pain. "I don't like being pampered much, anyway." He peered up at the angled ceiling and snorted. "I ought to be able to handle low ceilings. I've had some experience living in attic rooms."

Daphne knew where he'd gotten that experience: in college, in his fraternity house, in his top-floor bedroom. She'd been there; she'd seen the ceiling.

Her immediate instinct was to avoid looking at him. But he was standing too close to her, with the slope of the ceiling behind her denying her the space to back away from him. She couldn't prevent herself from meeting his knowing gaze.

"You still feel funny about it, don't you," he murmured, not bothering to spell out what was on both their minds. Not having to.

"Do you?"

"Yes." He ran his index finger along the edge of her jaw. Despite the tenderness of his caress, Daphne sensed that he was holding her chin to keep her from averting her eyes. "Maybe apologizing to each other wasn't enough."

"I don't know what else we can do," Daphne whispered.

He smiled crookedly. "Find ourselves a time machine?" he suggested.

Although his hand was the only part of him touching her, she was once again uncomfortably aware of his body's nearness. In the enclosed space of the bedroom she could feel his warmth, smell the faint traces of his after-shave, see the individual black lashes fringing his eyelids. And she could detect no answering awareness on his part.

"If you really want to go back in time," she joked, desperate to lighten the moment, "then let's go eat some Italian food. Maybe I can gain back my 'freshman twenty.'"

"I wouldn't let you do that," Brad argued, sliding his finger under her chin and down to the delicate gold chain circling her throat. He let his hand drop and started toward the door. "Three pounds maximum, Daffy, or there's no zabaglione for you."

IT DIDN'T SEEM FAIR to him. She was so damned right in so many ways. Her professional achievements were dazzling, her flair for selling houses impressive. She was smart and funny; he truly enjoyed her company. Jokes about her weight notwithstanding, she had a good figure, a bit scant in the chest area but basically well proportioned and healthy looking.

So why was it that he could stroke the smooth, clear skin of her face and feel nothing more than a tremendous affection stirring inside him? Why was it that he could gather her into his arms and hug her, even kiss her, and not feel all the usual responses? He didn't want to think some residual guilt was dampening his libido. But if that wasn't the problem, what could it be?

The obvious one; she was homely. No matter how tastefully she dressed, no matter how poised and pleasantly she behaved, she still had a plain face, half concealed by those distorting eyeglasses. She had a button nose, pale lips, nearly invisible eyelashes and kinky hair. She had a collection of features which, while far from grotesque, simply didn't work any magic on Brad.

Objectively, he was willing to concede that Daphne did the most with what she had. He was willing to concede, as well, that some men might find her cute and appealing in an eccentric way. Subjectively, he was willing to accept that he liked her a great deal. But she wasn't the kind of woman who could ignite fires within him, who could drive him to distraction with her feminine charms, who could reduce him to a seething sense of yearning with a smile and a wink.

She was a lovely woman, but Brad didn't love her. He was saving his love for the right woman, the perfect partner. And Daphne wasn't it.

He studied her across the small circular table at the rear of the restaurant's dining room. A candle encased in a cut-crystal glass lit the table, and its dancing flame threw ethereal shadows across Daphne's cheeks and brow. Maybe it *was* guilt, Brad thought, because even if he wasn't able to fall in love with her, he ought to be able to feel something more than what he was feeling for her.

She shook her head to refuse the cloth-lined basket of bread he extended to her, then asked, "How is your mother faring?"

"She's feeling very sorry for herself at the moment. My father has begun making noises about wanting to date a widowed neighbor of his."

"If I were your mother, I'd feel sorry for myself, too," Daphne defended Brad's mother. "Expressing a desire to take out other women isn't exactly a sign that your father's ready for a reconciliation.''

"That's exactly what he's ready for," Brad maintained, not really expecting Daphne to understand the convoluted dynamics of his parents' relationship. "He wants to make my mother jealous so she'll beg him to come back to her. She's feeling sorry for herself, but she's too proud to beg.''

"Speaking of jealousy," Daphne remarked with deceptive casualness, "how would you feel if I told you you might be a home breaker?''

"Me?" Brad froze in shock, his butter knife in midair. "What are you talking about?''

"Phyllis Dunn likes looking at you. Her Significant Other is apparently quite ticked off about it.''

"She likes *looking* at me?" Brad laughed. He recalled enough about Phyllis's muscular boyfriend not to want to be on the man's enemies list, but looking had never done anyone any harm. Phyllis hadn't been so horrible to look at, herself.

"I think she's searching for an excuse to end her affair with him," Daphne stated. "And I think you're the excuse she's looking for. Consider yourself forewarned.''

Brad shook his head and finished buttering his bread. As pretty as Phyllis Dunn was, he couldn't imagine relaxing over dinner with her the way he was right now with Daphne. Touching Phyllis's face would probably get his juices flowing in a way touching Daphne's hadn't . . . but he was honestly glad to be with Daphne. Much to his amazement, he didn't want his juices flowing at the moment. All he wanted was the unique enjoyment he experienced in dining with a good friend.

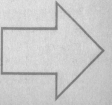

NO COST! NO OBLIGATION!
NO PURCHASE NECESSARY!

PLAY "LUCKY 7"
AND GET AS MANY AS SIX FREE GIFTS...

HOW TO PLAY:

1. With a coin, carefully scratch off the three silver boxes at the right. This makes you eligible to receive one or more free books, and possibly other gifts, depending on what is revealed beneath the scratch-off area.

2. You'll receive brand-new Harlequin American Romance® novels, never before published. When you return this card, we'll send you the books and gifts you qualify for absolutely free!

3. And, a month later, we'll send you 4 additional novels to read and enjoy. If you decide to keep them, you'll pay only $2.49 per book, a savings of 26¢ per book. There is no extra charge for postage and handling. There are no hidden extras.

4. We'll also send you additional free gifts from time to time, as well as our newsletter.

5. You must be completely satisfied, or you may return a shipment of books and cancel at any time.

FREE—digital watch and matching pen

You'll love your new LCD quartz digital watch with its genuine leather strap. And the slim matching pen is perfect for writing that special person. Both are yours FREE as our gift of love.

PLAY "LUCKY 7"

Just scratch off the three silver boxes with a coin.
Then check below to see which gifts you get.

YES! I have scratched off the silver boxes. Please send me all the gifts for which I qualify. I understand I am under no obligation to purchase any books, as explained on the opposite page.

154 CIH NBDY

NAME

ADDRESS   APT

CITY   STATE   ZIP

7	7	7	WORTH FOUR FREE BOOKS, FREE PEN AND WATCH SET AND FREE SURPRISE GIFT.
🍒	🍒	🍒	WORTH FOUR FREE BOOKS AND FREE PEN AND WATCH SET
●	●	●	WORTH FOUR FREE BOOKS
🔔	🔔	🍒	WORTH TWO FREE BOOKS

DETACH AND MAIL CARD TODAY

Their entrees arrived, and Brad noted with satisfaction that after blanketing her pasta in grated parmesan, Daphne dug into her high-calorie meal with gusto. Having spent the past couple of weeks with her, he could no longer remember how she'd looked when she was overweight. She really wasn't so bad looking, she really wasn't ...

Damn. It *was* guilt. Opening his soul to her last Sunday had helped, but it hadn't completely cured him. If he was ever going to recover from the disaster that blemished his past with Daphne, he was going to have to take more drastic measures. Especially since he was on the verge of becoming her neighbor.

He wasn't sure exactly when he'd made his mind up about the house, but now, sitting with Daphne in this quaint, unpretentious *ristorante* in Caldwell, he realized that he was already beginning to think of the region as his home. Assuming that Daphne was right about the seller's willingness to come down in price, Brad would buy the house. Hell, he'd probably buy it even if the seller didn't come down in price. In that price range, what was twenty thousand dollars one way or the other?

He liked it here. He liked this suburban village with its twisting, tree-lined roads and gentle hills. He liked the house itself, with its efficiently arranged kitchen and attractive yard. The house needed a little work—fresh paint on the porch, a new lighting fixture in the dining room— but nothing he couldn't handle. And he even liked the low ceilings. So what if he ran the risk of banging his head every now and then? Brad had never been averse to living dangerously.

He especially liked the notion of having Daphne living nearby. He could imagine asking her for advice about what flowers to plant in his flower beds, which supermarket to shop at, which trains ran closest to schedule. He liked the idea that he could call her up and talk to her whenever he wanted.

Except for the guilt, except for the awkward understanding that still existed between them. He had seen it in her flat green eyes when she'd stood beside him under the eaves in the bedroom he was already starting to think of as his. The air between them had grown electric, tense with something that approximated sheer panic, at least on his part.

He wanted to make it better. He wanted to make it go away.

All he needed was a time machine.

Chapter Seven

The elevator door slid open, and Brad found himself face-to-face with his father.

The two of them sprang back from each other in shock. But when the elevator door started to slide shut, Roger Torrance regained his bearings quickly enough to press the Door Open button and escape into the sumptuously decorated lobby of the Upper East Side apartment before the elevator whisked him away again. He smiled tensely, evened his tailored flannel blazer across his shoulders with a slight shrug, and said, "Dining with your mother, I take it?"

Brad had arrived at his mother's apartment building from the office, where he'd wasted the better part of the afternoon pretending he cared one way or the other regarding the selection of the new secretary and trying not to be too obvious about the fact that he was waiting for word from Daphne. She was supposed to have contacted the owner of the expanded cape that morning to make an offer on Brad's behalf—an offer that seemed insultingly low to him—and she had promised that she would call Brad with the seller's counteroffer, assuming the guy wasn't so offended by Brad's bid that he was unwilling to make one. But Brad's extension had never rung. Now he

was stuck fulfilling a dinner obligation to his mother,
during which he would continue to be distracted by
thoughts about whether or not he was going to be able to
buy the damned house and make use of his return ticket
to Seattle on the following Monday.

He was scarcely prepared for the onerous task of being
charming with his mother all evening; to see his father
emerging from the elevator left Brad at a complete loss.
When he didn't speak, his father filled the silence by
mumbling, "I stopped by the apartment to pick up a few
items, that's all."

Given his father's empty-handedness, Brad felt safe in
assuming that Roger was lying. Judging by the tousled
state of the older man's thick, silver hair and the lingering gleam in his blue eyes, Brad had a pretty clear idea of
what his father and mother had been doing together that
afternoon—and it wasn't picking up items.

He was elated. If his parents were willing to recognize
their compatibility in bed, they ought to be willing to
recognize the even more obvious truth that they belonged together. "Dad," he said, trying to sound calm
and impartial, "you don't have to pretend you and Mom
aren't still in love. You are, and I think it's great."

"Did your mother tell you we're in love?" Roger asked
indignantly. "If she did, I can assure you that she was
speaking for herself and not for me."

What a pair of stubborn fools, Brad thought with wry
amusement. His mother would never admit that she still
loved his father, either. If only they would stand side by
side in front of a mirror, they'd see the love emanating
from their own eyes—and from each other's. "Why can't
you two just sit down and work it out?" Brad asked with
what he considered supreme sensibility. "Why can't you
air your differences and admit that they aren't serious

enough to destroy your marriage? Why do you feel you're better off apart?''

Brad's father exhaled. He moved to the gold-veined mirror adorning one entire wall of the lobby, but what he saw in his reflection apparently wasn't love—it was a crooked necktie. He adjusted the knot, then turned back to Brad. ''I wish I could tell you that it's none of your business, Brad. But since you're our only child, I don't suppose I can fairly say such a thing. However, you'll just have to take your mother's and my word for it that we're pursuing the course that's best for us.''

''Even though you're still...?'' Unable to think of a tactful way to mention his parents' ongoing physical relationship, Brad tapered off and glanced toward the elevator from which his father had just emerged.

''Sex isn't everything,'' his father retorted dryly.

''It's a hell of a lot.''

Roger meditated for a moment. ''Your mother and I aren't divorced, Brad, and we happen to be ethical people. We aren't about to engage in extramarital affairs. Once our situation is legitimately finalized, I'm sure we'll both find other...outlets for our particular needs,'' he concluded.

''Outlets? Needs?'' Now it was Brad's turn to be indignant. ''Come on, Dad. After you and Mom spend one of these afternoons together, don't you feel close to each other? Don't you feel anything at all for each other besides animosity?''

Roger contemplated the question, then offered a grudging smile. ''I suppose we wouldn't bother at all with these occasional...afternoons,'' he said euphemistically, ''if we didn't feel something bordering on pleasant. I imagine that such pleasant memories help to make our separation less acrimonious. Your mother and I don't wish to hate each other, Brad—and an afternoon like this one does wonders on that account.'' He checked his tie in the mirror one last time, fidgeting with the knot even though it looked fine to Brad. ''Beyond that,'' Roger concluded, ''I have nothing to say on the subject.'' He smoothed his collar, then headed briskly toward the door, giving the doorman a perfunctory nod on his way outside.

Brad chased his father as far as the doorway and watched through the glass until Roger turned the corner and was absorbed by a throng of pedestrians on Park Avenue. Sighing, Brad turned away, walked back to the elevator, and wondered all over again why his parents insisted on being so damnably obstinate about their relationship.

In less than two minutes, he was upstairs, ringing the doorbell of the twentieth-floor apartment where his mother lived, and where he himself had spent the first eighteen years of his life. When his mother answered, her appearance revealed no hint of what she'd recently been up to with her estranged husband. Her white-streaked black hair was impeccably coiffed, her face carefully made up, her apparel staid and her tasteful jewelry in place. Penelope Torrance's usually expressive gray eyes, unlike her husband's, were totally emotionless, lacking any residual glow of passion.

''Hello, Brad,'' she greeted him placidly, brushing a maternal kiss across his cheek and ushering him into the apartment. Her nondescript welcome informed him that, even though she had to be able to guess that Brad had run into his father downstairs, she had no intention of mentioning his father's visit, let alone discussing what it did or didn't mean.

Brad dutifully followed her lead. If he was going to convince her to get back together with his father, he'd have to do it without mentioning the romantic interlude they'd just indulged in.

Almost as soon as Brad and his mother entered the living room, his mother's housekeeper appeared, carrying a crystal pitcher of martinis and two matching glasses. Brad didn't care much for martinis, but he accepted the cocktail Grace poured for him, offered his mother a silent toast... and thought about Daphne.

What shook him was not simply that she'd barged in on his thoughts when he hadn't expected it, but that he was thinking of her in the context of drinking. He wondered what would happen if he ever brought her to his mother's house for dinner. Penelope always insisted on serving martinis before dinner; it was a ritual about which she brooked no argument. Would Daphne accept a drink she didn't want for the sake of good manners, or would she politely refuse the drink, claiming that she never touched alcohol? How did teetotalers cope with social gatherings?

He probably shouldn't feel guilty about having driven Daphne to abstinence. For all he knew, he might have done her a big favor. But still... he would have preferred if he hadn't been the one to teach her, through wretched experience, what sort of scrape a woman could get into when she drank too much.

He realized that his mother was speaking, and he forced his attention to her. At the age of fifty-seven, Penelope Torrance boasted a fetching beauty. Her face was unlined, her throat sleek, her figure as lissome as a teenager's. Brad doubted that his mother had ever gained the "freshman twenty" during her years at Vassar.

"Brad, where are you? I'm talking to you," she scolded before sipping from her glass.

"Sorry."

"I was saying," she went on, "that this house you're planning to purchase sounds abysmal. I understand the time pressures you're facing, and your desire to return to Seattle next week—but that doesn't mean you've got to rush into such a major commitment. You're more than welcome to stay here with me until you find the house of your dreams."

"I've already found the house of my dreams," Brad said, surprising himself. He'd never viewed the expanded cape in Verona as the stuff of dreams—but now that his mother had mentioned it, he believed that maybe it *was* something of a dream house for him.

The apartment he was in right now didn't fit his image of a dream residence, even though he'd grown up there. Few of the furnishings had changed since his childhood. Several knickknacks had been rearranged, the torch lamps on either side of the sofa were a recent touch, but for the most part the decor had a certain nostalgic familiarity to it. He remembered spending hours constructing cabins with his Lincoln Logs on the plushly patterned Oriental carpet; he remembered devouring Mark Twain novels and chocolate-chip cookies on the couch—until Grace ordered him off with the admonition that he was getting crumbs all over the upholstery. He remembered gazing down through the window at the island of grass and flowers separating the northbound and southbound lanes of Park Avenue, and wishing he lived in a house with a yard.

Now, finally—if Daphne didn't blow it—that wish might come true. He might get his house and his yard, his flower beds and his tree-framed views of the sky. It was possible to make amends for the past, after all. It was possible, if one was willing to put forth the necessary effort, to compensate for the shortcomings of one's history, to overcome one's mistakes and disappointments, and put things the way they ought to be.

If only he could convince his parents of that, perhaps they'd work harder to repair their relationship, not just for sex but for love, for the sake of their marriage. Perhaps they could journey backward to the point where everything started to go wrong for them and do it over again, properly this time. If an afternoon of lovemaking could erase the hatred and the resentment, why couldn't it rekindle the love? Why couldn't it at least nourish the friendship?

THE SHRILL RING of the telephone jolted Daphne awake. As she cursed and groped blindly for the receiver, her brain staggered toward consciousness. Once her hand landed on the phone, she opened her eyes. Through a blur of sleepiness and myopia, she read the digits on the alarm clock next to the phone: one-one-two-eight. She cursed again, then lifted the receiver to her ear. "What?" she growled.

"Daphne, it's Brad. I just got back to Eric's apartment, and Andrea left me a note on the kitchen table, saying that you called. I'm sorry for getting back to you so late, but—"

"Oh." Daphne struggled into a sitting position and shoved a heavy tangle of blond curls back from her face. "Oh. Yeah." She knew she was communicating less than coherently, but there wasn't much she could do about it except wait until her brain clarified itself. After a minute, feeling semilucid, she managed to say, "Hello, Brad."

"I had dinner at my mother's this evening," he went on, his gabbiness giving her an opportunity to wake up more completely. "I had hoped to get back here earlier, but my mother was on a tear. All I did was say something about what a fine couple she and my father make, and she was off and running. For three hours I had to sit there, listening to a blow-by-blow description of every argument they'd ever had, every trivial disagreement, starting with whether to hold their wedding reception at the Pierre or the Plaza, on through whether they should have named me Brad Michael or Brad Roger, whether I should have gone to Collegiate as a day student or Exeter as a boarder, whether they should have bought a vacation house in the Hamptons or the North Fork... To go by what my mother said, there was not a single moment in their entire wedded life when they weren't at each other's throats."

At first, Daphne was nonplussed. When she'd left a message with Andrea to have Brad call her, she had presumed that he would be anxious to learn the outcome of her negotiations with the owner of the house he wanted to buy. Instead, all he wanted to do, apparently, was vent some steam about his mother.

That was all right with Daphne. If it made Brad feel better to talk to her about his mother, she had no objections. "Maybe her memory is more accurate than yours," Daphne suggested. "Or maybe she and your father tried to shelter you from their fighting when you were younger, so you were never really aware of it."

"I was always aware that they had their ups and downs," Brad insisted. "They never hid their arguments from me. But so what? People can disagree constantly with each other and still make a perfect couple. My parents belong together. They need each other; they're good for each other. They've been arguing for thirty-five years. I can't imagine why they want to stop at this point.''

"Brad." Daphne sighed, then allowed herself a weary smile. Despite her drowsiness, she was touched that Brad had chosen her, of all his friends, to unburden himself to, even if he was doing it at an ungodly hour. Besides being touched, she was still astonished to think of Brad as someone who would have to unburden himself at all. She'd never had any basis for assuming that he was as neat and well put together emotionally as he was physically, but given the externals of his life—the ingrown wealth, the career, the success, bedroom eyes and small buns and all the rest of it—Daphne was having trouble accepting that Brad, too, suffered from actual human anguish on occasion.

"You want me to shut up," he guessed, sounding appropriately contrite. "I know, it's late."

"I wouldn't mind the time," she assured him, "except that I've got to go to a closing at nine o'clock tomorrow."

"I'm sorry. I'll let you get back to sleep."

"Brad," she said swiftly, before he could hang up. "Don't you want to know about the house?"

"Oh—right! The house. What did the seller say?"

Daphne's smile widened and she drew her knees up under the covers, forming a tent with her sheet. "He said two thirty-five, take it or leave it."

"Two thirty-five?" Brad repeated, perplexed.

"Two hundred thirty-five thousand."

"But . . . but that's lower than we discussed, Daffy. That's much lower than I was willing to go."

"Take it or leave it," she said, smothering a laugh. "He doesn't want to haggle, he just wants to get the house sold. I swore you'd be a sure thing—no problems as far as your qualifying for a mortgage or anything like that. And he said he wanted to cut through the garbage and settle on a price.''

Brad let out a restrained hoot. ''No kidding? Daffy, that's fantastic! You're a genius.''

''I'm a businesswoman,'' she asserted. ''I want to see the sale go through, too. Shall I tell him you'll accept his price?''

''You mean you haven't already? Of course I'll accept his price.''

''I'll telephone him tomorrow. And I'll get a contract written up right away. You may have to do some of your application work for the mortgage long-distance, but I can help you with that if you and the bank need a go-between.''

''Thanks, Daphne,'' Brad said earnestly, his tone low and intense. ''I mean it. Thank you.''

''You're welcome. Now go to bed and dream about your soon-to-be new home.''

She heard a strange sound through the phone, something that might have been a cross between a gasp and a laugh. Then Brad said, ''You're clairvoyant, Daff. Go back to sleep—and thanks again.''

Before she could request an explanation for his cryptic remark, the line went dead.

She wasn't clairvoyant. She wasn't even that good a listener when it came to other people's problems. Whenever Phyllis embarked on one of her self-pitying discourses concerning Jim, Daphne invariably wound up making jokes. On those rare occasions when her sister Helen telephoned and griped about the constraints of her marriage to Dennis, Daphne seized whatever excuse was handy to end the call. She had little patience for people who had so much more going for them than she herself did, yet who constantly demanded sympathy from her.

But she honestly didn't mind listening to Brad talk about his parents. For one thing, he wasn't asking her for sympathy: his focus was totally on his parents' well-being, not on his own disappointment. For another, she liked knowing that his life wasn't as flawless as it seemed on the surface, that he cared deeply for his loved ones and ached for them. And for another, she was honored that he considered her trustworthy enough to confide in.

But clairvoyant? What on earth had he meant by calling her that?

A hectic day lay ahead for her, and she was too tired to puzzle out his strange comment. Besides the closing that she was supposed to attend the following morning, she had arranged to meet Bob Battinger for lunch and discuss with him the possibility of Horizon Realty's extending her a loan to finance her share of the partnership. Now that reality had set in, she was beginning to wonder whether she could afford to become a partner in the corporation. What with her mortgage, her car payments and two more years of a college loan to pay off, she was teetering on the edge of financial panic.

But she was too tired to worry about that, too, right now. So she plumped the pillow beneath her head, closed her eyes and drifted off almost immediately. One thing Daphne never had to worry about was her ability to fall asleep, regardless of the riddles and challenges that might be lying in wait for her when she rose.

IT WASN'T CLAIRVOYANCE that compelled her to drive past the expanded cape on her way back to the office from what had turned into a marathon luncheon with Bob Battinger the following afternoon. They'd met at one o'clock, tossed around various financial strategies during the course of their two-hour meal and then stopped in at a bank branch, where Daphne did a great deal of mortgage business, to discuss loans with one of the loan officers there. Bob seemed much more optimistic than Daphne about her ability to carry an additional loan—but then, it was always easy to be optimistic when someone else's money was at stake.

At four o'clock, she and Bob parted ways. She had no reason to return to her office, other than to drop off the paperwork from the morning's closing. Although realtors were sometimes required to work on weekends, they rarely had to work on Friday evenings. Nobody wanted to shop for a house after a long, exhausting week on the job.

Since she wasn't in a hurry, and since she wanted to think through what Bob had said about the value of the partnership, she decided to drive back to Bloomfield Avenue by a meandering back route, passing a raised ranch she had a listing on, a split-level she'd sold two months ago and a contemporary on a half acre that she'd sold last year—and could have sold for twice the price this year. Then she drove to the expanded cape she'd just sold to Brad. She found him standing in the driveway, his blazer slung over his shoulder and his shirtsleeves rolled up, his neck craned back so he could inspect the roof.

The fact that he happened to be visiting the house when Daphne cruised by didn't mean she was able to read his mind. It merely meant that this particular house was significant to both their lives at the moment. "The roof's fine," she called to him through the open window of her car.

Brad spun around, then grinned and waved as he recognized Daphne. She pulled her car to a halt behind the silver Ford Escort parked at the curb and climbed out. "How do you know it's fine?" Brad asked.

"It was reshingled last year. Didn't you read the M.L.S. write-up on it?"

Brad shrugged. "Should I care?" he asked, smiling hesitantly. "What I mean is, should I be thinking of it as *my* roof?"

Daphne strolled across the sloping front lawn and joined him on the driveway. "Meaning, is this your house? Assuming the bank approves, yes."

His smile grew wider, shimmering with delight. "I didn't dream about it last night," he confessed. "But I should have. It's a dream house, all right."

"Even if you're going to clobber your head on the sloping ceilings upstairs?"

"Even if," he confirmed. He turned back to examine the house some more, and slid his arm casually around Daphne's slender waist. "Daff...did I thank you for all this?"

"Several times last night," she reminded him. "More times than I would have liked. You must have kept me up at least thirty seconds longer than necessary with all your thank-yous."

"Oh, Daffy, I'm sorry about that, but..." His arm tightened around her for a moment, and then he let it fall to his side and took a cautious step away from her. "There was a whole lot more I wanted to talk to you about last night, but you were obviously too sleepy to take it in."

"Take what in?" she asked, eyeing him with curiosity. A necktie hung loose from his collar, implying that he'd once again spent time at his office in New York. Yet he didn't look frazzled or worn out. His eyes shone with a brilliance that put the clear May sky above the recently renovated roof to shame, and his smile cut long dimples into his cheeks.

It was not the kind of expression that made Daphne brace herself for a further analysis of Brad's parents' marital woes. What else might Brad have wished to discuss with her at eleven-thirty last night?

He extended his hand to take hers, and she let him lead her to the front steps of the house. He tossed his blazer down onto the concrete to protect her skirt, and she bit back the reflexive urge to make a wisecrack about his Sir Walter Raleigh brand of chivalry. Instead, she lowered herself to sit, pressing her legs together decorously beneath her A-line skirt, and interwove her fingers in her lap. Brad dropped onto the step beside her, balanced his elbows on his spread knees, and squinted into the late-afternoon sunlight.

His prolonged silence fed her curiosity. Finally, he asked, "Remember when we talked about a time machine?"

He was facing the lawn, not Daphne, but she understood the personal nature of his question. What he was really asking her was whether she remembered the discussion they'd had on her back porch. She believed they'd already said everything that had to be said on the subject; probing it further would in all likelihood only make her uncomfortable.

She didn't want to be angry with Brad, not when she was finally beginning to feel so warmly toward him. Talking about the unhappy incident marring their past was bound to make her angry. "I remember," she answered him curtly, hoping to close the subject before it was too late.

He shot her a quick glance, obviously sensing her edginess. "Then you remember that we both agreed if we ever got our hands on a time machine, we'd use it to go back to that night and do things all over again. Only we'd do them right this time."

"Uh-huh," she grunted impatiently. Her hands cramped in her lap, and her knuckles began to turn white. "So what?"

"I was thinking about it yesterday," he went on in an annoyingly leisurely manner. Daphne gritted her teeth. No matter how uninterested she made herself sound, he obviously wasn't going to stop. "I was thinking about it because when I visited my mother's apartment it was almost like going into a time machine. I grew up there, Daff. I spent my entire youth in that apartment. And there was my mother, dredging up the complete history of her relationship with my father, and..." The sentence went unfinished as Brad observed the breeze playing through the newly opened leaves of a red oak on the property.

Daphne forced herself to unclench her hands before her fingers went numb. If he didn't reach the point he was trying to make soon, she was going to get up and march back to her car, she decided.

"The attic ceiling in this house," he said abruptly.

"What about it, other than that it's too low for someone your height?"

"That's just it, Daff. It's low." At last he turned to her, his gaze penetrating her, cutting through her in search of a shred of evidence that she understood what he was getting at. His voice was soft and gentle when he continued. "We were both thinking the same thing when we were standing up there in the bedroom the other day, Daff. We were thinking about the last time we were together in a bedroom with a low ceiling. It's still with us, Daphne. The memories are still with us."

"All right," she conceded. "They're still with us. What about it?"

"Imagine a time machine," he said. "If only we could go back, we could undo the bad stuff." He paused to let his words sink in, then added, "We *can* do it right this time."

"Do what right?" she asked warily.

"Have our night together."

"What?"

"Make love."

"Now?"

"Not this minute, Daff—but the key is, we *can* go back, if we want to. We can relive that moment in time. We've got each other now, and we can relive it the right way."

She allowed herself a full minute to let his suggestion register. As soon as it did, she succumbed to a loud guffaw. "You're nuts!" she blurted out.

Brad appeared strangely wounded. "I am not nuts, Daff. I've been giving this idea some serious thought—stop laughing, Daphne," he said sternly.

She smothered her hysterics by clamping her hand across her mouth. A couple of hiccups slipped out, but she did a respectable job of regaining her composure.

Satisfied that she wouldn't dissolve into laughter again, he resumed speaking. "I've been thinking about it, Daff. We all go through our lives making mistakes and wishing we could go back and fix them. My parents keep dwelling on all the mistakes they've made with each other, instead of trying to fix their relationship. Never once did they try to go back, figure out what went wrong and make amends for it, or do it over the right way. And look at them now—bitter and sniping at each other. Well, for once in my life, I've got a chance to go back and fix the biggest mistake I've ever made. We've *both* got that chance, Daphne, and I think we'd be making even a bigger mistake if we didn't take advantage of the opportunity.''

"What opportunity?" Daphne asked, her amusement replaced by confusion.

"*This* opportunity. Eight years after we made asses of ourselves, here we are, good friends. We've talked the thing out, but it's still lying there between us." He stared defiantly at her, as if daring her to deny his assertion.

She couldn't, of course. It *was* still lying there between them. But even so, what he was implying... "I don't see how our making love is going to fix anything," she said, wondering if she was only imagining the tremor in her voice. "We may be friends, Brad, but we don't love each other."

"So much the better," he said enthusiastically. "That's what makes this thing so right. If neither of us loves the other, neither of us can get hurt."

"I don't believe that," Daphne refuted him. "And while we're at it, I don't believe we can go back in time. We're eight years older—"

"Exactly. Eight years older and wiser and more attuned to each other. That's the beauty of time machines, Daff—the time traveler returns to the past and brings his present perspective with him. We can't miss, Daphne. We're mature and sensible."

"If we were all that mature and sensible, we wouldn't be having this conversation," Daphne argued. Making love without being in love seemed so cold to her, so mechanical and arbitrary. Wasn't that part of the reason she and Brad had had such a bad experience last time? They'd made love without being in love.

No. They hadn't made love that time. They'd had intercourse, but they certainly hadn't made love.

She glanced at him, simultaneously intrigued and dismayed by his beguiling grin. Whether or not they loved each other, he was a hypnotically good-looking man, and she was a woman who hadn't been intimate with a man in a long, long time.

"You're tempted," Brad hazarded, interpreting her expression accurately.

"Well..." She smiled reluctantly, reminiscing about the many times she'd concluded she wouldn't kick Brad out for eating crackers in bed. "I think what you're proposing is...kind of dangerous."

"No, it's not. We're friends, Daff—and I promise you, it's going to be good. We'll set the past to rights, and it'll make us feel so much better afterward."

She felt a strange fluttering inside her, a warm, erotic tug when he said, "It's going to be good." She didn't agree with him that it wouldn't be dangerous, but she knew it would be good. She just knew it.

And as far as the danger... Phyllis and Andrea were always berating her for her tendency to opt for safety. Maybe they were right; maybe she spent too much of her life playing it safe. And where had that gotten her? She was a thirty-year-old single woman with a respectable career, a lot of debts, and the social life of an amoeba. A night of sex with a friend had to be better than that.

"I thought you were leaving for Seattle next week," she reminded him, groping for any justification to turn him down.

"Monday afternoon," he confirmed. "That still leaves this weekend—unless you're already busy."

She laughed nervously. Now it was her turn to inspect the purplish leaves of the majestic oak trees across the lawn. "I don't know, Brad. It seems so unromantic...."

"Talking about it makes it seem that way," he agreed. "But in actual practice, it's going to be the most romantic night of our lives. That's part of where we went wrong last time, Daff—we weren't romantic. This time we will be." He warmed to his subject, curling an arm around Daphne's slightly hunched shoulders. "We'll have an intimate dinner *à deux* first. Candlelight, mood music, the works. How does that sound?"

"Romantic," she admitted. "Are we supposed to have this romantic dinner at a restaurant, or am I supposed to cook it?"

"Whichever you prefer," he answered. "I'd cook it myself, except that I don't have title on this house yet, and I don't think it would be an intimate dinner if we did it in Manhattan, with Andrea and Eric in the next room."

"All right, I'll cook it," Daphne decided. If they were aiming for an intimate dinner, they couldn't go to a public restaurant. Daphne wasn't the world's greatest chef, but she would be able to concoct something reasonably romantic.

"What sort of music should we go with?" he asked. "Classical? Jazz?"

"Definitely not rock and roll," she said firmly. They'd had rock and roll the last time, and she wanted this time to be completely different. "I'd vote for classical, but nothing too high-brow. I could get some recordings of Strauss waltzes out of the library."

"Mozart's better than Strauss," Brad asserted.

"All right. Mozart." She laughed again, less nervously. It amazed her to think she was actually considering Brad's insane idea—more than considering it.

Somehow, without being aware of the precise moment, she'd crossed the line from considering to contributing to the plan.

But she had crossed it, that much was plain to her. She was not only contributing, she was actually looking forward to this romantic evening with Brad. For once in her life, she deserved to be romanced, to be reckless and sentimental and utterly swept away. If Brad was correct, one extremely romantic night would eradicate her memories of the least romantic night of her life. And even if he was incorrect, what did she have to lose? A few hours? A lonely Saturday night?

"This weekend, huh."

"Tomorrow. Six o'clock? No, let's make it five," he amended. "The earlier we start, the more time we'll have together."

If the evening was a flop, they wouldn't want to have more time together, Daphne pondered. But if the evening was a flop, they wouldn't be any worse off than they already were. She had enough faith in Brad to believe that their friendship would survive, even if they were as rotten in bed this time as they'd been last time.

"Five o'clock tomorrow," she confirmed. "I think maybe we're both nuts, Brad."

He pulled her toward himself and landed a light, surprisingly tender kiss on her lips. "We're going to go back and conquer the past, Daff. If that makes us nuts, so be it." He touched his lips to hers again, then slid her eyeglasses back up her nose to their proper place. "Between you and me, Daffy, I think we're doing something downright rational."

"Romance isn't supposed to be rational," she argued, just for the hell of it.

Brad grinned. "If that's the case, Daff," he said resolutely, "we'll just have to redefine romance."

Chapter Eight

Daphne lifted the lid and peeked inside the pot. The simmering clam sauce looked savory and smelled even better, but she couldn't resist adding another pinch of oregano to compensate for the fact that she'd used only about half the amount of garlic the recipe called for. No matter how much she relished the flavor of garlic, she wasn't about to put a hex on her romantic evening by cultivating bad breath.

Linguini with clam sauce wasn't terribly exotic, but Daphne figured that it was a meal she couldn't ruin. She'd spent well over an hour Friday night thumbing through her various cookbooks in search of the perfect dinner menu for her tryst with Brad, but anything that sounded even remotely romantic—soufflés, pressed duckling, assorted meats marinated in cognac and set aflame—were well beyond the limits of her culinary talents. Linguini was fattening, but a gain of three pounds wasn't going to make that much difference, considering how much thinner she was now than she'd been eight years ago. And anyway, she'd prepared a huge tossed salad. She could fill up on that while Brad gorged on the pasta.

Satisfied that the extra oregano added the requisite zest to her sauce, she set the lid back in place, checked the wall clock above the sink, and let out a slow breath to calm herself. Brad was scheduled to arrive in ten minutes. Her strategy was to avoid any strenuous mental activity in those ten minutes. If she thought too much—if she thought at all—she would probably wind up thinking about what a ludicrous plan this was.

Instead of thinking, she left the kitchen to check the dining room table setting one last time: beige linens, brown Ironstone place settings, two brown tapers protruding from silver candlesticks. Then she wandered to the living room and slipped onto the turntable of her stereo one of the records she'd signed out of the library that morning—a Mozart piano concerto. From there she journeyed to the bathroom to appraise her appearance one final time.

She'd fretted over her outfit even longer than over the menu, but all in all she wasn't dissatisfied with her choice. The blouse she had on was a shiny cream-colored satin, and she'd left the top several buttons unfastened to offer an alluring glimpse of what passed for cleavage on her small-bosomed torso. She had tucked the blouse into a pair of loose-fitting gray trousers that would have looked fabulous on Katharine Hepburn in a thirties movie. Actually, Daphne decided, her build was a lot like Hepburn's—tall, broad-shouldered and reasonably leggy. Unfortunately, her face wasn't anything at all like Hepburn's, but Daphne had done her best to maximize her meager assets, adorning her eyes with a hint of green shadow and a tawny mascara, highlighting her cheeks with a pink blusher, blow-drying her hair before the curls had a chance to kink. She'd dabbed her throat with cologne, and put on earrings that dropped like two elegant gold tears past her jaw.

The doorbell rang. She endured a brief clutch of fear somewhere in her lower abdomen, then adamantly shook it off and strode from the bathroom, stopping in the living room to turn on the stereo before she answered the door.

All she saw at first were flowers: red roses, pink roses, baby yellow roses, white lilies, several sprays of lilac and a few other blossoms she couldn't identify, all bunched within a feathery nest of green ferns. A hand held the enormous bouquet, so Daphne felt it reasonably safe to assume that a human being was somewhere in the vicinity. She curled her fingers around the tissue-wrapped stems and pulled the bouquet aside to find Brad behind the flowers, grinning.

He was wearing a navy-blue blazer, a pale blue shirt and khaki trousers. The effect was preppyish in the extreme, but Daphne liked it. She liked the way the skin of his neck glowed a healthy golden color beneath the open collar of his shirt, and the way the fading light of dusk played mysteriously over the sharp lines and planes of his face. She liked the dark density of his hair, the intriguing shimmer of his eyes, the minty scent of his aftershave, the stark white evenness of his teeth as his smile expanded.

Some distant corner of her brain rattled to life with the abrupt understanding that in a matter of hours, she was going to be in her bed with Brad, naked, making love with him. But she shunted the thought away. It was simply too disconcerting.

"Are all these flowers for me?" she asked, pleased by her breezy tone.

"No, just half of them. The other half are for Steve and Melanie Persky, up in Armonk. I figured if things got boring here, we could always take a drive up there to visit them..." Noticing the way she stiffened slightly at his joke, he laughed and rested the bulky bouquet within the cradle of her arm. "Don't worry, Daff," he whispered, brushing his lips against her forehead. "Things aren't going to get boring here."

His promise only increased her anxiety. She labored to disguise her tension behind a hesitant smile. "Come in," she said, realizing at once that she sounded more like a Marine sergeant barking orders than a seductress luring a willing victim into her lair.

Brad bent to lift a bottle-shaped paper bag from the step before following her inside. After commanding Brad so brusquely to enter her house, Daphne wasn't about to make matters worse by reminding him that she didn't drink wine.

"You're nervous," he observed, trailing her into the kitchen.

She busied herself laying the flowers on a counter near the sink and then pulling a porcelain vase from a cabinet. "Who, me?"

He chuckled. "I'm nervous, too, Daffy, so don't feel bad about it."

She spun around, startled. "Why are you nervous?" she asked, thinking that, for someone who claimed to be nervous, he appeared remarkably relaxed.

He smiled again, and she responded to his luscious dimples with a discernible tightening in the pit of her stomach. His gaze roamed around her kitchen before coming to rest on the extravagant floral arrangement. "I'm nervous because these flowers aren't going to fit in your vase," he told her.

She cracked a grin and turned to examine the vase. "You're right, Brad. They're not. I guess we'll have to make a delivery in Armonk, after all."

"I admit I got a little carried away," he apologized, setting the paper bag containing the wine on the breakfast table and joining her at the sink. "I couldn't make up my mind which flowers to buy, so I bought them all. Maybe we could just fill the sink with water and leave them there."

Daphne dismissed his suggestion with a vague shrug. "I'm sure I've got something they'll fit into," she said, swinging open cabinet doors in search of a larger vessel. She found an empty mayonnaise jar. "How's this?" she asked, filling it with water.

"Ugly."

"The flowers are so pretty, they'll make up for it," she assured him as she tried to jam the stems through the neck of the jar.

"Don't stuff them all in," he cautioned her—too late. Her attempt to squeeze too many stems into too small an opening caused the jar to skid off the counter and land with a crash on the linoleum floor.

Daphne shrieked and jumped back, trying to elude the splatter of water. Brad jumped back, too, then stared at the mass of broken glass, puddling water and ferns strewn across the floor between himself and Daphne. He laughed.

"It's not funny!" Daphne roared before submitting to a reluctant smile herself. There was something so ridiculous about the size of the bouquet, and something so utterly unromantic about a mayonnaise jar. There was, Daphne had to concede, something perversely appealing about getting down on her hands and knees with Brad and swabbing up the mess.

By the time the last sliver of glass had been disposed of and the water mopped up with a sponge, Brad's jacket was off and Daphne's sleeves were rolled up. "The florist warned me I was buying too many flowers," Brad said, still grinning. "Can we divide them into two jars or something?"

"I don't even know if I have two empty jars left," Daphne informed him, selecting a couple of roses for the vase. "There's a limit to how much mayonnaise I can eat in any given year." She wrung out the sponge, accepted the remaining flowers from Brad and dumped them into the sink, which she filled with water from the tap. "I'll figure out something to do with them later. Right now, I've got to get the dinner heated up."

"Whatever you made, I hope it goes with red," he said, pulling the bottle of wine from the bag. "I picked up a Bordeaux—"

"It goes with red, all right," Daphne said, lighting the burner under a kettle of water for the linguini. "But you'll have to drink the wine alone, Brad."

He stared at her for a minute, then at the bottle. "Oh, brother," he grumbled.

Daphne was perplexed by his apparent annoyance. "You don't have to drink the entire bottle, Brad," she reassured him. "You can have as much as you like here, and then you can take the rest home with you."

"It isn't that," he swore, glaring at the bottle again. "It's just..." He sighed. "I had it in my head that when you romance a woman, the traditional offerings are flowers and wine. I brought too many flowers, and I shouldn't have brought any wine at all. I'm sorry, Daff. I seem to be screwing the whole thing up."

"Don't be sorry," she consoled him. "I like the flowers—in fact, I like them a lot more than I liked that jar I broke. And seriously, Brad, you can have wine without me. Just because I'm a stick-in-the-mud—"

"You aren't a stick-in-the-mud," he said quietly as he carried the unopened wine bottle to the garbage pail. Without any fanfare, he tossed it in.

Daphne opened her mouth to object, then shut it. Throwing out the bottle of wine was quite possibly the most romantic thing Brad had done so far. "You're going to be rewarded for your temperance," she promised, hearing the bubbly sound of the water for the pasta beginning to boil. She lowered the heat and beamed at him.

His answering smile was unnervingly sexy. "That's what I'm hoping, Daff."

"I was referring to *dinner*," she said sternly, although she felt her innards thawing into a warm pool of yearning beneath his uninhibited gaze. The blatant message in his eyes ought to have made her even more nervous, but for some reason it didn't. If she and Brad could laugh about broken jars and wasted wine, they could surely hang on to their sense of humor for the remainder of the evening's agenda.

"It does smell good," Brad said, steering his hunger from Daphne to the pots on the stove. "As a matter of fact, it smells like spaghetti."

"Linguini," she told him. "Equally fattening."

"I love it." He lifted the lid on the kettle of boiling water, then the one on the smaller pot. "Homemade sauce? How domestic, Daphne. I didn't know you had it in you."

"It's only about half homemade," she confessed, dumping a fistful of dry pasta into the boiling water and then giving the sauce an unnecessary stir. "The basic sauce comes out of a can, but I added lots of spices. Of course, the clams came out of a can, too."

"Clams," Brad muttered, recoiling from the stove.

Daphne eyed him apprehensively. "You don't like clams? Oh, Brad, I'm sorry. We can pick them out of the sauce if you'd like—"

"That won't do, Daff," he said, staring at the sauce with brooding suspicion. "It's not that I don't like clams—it's that I'm deathly allergic to them. Even if I picked every last clam out of the sauce before eating it, I'd still break out in hives."

"Oh." Daphne focused on the carefully seasoned contents of the pot and grimaced. Just one more mistake to add to the mayonnaise jar and the wine. "I bet you hate that piano concerto, too," she said glumly, reaching the depressing conclusion that the entire evening was doomed to be as disastrous as the last evening she'd wound up spending alone with Brad. "I know I'm not wild about it."

She heard what sounded like a low chuckle behind her. She couldn't believe Brad found anything amusing in the fact that, on top of everything else, the dinner itself was a complete bomb. But when she turned around, she saw him practically doubled over with laughter. He was leaning against the breakfast table, his shoulders convulsing and his eyes closed, with tears of laughter leaking through his thick eyelashes and streaming down his cheeks. "Daff—" he gasped, "Daffy... you look so serious! Come on, honey, admit it... we're really on a roll here!"

Even if she didn't find the situation as funny as Brad did, she was unable to resist the infectious rumble of his laughter. She shot a glance toward the sink filled with soggy flowers, and then toward the garbage pail harboring the shattered mayonnaise jar and the wine, and then toward the stove with its poisonous pot of sauce.

She started to laugh, too.

As soon as he heard the counterpoint of her laughter against his, Brad reached for her hands and pulled her toward him, steering her between his outstretched legs. "Would it make you feel any better if I told you I adored the music?" he asked once he'd regained control of himself.

"I don't know," she replied. "I think it's kind of stodgy."

"I think you're an idiot."

"I think you're a boor."

"I love it when you talk dirty," Brad murmured before grazing her lips lightly with his. He drew back, allowing his gaze to meet hers. If anything, he looked even sexier than he had earlier. Daphne's laughter stuck in her throat as she comprehended the message inherent in the smoky radiance of his eyes.

"I don't usually talk dirty," she whispered breathlessly.

"You don't have to."

"Do you want to skip dinner?"

"I'd rather skip dinner than get hives."

She inhaled deeply, keenly aware of what they would wind up doing if they didn't eat.

When she'd contemplated the evening ahead, she had expected that they would build up to the ultimate event with a couple of hours of genial conversation, filling food and sweetened coffee. She had anticipated having time to accustom herself to the idea of Brad as a lover.

Perhaps it was better this way, without the preliminaries, without the opportunity for them both to reconsider what they were planning and come to their senses. As she stood just inches from Brad, with his long-fingered hands resting on either side of her waist and his unswerving gaze piercing her defenses, all she could think of was how delectable his throat looked to her, how much she wanted to kiss it.

She didn't have the nerve, not quite yet. "I was going to—I mean, I thought—in the interest of romance and all..." She pressed her lips shut to keep herself from babbling anymore.

"You thought what?"

"I thought I should slip into something more comfortable," she said, then grinned crookedly at the banality of her statement.

"That would be very nice," Brad murmured.

Daphne slid from his light embrace and darted out of the kitchen. In her bedroom, she closed the door, leaned against it and gulped in a few more frantic breaths.

All right. They'd get this part over with, and if it was awful they'd call it an early night and get as far away from each other as they could. And if it wasn't awful, then none of the mishaps they'd suffered so far would matter.

She undressed, forcing herself not to dawdle, and hung her blouse in the closet. She noticed that her slacks were damp around the ankles from the water that had spilled when she'd dropped the jar, so she arranged them over the back of a chair to dry. Then she pulled on an embroidered silk caftan she'd bought on a whim when she'd vacationed in the Bahamas last winter. She hardly ever wore it, but she thought it would serve nicely tonight, draping over her modest curves in what she hoped was an alluring way. As with her damp clothing and her hive-inducing dinner menu, she'd spent a great deal of time last night analyzing whether she ought to wear this caftan for Brad. What had persuaded her to make use of it was her mental picture of him easing down the zipper one inch at a time, gradually revealing her body to his eyes and his touch. In her imagination, such a languorous disrobing had seemed incredibly romantic.

In reality, she wasn't so sure it would be.

Before leaving the bedroom, she removed her eyeglasses and fluffed her hair out. Then, sucking in one last, panic-stricken breath, she went to find Brad.

He was seated on the living room couch, listening to Mozart. He'd removed his shoes and kicked his legs up onto the table in front of the couch, but he immediately swung his feet back to the floor and stood at her entrance. His eyes widened as he surveyed her. "You look very nice," he said.

"You sound surprised," she shot back, then bit her lip. Now was not the time to remind Brad of her shortcomings in appearance.

Brad accepted her words without flinching. "Maybe I am, a little," he granted, crossing the room to her. His honesty moved her in a way empty compliments never would have; if there had been any doubt about her ability to trust him, it was gone now. She smiled shyly as he cupped his hands over her shoulders and drew her to him. His mouth covered hers, teased it, coaxed it open. He traced the edges of her teeth with the tip of his tongue, then slid his lips from hers. "Am I rushing things, Daff?" he asked solicitously.

"No," she said in a rusty voice. His tongue had felt wonderful inside her mouth. She wished he'd go right ahead and rush things some more.

"I want you to tell me," he implored her. "This time, I want you to tell me what feels right, what doesn't . . . I want it to be as good as we can make it—"

"Then kiss me again," she requested, lifting her hands to the back of his head and guiding his mouth back to hers.

He wrapped his arms around her, pulling her body to his, and angled his lips against hers to afford him greater access to the inner recesses of her mouth. His tongue lunged deep, searching for its partner and sliding sensuously around it.

Daphne was astonished to feel the instantaneous effect of her kiss on him, his beginning erection as he leaned into her hips. His hands skidded upward to her hair, his fingers twining through the loose blond curls, and he groaned. "Where the hell did you learn to kiss like that?" he asked, his tone gravelly as he leaned back from her.

Daphne didn't recall having learned it anywhere. It was more a matter of inspiration, she believed, the inspiration of Brad's equally transporting kiss. It wasn't anything like the kisses she remembered him giving her the last time—kisses she'd tried for the last eight years to forget. "I was going to ask you the same thing," she mumbled.

"I haven't got the answer," he admitted. "Let's try it some more—maybe we'll figure out what we're doing right." He took her mouth with his again, and let his hands glide forward to cup her cheeks. His thumbs stroked down along the angle of her chin as his tongue danced with hers, and his hips surged against hers again. "Maybe it's the Mozart," he whispered, his breath tickling her lips.

"I highly doubt that," Daphne countered with a grin.

"You should have told me you didn't like Mozart."

"I never said I didn't like the music. I just said it's stodgy. But," she concluded, emboldened by the rapturous effects of Brad's kisses, "it doesn't matter. We probably won't be able to hear the record in my bedroom."

Brad groaned again. As if he'd read her mind—as if his sole desire in life was to fulfill her fantasies—he located the zipper of her caftan and tugged it down an inch. Bowing, he pressed his lips to the newly exposed skin at the base of her throat. "I want you undressed," he announced, stating the obvious. "Is that all right?"

"It beats eating clams and getting hives," she joked.

Brad laughed briefly. He slid the zipper down another couple of inches, then stopped. He wiggled the tab, jerked it, tugged it and scowled. "It seems to be stuck," he said, straightening up.

Daphne lowered her gaze to the zipper, which had opened to about the middle of her sternum. She zipped it up a bit, then down again. It refused to budge past that point. "It *is* stuck," she wailed.

Brad was besieged by fresh laughter. Daphne joined him. Even as she jiggled the tab futilely and watched yet another romantic moment stumble into calamity, she couldn't keep the giggles from spilling out.

"What's the verdict?" Brad asked as his laughter waned. "Are you going to have to spend the rest of your life in this thing, or do you want me to hack it off with a chain saw?"

"We might be able to pull it off over my head," Daphne suggested.

Brad bowed to gather up the hem of the robe. He raised it, allowing his hands to run along the backs of her legs. When he reached her hips, he sucked in a shaky breath. "You're not wearing anything underneath," he noted.

"I thought...I mean, isn't that supposed to be the general idea?" Daphne mumbled.

"Oh, God..." Shoving the bunched fabric out of his way, he molded his hands to the soft, round flesh of her bottom and pressed her to himself. "You are one hell of a turn-on, Daphne," he whispered hoarsely.

"I thought that was supposed to be the general idea, too," Daphne murmured, secretly thrilled that her attempt at playing seductress hadn't been a total failure, after all.

For a long moment he held her, sketching circles over her skin with his fingertips, urging her higher against him so her body would accommodate the increasing hardness of his. "Something tells me this evening is going to turn out to be one of the best ideas I've ever come up with," he said, his tone still rasping as he lifted Daphne into his arms.

"Don't carry me," she cautioned him, gripping his shoulders as he staggered beneath her weight. "You're going to hurt yourself."

"Not if we move fast. Where's your bedroom?"

"Down the hall and to the left. Brad—"

"It's a good thing we didn't eat first," he teased, stalking down the hall with her. "If you'd gained your three spaghetti pounds, I wouldn't be able to do this." He raced across the bedroom to the bed, where he dropped Daphne and collapsed onto the mattress beside her, panting. "There," he gloated, once he'd caught his breath. He flexed his arm muscles proudly. "You're dealing with a pretty tough specimen."

"If you're so tough, you ought to be able to open an itty-bitty little zipper," she challenged him.

"I'm so tough, I'll open it with my teeth, Daff." He didn't quite follow through on that boast, although his teeth weren't far from the zipper as he attempted to wrestle it down again. When the zipper refused to give, he ignored it and kissed her breast through the silk of the caftan.

Daphne moaned. She felt as if she were teetering on the edge of too many emotions—amusement, affection, ravenous passion and something else, something she wouldn't dare to call love. It was confusing, dizzying, and very, very dangerous. And she didn't want it to end.

Just because Brad hadn't yet succeeded in undressing her didn't mean she couldn't start to undress him. She groped for the buttons of his shirt and opened them. Brad assisted her by shrugging his shoulders free of the shirt, then sweeping it down his arms and flinging it across the room. For someone who had always struck Daphne as fastidious, who would never consider tackling the dirty work of renovating a handyman's special, who even in college had kept his fraternity house bedroom tidy, the careless manner in which he'd disposed of his shirt took Daphne by surprise.

She was also surprised by the firm, gloriously virile lines of the chest he'd bared. His streamlined muscles stirred beneath bronze skin that was enhanced by a sparse mat of dark hair. His shoulders were solid, rounding into taut biceps in a gracefully masculine way. The stretch of skin above his belt was flat and well toned, and his neck was even more inviting than she'd realized. Daphne hadn't remembered him having such a gorgeous physique—but then, she'd remembered nothing positive about the one time she'd seen his body.

Tonight she suspected that she'd remember nothing negative. The mishap with the mayonnaise jar, the threat to Brad's health posed by the dinner, none of it—with the possible exception of her jammed zipper—could alter the pleasure she believed she and Brad were destined to experience together. "Let's try over my head," she said, not bothering to waste her breath by shaping a grammatically correct sentence.

Brad understood what she was attempting to say. He gathered her caftan by the hem again, lifted Daphne toward him, and pulled the robe upward. She raised her arms and sparred with the cloth; he yanked it around her head; she opened her mouth to complain about her inability to see and wound up with a clump of fabric trapped in her lips. But somehow, thanks to Brad's patience and a bit of well-timed wriggling on Daphne's part, she was liberated from the caftan.

Brad tossed it aside and turned his attention back to her. He ran his gaze over her long pale body, taking in her small breasts with their nipples already taut and flushed, and then the slender span of her waist, the spread of her hips, the triangle of blond hair between her thighs. His breath was even but shallow, as if he were exerting himself mightily to maintain his self-control.

He seemed on the verge of speaking, but instead he lowered his hand to her, combing his fingers through the golden thatch of curls and discovering the moistness of her flesh beneath it. Both he and Daphne flinched. He issued a strange, broken sound, then whispered, "You feel so good, Daphne."

He refused to take his hand away when she reached for his belt. She wasn't about to ask him to move, even though his position made stripping off his trousers difficult. She wanted his fingers exactly where they were, holding her, arousing her, tantalizing her with delicate caresses and almost indiscernible pressure.

He helped her as much as he could in the removal of his slacks, shifting his hips so she could pull them off, kicking his feet to free himself from his briefs. And then her hand found him, full and eager, and she held him as he held her.

He kissed her with unexpected tenderness. "Daff," he whispered, gripping her wrist and easing her hand from him. She must have looked hurt or bewildered, because he explained his action: "Not yet. It's too intense, it feels too good." He lifted her hand to his lips and grazed the tips of her fingers. Then he set her hand free on his shoulder. "Touch my back, instead," he suggested before conquering her lips with another, deeper kiss.

At first Daphne wasn't sure what to make of his talkativeness. Even during her first clumsy attempts at sex with Dennis, she would never have had the audacity to tell him what to do—or to ask him what he wanted her to do. And when she'd been with Brad the last time, from the moment he'd handed her a Cornell mug filled with wine to the moment she'd fled from him, they hadn't spoken a single word to each other.

Now, here he was, chatting away. "Do you always talk during sex?" she asked as her hand obediently kneaded the ridge of his shoulder and then crept down to the warm, supple skin of his upper back.

He groaned happily, leaning back to savor her massage. "Do you always ask men what they always do during sex?" he parried.

It took her a moment to sort through his convoluted question. "I'm not asking to be nosy," she clarified. "I don't care what you do with other women, Brad. It's just . . . last time, we didn't talk."

"Maybe that was another big mistake we made," he commented. "This time . . . ohh . . ." He closed his eyes and sighed as her fingers roved down toward the knotted muscles of his lower back. "God, Daff—that feels too good, too. What are you doing to me?"

She wasn't conscious of doing anything special. What she was doing was exploring his back with her fingers, sliding her knee against the inner surface of his thigh, gazing up at him from the pillow on which she rested her head. She was smiling at him and wanting him, and gasping as his thumb scaled the rise of her breast to rub her nipple. She was crying out softly as his tongue followed in the wake of his thumb, twirling hot and wet over the swollen red skin, sucking hard.

Whatever hazy thoughts she had left of the last time she'd been with Brad burned away in the fierce ecstasy of the present. Even if they went no further than this, she believed she would be satisfied.

But there was no question of stopping. As Brad shifted his mouth to her other breast, she lowered her hands to his hips and arched against him. He shuddered. She slithered down under him, aligning their bodies, and he braced himself above her. "Kiss me," she whispered, astonished to hear herself verbalizing her desires as directly as he had.

He obliged, devouring her mouth with his. She bent her knee between his legs again, and he flexed his thigh against her. Their movements seemed to pick up momentum, urgency, drive. When he rolled onto his back, bringing Daphne up onto him, she accepted the new position, not bothering to wonder at the uncharacteristic aggressiveness that compelled her to kiss his chest as he'd kissed hers, to run her teeth and tongue over the small brown nubs of his nipples and her fingers over his ribs and abdomen. Not bothering to protest when he wedged his hand between her legs and stroked her. It was too intense, everything was too intense—and she wanted it to go on forever.

"Daff." His voice was scarcely audible. "Daphne..."

She reached down to touch him again, aware that this time he wouldn't ask her to stop.

He surged against her palm and groaned something unintelligible. Opening his eyes, he fixed her with a dazed smile. "Do you want to be on top?" he asked thickly.

She laughed, astounded that at this point he was still capable of shaping a coherent question, and equally astounded that he wasn't too swept up in his own rapture to care about Daphne's preferences. "No," she answered, descending to the mattress, careful not to lose the precious contact of his hand on her. "You."

He rose, balancing himself above her, sliding against her palm again. "Now?"

She nodded, bringing him to her, circling his hips with her legs as he thrust into her. They moaned in unison. Brad relaxed onto her for an instant, then thrust again, slow and deep, filling her completely.

She curled her arms tightly around him, distantly aware that her fingernails were carving up his back. He didn't seem to mind. His fingers became lost in the wild blond halo of her hair, and his lips danced from her forehead to her chin before settling on her mouth. His body rocked hers in a steady, pulsing rhythm, sliding, stroking, taking and giving.

She felt the spinning storm of emotions gathering once more inside her, less amusement now and more passion, more affection, more hunger and love and need, funneling down through her body in a contracting coil until the thrill of it grew nearly painful. She sobbed an inchoate plea, her garbled words absorbed by Brad's kiss—and then ecstasy came in a great, consuming rush, throbbing through her body and her soul before capturing Brad, hurling him down into the center of the storm with her.

Minutes passed, an immeasurable stretch of time during which they lay fused together, clinging to each other with an almost deranged desperation. Their chests pumped savagely against each other, their breathing rough and ragged, their hearts beating clamorously. Slowly, gradually, Brad lifted himself up. His eyes took a while to focus on Daphne; his mouth was curved in a dazed grin. "Well," he whispered huskily, "I think we've finally gotten the hang of it."

"And it only took us eight years," Daphne quipped, mirroring his blissful smile.

"Believe me, Daphne—if it had been like this last time, I wouldn't have waited eight years to do it again." He brushed a few curling tendrils back from her cheeks and kissed her lovingly. "It was spectacular, Daff. Unbelievable."

She wrapped her arms around him and pulled him back down to her. He willingly returned her hug, then cushioned his head on the pillow next to her and nuzzled the skin below her earlobe. She closed her eyes, praying that the thoughts she'd managed to hold at bay so far would continue to keep their distance for a while longer.

If she let them sneak up on her, she knew what they'd tell her: that making love with Brad *had* been spectacular, more than spectacular. That her feelings about what had happened this time were just as overwhelming as they'd been last time—only this time she wasn't burning with hatred. That the ground rules Brad had established for this evening—that he and Daphne were friends, and that no one would get hurt—might define his position much more accurately than hers.

If she hadn't done something as stupid as fall in love with Brad, she had come damned close. And if she *had* fallen in love with him, she was going to get hurt, all his promises to the contrary.

But she wouldn't think about that now. For the moment, the only thing she intended to do was curl up in the protective warmth of his body and pretend that nothing—no uneaten dinner, no waterlogged flowers, no past or future—existed beyond the bedroom door.

Chapter Nine

"You must be starving," she said.

Brad groaned. At the moment, he was too mellow to be starving. His entire body resonated with the tranquil afterglow of their lovemaking; every cell in his body was serenely still.

The only thing he could imagine doing with his mouth right now was kissing Daphne—if she could bear to be kissed again. Her lips were a dark, rosy color, slightly puffy from the workout he'd already given them. He considered asking her whether she'd object to more exercise, then thought better of it and kissed her without obtaining her permission. Her response was sluggish—but then, his kiss was sluggish, too. He doubted either of them had enough energy to embark on an activity as strenuous as eating.

"Maybe later," he mumbled, nestling contentedly into the pillow and forcing Daphne's head down to his shoulder. "We'll eat later."

She cuddled up to him, tucking one of her legs between his and letting her lips brush against the hollow of his throat. From this position, he could see only the delicate slope of her shoulder and the fuzzy mop of yellow curls crowning her head.

The peaceful warmth began to ebb from his flesh, replaced by something equally pleasurable but harder to identify. Some sort of giddy bafflement, perhaps, something that both bewildered and tickled him: the astounding realization that Daphne Stoltz *was* dynamite in bed.

Who would have thought it? Who would have thought that this flat-chested, four-eyed woman with the Harpo Marx hairdo could do such incredible things to him? He hadn't imagined that his discovery of her nakedness under that weird silk bathrobe had stricken him with all the force of a bolt of lightning, or that her tongue had engaged his in the most unabashedly wicked foreplay he'd ever known, or that her touch had somehow managed to throw his entire nervous system out of whack. He hadn't imagined the ferocious urges she'd unleashed in him with her neatly manicured hands, her teeth, her bony pelvis colliding with his, her body—that strange, imperfect body of hers surrounding him, carrying him somewhere he'd never been before.

He had told her it was spectacular and unbelievable. Reflecting on the experience, he decided that those two feeble adjectives hardly began to do justice to what he'd just undergone with Daphne.

"Let's make love again," he suggested, aware even as he spoke that he'd probably need a bottle of megavitamins and an hour of rest to get his system back in functioning order.

Daphne laughed, her breath warm and dry against his chest. "Right. And then we'll notify the *Guinness Book of World Records*."

"You, too?" he half asked, understanding at once that she was as blissfully depleted as he was. He smiled inwardly, delighted to know that he wasn't alone in his thunderstruck response to what they'd shared, that what had been the epitome of physical fulfillment for him had been no less awesome for her.

He combed his fingers gently through the wheat-colored mop of her hair, careful not to get snared by the dense curls, and angled her head away from his arm so he could peer into her unfocused green eyes. They weren't truly pretty eyes—the irises reminded Brad of the olives with which his mother garnished her martinis—but there was something incandescent about them right now, the glow of a woman totally and wondrously sated. The last time Brad had been intimate with Daphne, he hadn't seen that glow. He had been smart enough not to look for it. But he looked for it this time, and discovering it gratified him in a way that went well beyond the implied compliment regarding his prowess in bed.

Sex hadn't been great just now because *he'd* been great. It had been great because Daphne had been great—because they'd been great together.

"Just a warning, Daff," he murmured, leaning toward her and kissing the undefined tip of her nose. "Sooner or later, we're going to have to make love again. That's the way it is with any proper experiment: if you can't believe how good the results are the first time, you're supposed to repeat the experiment to make sure."

"I'm not arguing," she said languidly. "All I'm saying is, we'd better eat something first."

"Ah, so *you're* starving."

"Mmm-hmm. Can I interest you in some clams?"

"That was low, Daffy," he said, presenting her with a wounded expression. Then he leaned forward to kiss her again. "I'll settle for the linguini with a little melted butter on top."

"Forget it," she declared. "The linguini's been sitting in a pot of hot water for well over a half hour, which means it's probably got the consistency of cream of wheat by now. And to tell you the truth, Brad, I'm not in the mood to cook another batch.''

He didn't blame her. ''Have you got any peanut butter?'' he asked, deciding their best strategy was to keep their snack quick and simple. The sooner they ate and replenished their reserves of strength, the sooner they could be making love again.

She grinned and swung her legs off the bed. ''With or without jelly?''

''You're the hostess. I'll leave it up to you.''

He pushed himself away from the mattress to sit, but a sharp glance from her kept him in place. ''We're going to eat in bed,'' she explained as she crossed the room to her robe, which had landed in a rumpled heap on the floor near her closet door. She picked it up, examined the snagged zipper and snorted. After throwing the garment onto a chair, she opened a drawer of her dresser and pulled out an oversize man's shirt. She buttoned it on. ''You stay right where you are, Brad. I'm going to serve you in bed. How's that for romantic?''

''It sounds more romantic than cream-of-wheat pasta,'' he answered. He could think of only one thing more romantic that he'd rather do in bed with Daphne than eat—and they'd already established that they needed to refuel for that.

''Well, I figure, one way or another, something's going to go right tonight in the romance department.''

''Something already did,'' he reminded her, his smile a hybrid of lecherousness and gratitude.

She laughed. ''Something besides that,'' she said, slipping her eyeglasses on and then heading for the door in a loping stride.

"I might get bread crumbs on the sheets," he called after her in a warning.

"I wouldn't kick you out of bed for that," she swore before vanishing down the hall.

Temporarily abandoned, he propped the pillows against the headboard, fashioning a more comfortable seat for himself. Then he contemplated the woman who'd just left the room. He thought about her lanky legs, her shapeless nose, the angular protrusions of her shoulder blades, the milky pallor of her skin, the inexplicable drabness of her eyes... the way her questing mouth had felt on his chest, and her fingernails when she'd scraped them across his back, and the way he'd sensed as much as heard the low, purring sound of rapture that filled her throat the moment she'd peaked....

Even without an emergency dose of megavitamins, he felt himself getting hard again. Twisting to examine the back of his shoulder, he saw a long pink scratch where her fingernails had raked his skin—and the sight aroused him even more. If she didn't look so much like an improved version of the dowdy coed with whom he'd botched things so badly in college, he would have been convinced that the Daphne Stoltz he remembered and this one were two completely different creatures. It didn't seem possible to him that the same woman could have been responsible for both the worst and the best sex he'd ever experienced in his life.

The best? Well, no, he and Daphne had just had a terrific time, but it hadn't really been the *best* he'd ever had, had it? Back in Seattle, he'd been seriously considering marriage to Nancy, for heaven's sake. He had loved Nancy, revered her, been overwhelmingly infatuated with her. He had spent over two years courting her and untold hours meditating on her perfectly shaped hazel eyes, the lustrous auburn waves of her hair, her peaches-and-cream complexion, her voluptuous breasts and microscopic waist and soft, sultry lips...

But the God's honest truth was, sex with Daphne just now had been better than anything he'd ever known with Nancy.

It must have been a fluke, he concluded, the orgasmic equivalent of an optical illusion. Surely he and Daphne would never be able to scale such heights a second time... although his insistently aroused body seemed more than ready to deny that prediction.

Daphne returned to the bedroom carrying a tray of food, and Brad discreetly pulled the blanket around him so she wouldn't notice his condition. She lowered herself onto the bed next to him, then balanced the tray between them on its fold-out legs. It held two plates, a loaf of whole wheat bread, a jar of peanut butter, one of strawberry jam, knives and paper napkins. "I don't know whether you want something to drink," she said, crossing her legs squaw-style and reaching for the peanut butter jar, "but while I don't mind crumbs in bed, I do mind spilled beverages."

"That's understandable." Brad watched her smear peanut butter onto a slice of bread and fantasized about her naked body beneath the baggy shirt. The fantasy was so stimulating he had to shift his legs and rearrange the cover around him, but Daphne appeared to be unaware of his discomfort. She handed him the sandwich she'd begun, and he topped a second slice of bread with jam to complete it.

"I was right about the linguini," she reported, preparing another sandwich for herself. "It was disgustingly mushy. I had to take the flowers out of the sink in order to soak the pot. They're all mushy, too."

"Ask me if I care," Brad said nonchalantly.

"The roses I put in the vase are beautiful, though," she said, offering Brad a sincere smile. "Did I tell you how much I appreciate them?"

He wondered how often—if ever—Daphne received roses from men. The possibility that she never did saddened him, and he shoved the thought away. "If I'd known you liked roses, I would have brought you more of them."

Daphne chuckled. "You brought plenty of flowers, Brad," she assured him. "More than I know what to do with, obviously."

He was listening to her with only half his mind. The other half continued to scrutinize her as she bit into her jamless peanut-butter sandwich, chewed, swallowed and ran the tip of her tongue over the corners of her mouth to capture the stray crumbs. It vexed him to think that Daphne wasn't showered with roses from male admirers on a regular basis. She ought to have boyfriends by the dozens, by the hundreds. But she didn't—for the simple reason that she was not pretty. The comprehension infuriated him, and yet there he himself was, no better than any other man, wishing that she were more attractive so he could think of her as a suitable partner for himself.

He gently lifted her eyeglasses from her face and set them on the night table behind her. "Why did you do that?" she asked, blinking.

"You took them off before. I'm just trying to get used to the way you look without them." He skipped mentioning that she looked marginally better when she wasn't wearing them, and chose instead to ask, "Have you ever considered wearing contact lenses?"

She nodded and scowled at the memory. "Right after college, when I moved to Chicago I bought a pair. They were never comfortable, though. Dust kept blowing into my eyes—believe me, they don't call Chicago the Windy City for nothing. Then I scratched my cornea taking one out, and I was in a lot of pain from it." She bit into her sandwich, reminiscing. "Some people just can't wear contacts. I wish I could. I can still remember one night when I forgot to take them out before going to bed. When I woke up the next morning and opened my eyes, my vision was kind of cloudy, but I could *see* things. I could read my alarm clock without squinting, and make out the slats on the Venetian blind on my window. I thought I'd been the beneficiary of some sort of overnight transformation, and my eyesight had been miraculously cured. That's always been one of my lifelong dreams—to wake up one morning and discover that I had perfect vision."

Brad lowered his empty plate to the tray and slung his arm around Daphne's shoulders. It had never occurred to him that for nearsighted people, the worst thing about their situation was not having to wear eyeglasses, but having to contend with poor vision. Instead of feeling sorry for Daphne for being saddled with spectacles that detracted from her appearance, he ought to feel sorry for her for being saddled with a blurry view of the world.

"What are some of your other lifelong dreams?" he asked, suddenly frustrated by how embarrassingly little he knew about her.

She popped a corner of crust into her mouth and then snuggled more cozily against him. Her elbow poked into his rib cage in a way that ought to have hurt him, but it didn't. He wanted her close to him, as close as it was possible to be. Once she had arranged herself comfortably he tightened his hold on her, pinning her to him so she wouldn't be able to move away.

"My lifelong dreams, huh," she echoed. "Other than waking up with perfect vision?" She ruminated for a minute. "I'd like to be able to buy my partnership in Horizon Realty without having to sign for any more loans."

"That doesn't count," Brad criticized good-naturedly. "One week ago, you weren't even thinking in terms of a partnership in the company. I mean your *lifelong* dreams, dreams you've been dreaming for a long time. Like perfect vision."

Daphne acquiesced with a nod. "World peace, of course, and a cure for cancer—along with a cure for myopia. And I wouldn't mind finding Mr. Right someday, and having a child. How about you?"

"Pretty much the same," Brad told her. "World peace, a cure for cancer... and a cure for myopia if you want it, Daffy." He twirled his index finger through a ringlet of her hair as he thought. "I dream that my parents will stop their silly bickering and get back together again. And, sure, the rest of it—a beautiful wife and a couple of kids."

He detected a subtle tension rippling through her, causing her shoulders to hunch slightly. Why was she suddenly shying from him? What had he said wrong?

A beautiful wife.

Surely Daphne didn't expect Brad to propose marriage to her just because they'd made love. She was a savvy woman, smart and mature. She and Brad both understood the reason for this get-together. It had to do with preserving a friendship, not fostering a love or exploring marital options. They both knew that.

Gradually it dawned on Brad that Daphne hadn't been reacting to the word *wife*. What she'd reacted to was the word *beautiful*.

A full minute after he'd spoken, she still hadn't relaxed within the curve of his arm. He cursed silently, then twisted to peer at her. "Daff?"

She raised her eyes from the tray to his face. They were willfully dry and empty, refusing to reveal her emotions.

"Can we talk about this?"

"About what?" she asked with false ingenuousness.

"About why your body's just dropped twenty degrees in temperature."

She turned to stare at the tray again. She pinched the ruffled trim edging the blanket with her fingers, then let her hands go slack in her lap. "It seems to me," she said slowly, in a muted voice, "that far too many men—the vast majority of them, no doubt—are looking for *beautiful* wives."

It pained Brad to think of how much his tactless comment must have hurt her—especially since she was brave enough to answer him truthfully when he'd goaded her into saying something she clearly didn't want to say. "Don't think you aren't beautiful," he reassured her, hoping he wasn't digging himself even deeper.

She smiled wryly. "Please don't be a hypocrite, Brad. One thing we seem to have going for us is honesty. Don't blow it, okay?"

Her tone was less bitter than beseeching. She was right, of course—honesty was important, an essential part of their burgeoning friendship. Brad had no intention of spoiling that friendship by resorting to hypocrisy.

Yet when he'd told her, however obliquely, that she was beautiful, he hadn't been hypocritical. At least at that moment, when a measure of emotion had crept into her face, the faintest glimmer of anguish and fear, he *had* considered her beautiful. No matter how unattractive she was from an objective standpoint, she was beautiful, too.

He sighed. "Daphne," he murmured, stroking his finger absently behind her ear and wondering how to restore the closeness between them. Abruptly he realized that they'd never lost that closeness. Talking to Daphne was, in its own way, as intimate an act as making love to her. "Daphne, listen to me. You are beautiful."

She chuckled—and, again, he detected not a trace of bitterness in her quiet laughter. "Maybe you're the one who needs glasses," she suggested. "I'll grant you that my face isn't so horrible it's going to shatter any camera lenses. But I'm no cover girl, either."

"You don't have to be a cover girl."

"Thank heavens for that," she said, indulging in another pensive laugh. "If I *did* have to be one, I'd be in a whole lot of trouble."

"What I meant—" he felt suddenly desperate to make her believe him "—is that beauty is in the eye of the beholder."

"No!" she gasped with phony surprise. He recognized that she was mocking him, but she went on before he could defend himself. "I thought it was only skin deep. Or is it 'Beauty is as beauty does'?"

"Daff—"

She softened, apparently sensing that he needed reassurance even more than she did. "Let me fill you in on a little secret, Brad: believe it or not, most women really do know what they look like. We know that we have our good days—and our bad days, too—but by and large, we've got a pretty clear handle on what we look like. When I was growing up with my pretty little sister, my parents were always reciting all those charming sayings to me so I wouldn't feel bad about being so much less attractive than Helen. It was all very sweet and well intended on their part, but none of it changed the fact that

I'm a plain-looking woman. Most men look at me and think I'm too tall or too gangly or too blah, or my hair is all wrong or I squint too much. If they take the time to get to know me, they decide that I'm not such terrible company. But they sure as hell don't think I'm beautiful."

Her bluntness flabbergasted Brad. He had never heard a woman speak so frankly about herself, and he wasn't quite certain what to do about it. "Why don't they fall in love with you?" he asked, too fascinated by her words and her attitude to worry about diplomacy. "You're wonderful company and—depending on the eyes of the beholder—you're beautiful, too. Why haven't you found Mr. Right?"

"Why hasn't he found me?" she rejoined with exasperating logic. "Whenever I begin to suspect that I've met him, he winds up telling me he thinks of me as a sister."

"I don't think of you as a sister."

Daphne's smile grew wistful. "Not at the moment," she guessed. "Not today. But I wouldn't be surprised if you did yesterday, and I'd wager good money that you will again tomorrow."

"No, Daff," he argued. "I don't think I will."

She shook her head. "You aren't my Mr. Right, Brad, so it doesn't matter, does it?"

He wanted to grab her by her shoulders and shake her until her teeth rattled. He wanted to scream at her that she was completely off base, that she didn't know what she was talking about, that she was beautiful and sexy and perfect in every respect.

But the thing that made her seem so perfect to him right now had nothing to do with her debatable beauty or her sexiness. It was her candor, her openness, her total lack of guile. It was, above all, her refusal to deny the truth about herself. Brad wasn't her Mr. Right and he never would be. Regardless of how splendid making love to her had been, he wasn't going to marry her. She wasn't his ideal mate, the woman with whom he intended to build a future and a family—and she wasn't going to kid herself about it by pretending that she was.

He carefully removed the tray from the bed and placed it on the floor. Then he turned back to Daphne, closing his arms around her, urging her down to the pillow with him. He slid one hand under her hair to the nape of her neck and stroked through the soft wisps of hair there.

"You seem to be deep in thought," she observed quietly.

"Mmm," he said, struggling to clarify his mind before he spoke. "I'm thinking...I'm thinking that you're one of the gutsiest women I've ever met."

"I'm not so gutsy," she argued. "I'm just realistic."

"Whatever you are," he whispered, touching his lips to her brow, "it's turning me on."

She slipped her hand beneath the top sheet, skimming her fingers over his abdomen and below to feel for herself the evidence of his arousal. As her fingers ringed and then ran the length of him, he moaned.

He itched to unbutton her shirt, to kiss her breasts and inhale the lingering fragrance of her perfume. Yet he held back, strangely protective of her. He waited for a sign, any sign from this brave, magnificent woman, that she could possibly desire him as much as he desired her. "Do you want to make love again?" he asked when her silence extended beyond a minute.

"Yes."

"I would like to spend the night with you," he went on, hoping he wasn't pressuring her. "I know we didn't discuss that, Daff, but—"

"I'd like for you to stay."

"Because—because I don't really think the first time was a fluke."

"A fluke?" She laughed hesitantly.

He probably shouldn't have said that, either. But he'd said so many wrong things already, he would let this one pass. Instead of bothering to explain himself—and risking making matters even worse—he worked open the buttons of her shirt, slid it over her shoulders, and kissed her exactly as he'd wanted to, touching his tongue to the dainty indentation between her collarbones, filling his nostrils with the scent of her and his hands with the roundness of her breasts.

As her response intensified, as her flesh warmed and her breath shortened and her body grew damp with readiness for him, he found himself thinking about how peculiar it was that, just as it had been with the house Daphne had sold him, one didn't always realize something was the answer to a dream until the dream was already within one's grasp.

INTELLIGENT THOUGH SHE WAS, Daphne knew that there were certain times when thought was your enemy. If she entertained any thoughts about what was going on between her and Brad while he was with her, she'd ruin the weekend.

So she didn't think. She simply allowed herself the conceit that the whole thing was nothing more than an exorcism of the past, a whimsical way to counter the eight-year-old curse hanging over their friendship. After making love with Brad a few times, she would be hard-pressed to remember what that wretched experience had been like back in college. And that was the point—to replace miserable old memories with happy new ones. That was what Brad had had in mind when he'd proposed this weekend; that was what was going on.

She refused to be overwhelmed by how lovely it was to wake up beside him. She refused to become sentimental over the pleasure of his company at breakfast. They were friends, not lovers, and friends didn't wax rhapsodic about how delightful it was to gaze into each other's sleepy eyes over the morning's first cup of coffee.

Stifling her emotions, stifling her urgent desire to think, she lowered her eyes from Brad's face to her nearly empty cup and calmly asked, "When does your plane leave tomorrow?"

Brad seemed startled by the down-to-earth tone of her conversational gambit. It was the first cogent statement either of them had made since around two o'clock that morning, when Brad had awakened Daphne from a dream-filled slumber to make love to her again.

She hadn't objected. After making love to Brad twice with the bedside lamp on, she found making love to him in the pitch dark something of a novelty. Not that it was any more resplendent an experience than the first two times—or any less resplendent, for that matter—but it was different. Brad's kisses had been hungrier in the dark, his touch more decisive, more demanding. When he'd rolled her on top of himself she had accommodated his tacit request and remained there, straddling him and taking him, dominating their motions and setting her own pace.

Whatever it was that exploded between them, it certainly hadn't been a fluke.

When it was over, they'd found themselves too invigorated to go back to sleep. They had decided to burn off their excess energy by showering and then cleaning up the kitchen. Brad had refused to go near the pot of clam sauce, but he'd dutifully thrown out the textureless pasta and the waterlogged flowers, tied up the trash bag and lugged it to the garage, while Daphne had scoured the pots and put away the unused dishes and flatware. Then she'd lit the candles, flipped over the Mozart record, turned on the stereo and served the fruit and cheese she'd purchased as a romantic dessert for their would-be romantic dinner.

Gouda, pear slices, grapes and a piano concerto—even at two-thirty in the morning—had proven to be exceptionally romantic.

"My plane?" he asked, after taking a sip of coffee.

"What I was thinking," she clarified, nudging the box of corn flakes toward him after filling a bowl for herself, "was that if your plane doesn't leave until the afternoon, you could stop by one of the banks in town and get your mortgage application started."

He nodded, accepting the sensibility of her advice. Shaking a heaping mound of corn flakes into his bowl, he said, "It's a two-o'clock flight. But I thought I couldn't apply for a mortgage without a signed contract."

"You can start the ball rolling with an unsigned copy of your contract, and once it's signed, the bank will already have all your application materials in place. They don't usually like starting things without the contract, but I have friends in the mortgage departments of some of the banks. They'd do it as a favor for me."

"I don't want you using up your favors on me," Brad remarked.

If she were permitting herself to think, Daphne would have indulged in a thought about how, for Brad, she'd gladly use up every favor she had coming to her. But that was the wrong approach to take on this cloudy Sunday morning, and she avoided it. "The sooner you close on the house, the sooner I get paid my commission, Brad. You'd be doing me a favor if you got things started before you left."

He nodded. "All right. Which bank do you recommend?"

She named a few that operated branches in the area and informed Brad which were currently offering the lowest rates. "I've got a ten-o'clock appointment with another client tomorrow morning, so I may not be in the office. I'll leave a copy of your contract with Margaret," she told him.

"Running off with another client, are you?" he muttered with pretended dismay. "Love 'em and leave 'em, huh. Now that you've found me a house, you don't want to waste any more of your time with me."

Daphne smiled, refusing to take his griping seriously. "If it were just any client, I'd give you priority, Brad. But the appointment's with somebody who wants to look at the estate in Upper Saddle River."

"Ah," he said, properly impressed. "Sell that house, and you'll be able to use your commission to pay for your partnership."

"Just about," Daphne confirmed.

A dull gray light filtered through the layer of clouds to enter the kitchen. Lapsing recklessly into thoughtfulness for a minute, Daphne pondered how appropriate the light seemed to her mood—bright enough to illuminate her surroundings, but not bright enough to warm them.

Perhaps that was just as well. If the kitchen were too
bright, she'd be forced to see Brad more clearly than
she'd care to. As it was, she couldn't resist the temptation to let her gaze linger on his strong, symmetrical features, his jaw shadowed by an overnight growth of beard,
his eyes clear and lively despite his interrupted sleep last
night, his dark hair haphazardly arranged around a
crooked part. He'd borrowed Daphne's hairbrush to
groom it, but he'd rushed the job as if he didn't want to
spend too much time with her bristles in his tresses—as
if sharing her hairbrush were too intimate an act.

Well, that was where thinking got you, Daphne mused
glumly. Shoving those troublesome thoughts from her
skull, she manufactured a crisp smile for Brad and said,
"Can I get you some more orange juice?"

An hour later, he took off. He departed with chipper
words about how great it was going to be to have Daphne
as his neighbor, how much he was looking forward to
returning east and spending more time with Eric, how
eager he was to tackle his new job and how fervently he
hoped his parents would have worked out their differences by the time he was settled in his new home.

Daphne smiled, nodded, interjected words of agreement at the right times, and waved him off. Then she shut
her door and indulged in a mournful sigh.

She should have grown wiser over the past eight years.
But if she was so damned wise, how could she have managed to make a mistake at least as catastrophic as the last
one she'd made with Brad?

She loved him. He was gone; she didn't have to bury
her feelings anymore. The previous night had proven to
her that she loved him.

And to him, the previous night had represented nothing more than an opportunity for him and Daphne to tie

up loose ends and free themselves from the past. As far as he was concerned, they could now go their own ways, unconstrained by unfinished business. He could find himself the beautiful wife of his dreams, and sire himself some beautiful children.

As for Daphne's dreams...well, world peace was beyond reality's grasp. A cure for cancer seemed nearly as elusive as did one for myopia. She'd undoubtedly have to live the rest of her life in eyeglasses.

And Mr. Right...Mr. Right was planning to move to Verona and be her pal. If Daphne hadn't missed her bet, he was probably already thinking of her as a sister.

Chapter Ten

"Jim and I are through," said Phyllis.

She was standing on Daphne's front porch, dressed in a stone-washed denim jacket, matching tapered jeans, a pink-and-white checked shirt and white calfskin boots. Her hair was artistically windblown and her eyes were adorned with a subtle frosted shadow. At her feet stood a soft-sided leather valise. Daphne found it truly amazing that, even during what was evidently a domestic upheaval of critical proportions, Phyllis managed to look devastatingly chic.

Daphne was thankful for the distraction offered by Phyllis's unexpected appearance Sunday evening. She ushered Phyllis inside and closed the door.

"I know I should have telephoned you first," Phyllis rambled contritely. She dropped her valise onto a chair, then paced the length of the living room in agitation, trying to burn off her nervous energy. "But by the time I thought about calling you I had already reached the exit off the interstate, and I figured I might as well just come. You can throw me out if you want."

"Why on earth would I want to throw you out?" Daphne asked. "Give me your jacket, Phyllis, and sit down and tell me what happened."

"What happened?" Phyllis railed, marching freneti-
cally to the picture window and then spinning around to
face Daphne. "I told him I'd had it up to here," she said,
indicating the top of her head. "I told him to get the hell
out. That's what happened."

If Andrea were present, she would be smothering
Phyllis in a congratulatory hug right now. But Daphne
was too emotionally drained to hug anybody. She was
running on only five hours of sleep—and a lot of erotic
memories. She scarcely had enough strength to acknowledge Phyllis's announcement with a nod. "If you
told him to get out, how come you're here?" she asked,
staring pointedly at the valise.

"I would have gone to Andrea's, Daff. I mean, who in
their right mind would want to spend the night in Jersey—no offense intended, Daffy, but, I mean, *really*. But
Andrea's already got a house guest. She hasn't got room
to put me up, too. Unless she put me and Brad in the
guest room together, which... believe me, the idea has
enormous appeal, but—"

"Phyllis," Daphne cut her off, "what I was asking
was, if you kicked Jim out, shouldn't you be home and
he be on some friend's doorstep with a suitcase in his
hand? Why did *you* leave the house instead of him?"

Phyllis sighed. "Well, I've got to give him a chance to
pack his things, don't I? I mean, the house is in my name,
so I'm going to end up with it. But I had to let him collect his stuff and cart it someplace else."

"Uh-huh. And how long do you suppose that's going
to take?" Daphne had visions of Phyllis camping out in
the spare bedroom for weeks while Jim moved his belongings out of her house one sock at a time.

Phyllis bristled. "Look, Daff, if it's a problem, I'll find
somewhere else to stay."

"It's no problem," Daphne swore, crossing to Phyllis and tugging the denim jacket off her shoulders, an act of nearly aggressive hospitality. "You can stay with me as long as you like. I've got the room. I was only thinking about Jim, though. As long as he's still got access to your house, he can stall. Possession is nine-tenths of the law and all that."

"Is this what they taught you in real-estate school?" Phyllis asked, her expression a mixture of irritation and fear. "If he isn't gone by tomorrow, I'll go back with a policeman and have him evicted."

"You can't have him evicted," Daphne explained patiently. "He's not your tenant. But don't worry about it," she added hastily as she read the panic in Phyllis's eyes. "I'm sure he'll clear out as soon as he can." She hung the jacket in the closet and scrutinized her friend. "Why don't you tell me what happened?"

"I need a drink," Phyllis declared, plopping herself onto the sofa with such force the cushions bounced around her. "I'm sorry, Daff, but I'm really a wreck. Have you got any booze? I'm not picky—anything will do."

"I have some Bordeaux," Daphne said, remembering the unopened bottle of wine Brad had brought her, which was currently sitting in a trash bag in her garage. She had no other alcoholic beverages in her house, but after having kept her abstemiousness a secret from her friends for so many years, Daphne didn't think that now was the proper time to reveal to Phyllis that she never drank liquor.

"Thanks. That sounds great."

"Have a seat," Daphne ordered her. "I'll be right back." She didn't want Phyllis following her to the garage and learning that the closest thing Daphne had to a wine rack was a three-ply Hefty bag full of overcooked pasta.

It took her several minutes to exhume the bottle from the trash bag, and several minutes more to rinse off the clam sauce that clung to the smooth green glass, gluing a few limp lilac petals to the label. Drying the bottle with a paper towel, she gazed through the kitchen window at the late-evening sky. It was still overcast. Even though she was wearing her eyeglasses, the moon looked murky and dim to her, a blurred semicircle of gray struggling futilely to shed its light through the layers of clouds and mist.

Daphne didn't believe that the heavens exerted any mystical powers over the earth, but she found it apt that such a dismal, gloomy sky was doming her corner of the planet on this dismal, gloomy night.

All day she had tried to keep herself busy. She had done a little gardening, swept the enclosed back porch, read assorted sections of the Sunday newspaper, ironed a few blouses. It had been a Sunday like any other, except for the fact that it had followed a Saturday night that didn't resemble any other night in Daphne's life.

It didn't matter how many blouses she ironed, or how many weeds she yanked out of the flower beds, or how many times she brushed a broom over the back porch. It didn't matter that she and Brad were mature and sensible, as he'd claimed they were when he had proposed that they spend a night in each other's arms, or that he believed setting the past to rights was going to make them both feel so much better afterward. Daphne didn't feel better. What she felt was a deep, implacable love for Brad—along with the painful understanding that her love wasn't returned.

She had known going in that Brad didn't love her. She had known that he didn't love her the last time they'd gone to bed together, too—only this time, she'd gotten tripped up on her own emotions. This time, she'd made love to Brad because he was Brad, not because he was a good-looking, congenial acquaintance who happened to have wandered away from a fraternity party at the same time she did.

The only corkscrew she owned was attached to a bottle opener, and she nearly cut her finger on the point when she snapped open the hinge. She reproached herself for allowing her thoughts to drift to last night instead of remaining in the present. Phyllis needed someone to talk to right now, and Daphne needed someone to divert her attention from her heartache and her anger with herself over her stupidity. As sympathetic as she was to Phyllis's travails, she was almost a little bit relieved by the thought that someone else's life was in an even bigger mess than her own.

Poor Phyllis—one more woman trapped within the spell of this dismal, gloomy night sky, Daphne pondered dolefully as she poured some wine into a glass and carried it into the living room. She considered asking Phyllis whether she believed in the power of weather to influence people's moods, but that might arouse Phyllis's curiosity about Daphne's dreary temperament, so she refrained.

"This wine is delicious," Phyllis said after taking a sip. "What is it?"

"It's a Bordeaux," Daphne told her.

"I know that. I meant what vintner, what year..."

Stymied, Daphne shrugged. "The bottle's in the kitchen if you want me to check." At Phyllis's puzzled look, she added, "To tell you the truth, Phyllis, it was a gift. I don't drink red wine, and I don't pay attention to the vintages."

"So you're foisting your unwanted gifts on me. That's okay, Daffy. I don't mind. As I said, it's delicious." Phyllis took another taste, then lowered the glass to the coffee table and sighed. "So. I finally did it."

She no longer seemed terribly upset—or even particularly frazzled. Perhaps a few sips of wine were all it took to put her feelings into perspective.

Perhaps a few sips of wine would have a similar effect on Daphne, enabling her to view her night with Brad for what it was: a sexual romp, mutually satisfying on a physical level and utterly devoid of commitment. She contemplated jumping off the wagon for about ten seconds, then came to her senses. "What made you decide to call it quits with Jim?" she asked, slouching in one of the easy chairs and slinging one leg over the arm of the chair.

"Brad," Phyllis said simply.

Hoping her face didn't betray her discomfort at hearing his name mentioned—let alone mentioned as a co-respondent in Phyllis's breakup with Jim—Daphne waited for her friend to elaborate.

Phyllis drank a bit more wine first. Then she settled deeper into the sofa's upholstery and tossed a wavy lock of her ash-blond hair back from her face with a graceful flick of her head. "Jim hasn't shut up about Brad, ever since the party at Andrea's."

"Because of the way you looked at Brad?"

"Well...I admit I did more than look," Phyllis whispered with a coy smile.

Daphne took a moment to collect herself. Were Phyllis and Brad having an affair? Why hadn't Brad said something about it? How could he have been fooling around with Daphne's close friend behind Daphne's back? Not that he owed her any explanations for his behavior, not that he was obligated to her in any way, but . . . she trusted him. She trusted him, and he was apparently doing something more with Phyllis than merely letting her look at him.

Daphne should have expected as much. When a woman as ravishing as Phyllis looked at a man, he would have to be comatose not to notice, and not to want to return the compliment. Maybe Brad had been lusting after Phyllis as avidly as she'd been lusting after him. Maybe after Daphne and Paul had made their early departure from Andrea's party a couple of weeks ago, Phyllis had found some willing soul to take Jim for a stroll around the block, and then she'd cornered Brad and propositioned him. . . .

"And he was eavesdropping on me, Daff," Phyllis complained, affecting her adorable little-girl pout. "That's what hurt so much."

"Huh?" Daphne scrambled through the thicket of suppositions that had sprung up around her, trying to find her way back to her conversation with Phyllis. "Brad eavesdropped?"

"Not Brad, Jim," Phyllis explained, too caught up in her self-righteousness to mind that Daphne wasn't paying full attention to her. "I mean, the guy had the nerve to listen in on an extension when I called Brad. Not that he had anything especially juicy to listen to. All I did was ask Brad to meet me in the city for lunch. It's not as if I'd asked him to run off to Tahiti with me. But the way Jim was carrying on, well, you'd think—"

"When did you and Brad have lunch?" Daphne asked, hoping she didn't sound too anxious. "Where did you go?"

"We didn't go anywhere," Phyllis said. "Brad said that his schedule was really hectic, but that maybe once he was moved into his new house and working at his new office in the city, we might be able to work something out and get together. So, when Jim started hurling his filthy insinuations at me, I figured it was time to throw the bum out."

Despite Phyllis's tough talk, despite the courage the wine seemed to give her, Daphne noticed a faint haze of tears collecting along her eyelashes. If Daphne could feel so blue about saying goodbye to Brad after spending all of one night with him, how must Phyllis feel about saying goodbye to a man she'd lived with for over a year?

"I'm really sorry," Daphne said sincerely.

"So am I," Phyllis chimed in. "It kills me to think how much time and energy I wasted on Jim."

"That's not what I meant," Daphne insisted. She wasn't fooled by Phyllis's stoicism. "Ending a relationship like yours and Jim's must hurt, even if it's the right thing to do. You did love him, after all. It always hurts to realize that a love affair is over."

Phyllis's gaze narrowed suspiciously on Daphne. "Oh, Daff," she said, suddenly compassionate. "You sound like you're speaking from personal experience."

Daphne hadn't meant to be so transparent. But Phyllis had known her a long time, and Daphne couldn't hide her feelings completely from her old friend. However, she couldn't very well tell Phyllis that she was grieving over her ill-fated fling with Brad, not when Phyllis herself had designs on him.

"Tell me about it," Phyllis demanded sympathetically. "I feel so much better after getting everything off my chest about Jim. You'll feel better if you get everything off your chest, too." When Daphne didn't speak,

Phyllis added, "I'm your friend, Daff. Talk to me. Tell me about it."

Daphne exhaled. Phyllis was her friend, and she was undoubtedly right in claiming that Daphne would feel better if she didn't keep her emotions locked up. "All right," she said carefully. "I'm . . . it's no big deal, Phyllis. I'm just . . . a little brokenhearted, that's all."

"A little?" Phyllis scoffed. "Brokenheartedness is an absolute, Daffy. Either you're brokenhearted or you aren't."

"Okay," Daphne conceded, unwilling to get into a debate about semantics with Phyllis. "I'm brokenhearted."

"Who's the bastard?" Phyllis asked, automatically taking Daphne's side. "That redheaded guy, Paul?"

Daphne appreciated her friend's unquestioning loyalty. "No, it isn't Paul," she replied. "It's . . . nobody you know." She hated having to lie, but there was a limit to how much she could confide in Phyllis.

"And what did he do to you?"

He made me fall in love with him, Daphne almost said. *He stole my heart, and he thinks of me as a sister.* "Nothing, really," she hedged. "It's just one of those things. I love him, and he doesn't love me."

"Why doesn't he love you?" Phyllis asked indignantly.

"He never has. He was always up front about it, Phyllis. It's my fault, really." She forced a weak smile. "There isn't a whole lot to say about it, Phyllis. I wouldn't have even brought it up, except—"

"I'm glad you did," Phyllis asserted. "You always keep your social life such a deep, dark secret, Daff. You ought to open up more, and let your friends help you through the rough spots. I know you and Andrea have helped me through more rough spots than I can count, and I appreciate it."

By Daphne's estimation, Phyllis's love life underwent more rough spots in any given month than Daphne's love life had undergone since she'd first become aware of the opposite sex. But Phyllis had a valid point. It did feel good to vent some of her misery, to share her pain with a friend. Even though Daphne could never divulge the specifics, the basics were true: she loved a man who didn't love her, and it hurt.

"Have you told him anything about your feelings?" Phyllis asked.

Daphne shook her head. "He thinks we're just friends."

"Well... how intense is this friendship? How do you even know that what you feel for him is love and not just deep affection?"

Daphne winced. "We slept together."

"He slept with you, and he thinks of you only as a friend?" Phyllis erupted. "What kind of jerk is he, anyway?"

The kind of jerk you want to take up with, once he moves to Verona, Daphne answered silently. "It was... an experiment," she explained, recalling Brad's remark about how researchers often had to repeat their experiments to make certain the results were accurate.

Phyllis shook her head. "I'd stay away from this creep if I were you," she advised. "He sounds like the kind who enjoys playing with fire—and you're the one getting burned. Steer clear of him, Daff. Fall out of love with him as fast as you can."

Daphne couldn't dispute Phyllis's advice. She wasn't going to be able to steer completely clear of Brad, but her wisest strategy would be to get over him as quickly as possible. Her love was doomed to remain unrequited. There was no point in clinging to false hopes, wasting time and energy on a man whose biggest dream in life was to find himself a beautiful wife.

"You're right," she agreed. "That's exactly what I intend to do, Phyllis. I'll survive this disaster—we'll both survive our disasters," she concluded with all the spirit she could muster.

Phyllis smoothly accepted the fact that the focus of the conversation had veered back to herself. "I know we'll survive, Daff. You'll probably go back to finding one of those safe, boring types you prefer—and I'll go after Brad. He'll be living in the area soon; maybe he and I can develop a relationship. I think we've got great potential as a couple, Daff. What do you think?"

"I think you'd look swell together," Daphne answered, wondering whether Phyllis would pick up on the heavy irony in her tone.

She didn't. "When is he going to be moving east?" she asked innocently. "Do you know?"

Daphne knew the approximate closing date on his house, assuming he ran into no trouble with the bank. But, out of professional integrity, she would never publicize the details of his house purchase. "No," she fibbed. "I really don't know."

"Well, whenever," Phyllis said, unconcerned. "I don't want to rush into anything with him. We'll just take it one step at a time, and let nature take its course."

"Phyllis." Daphne knew she couldn't keep Brad for herself—he wasn't hers to keep. But Phyllis seemed to be making too many serious decisions based on some half-baked notion that Brad might become her lover. She'd given Daphne some sound counsel; Daphne owed it to her friend to reciprocate. "Breaking up with Jim for the sole purpose of pursuing Brad seems awfully foolhardy to me," she commented. "You barely know Brad—you haven't even had that lunch date with him, yet. What if you don't like him? What if he doesn't like you?"

The odds were quite high, of course, that Brad would adore Phyllis. She had so much more going for her than Daphne did. How could he not fall head over heels for her?

Indeed, Daphne was too realistic to presume that things would evolve in any other way. Given his choice, Brad would select Phyllis over Daphne any day. All that blather he'd spouted about how beautiful Daphne was—that had been nothing more than the sort of speech a tactful man made to the woman he'd just had sex with. Brad would choose a beautiful woman over a funny-looking one. Any sane man would.

"Do you want his telephone number in Seattle?" she asked, resigned to the inevitable. She wasn't going to be selfish. Brad was beyond her grasp. If Phyllis wanted to try her luck with him, Daphne wouldn't stand in her way.

Phyllis perked up. "Have you got it?"

Nodding, Daphne unwound herself from her chair and crossed to the coat closet, where she'd left her briefcase from work. She pulled her "Brad Torrance" folder from the briefcase and jotted his Seattle number on the back of one of her business cards.

She handed the card to Phyllis, who slipped it into the breast pocket of her shirt. "I'm not sure I'll use this," Phyllis allowed, presenting Daphne with a sheepish smile. "I don't know what I would say to him if I called him out there. I can't very well invite him on a lunch date when he's three thousand miles away."

You'll think of something, Daphne muttered beneath her breath. Damn it, but she was jealous. No use denying it—she was jealous of her friend for being so pretty and desirable. Phyllis might become involved with too many cads; she might be single-handedly supporting the branch of the publishing industry devoted to books about superior women falling in love with inferior men. But her social life was much more exciting than Daphne's. At least those inferior men intermittently lavished attention on her.

Brad wasn't an inferior man—and he just might choose not to lavish attention on Phyllis. But he wasn't going to fall in love with Daphne. Of that much, she was certain.

"Good luck with him," Daphne said, lifting Phyllis's empty wineglass and carrying it to the kitchen for a refill. "He's all yours."

BRAD LOATHED PACKING.

Since his company was paying for his transfer, he had arranged to have most of his possessions packed by the movers. However, certain packing chores he reserved for himself: the books that had belonged to his grandfather that had antique value; some irredeemably out-of-fashion articles of clothing which he needed to sort through and set aside for Goodwill; the items stored on the upper shelf of the den closet, a treasure trove of miscellanea to which he was sentimentally attached.

He had already spent an hour in the closet that afternoon, hauling from the shelf a portfolio of letters he'd sent to his parents while he was at college, the cedar cigar box filled with his all-time favorite marbles, the grotesque Buddha-shaped brass incense holder his very first girlfriend had given him, with its gummy residue of balsam incense at the bottom of the Buddha's belly. The next thing to come off the shelf was an envelope filled with photographs of Nancy.

After dusting off his hands on his jeans, he carried the envelope to the sofa bed and took a seat. He shook out the photos, then stacked them into a neat pile and studied them one by one. There was Nancy standing on a dock at the marina, her glossy auburn hair dancing about her shoulders as she gazed toward a monstrously large sailboat; there she was at the beach in an R-rated strapless bikini; there she was, standing with Brad in front of her apartment building. They were both dressed elegantly, Brad in a dark suit and Nancy in a revealing cream-colored sheath that contrasted stunningly with her deep tan. Her hair was pinned off her neck in a dramatic sweep and her face was expertly made up. Brad had his arm around her in the photo; she had asked the doorman to take the picture for them.

They had gone to an engagement party that night, Brad recalled. One of the associates in Nancy's law firm had hosted it at a yacht club. Everyone had talked about how Nancy would be next, how she and Brad would be hosting their own engagement party soon enough.

Examining the photograph, Brad was struck by how wonderfully matched he and Nancy had been. She was petite and lovely, and he was tall and polished. They both knew how to wear their clothes well. They'd both been born with a certain implied destiny, and they'd both fulfilled their promise.

And it hadn't worked out. To this day, Brad still wasn't sure why, but it hadn't.

Restless, he tossed the photographs aside and wandered to the window. A fine drizzle was descending from the sullen gray clouds, the perfect counterpoint to his state of mind. Filling cartons with his belongings was boring, saying goodbye to neighbors and friends was a grim task, worrying about whether his pending mortgage application would be approved was nerve-racking, and the constant rain depressed him.

Ever since he'd returned to Seattle a week ago he'd been in a funk, apathetic about food and listless at work the few times he'd stopped by his old office or touched base with his West Coast clients. He was drinking too many beers at night, waking up with too many headaches, becoming short-tempered with his Seattle realtor whenever she called to learn whether he had a firm moving date yet.

Too much rain, he decided. Too much precipitation, too many clouds, too many things left to do before he moved. He could think of no other logical explanation for his touchiness.

He was on his way back to the sofa bed to gather up the photographs when he heard the telephone ring. He jogged across the hall to his bedroom and answered. "Hello?"

"Brad? Hi, this is Phyllis Dunn."

Phyllis. From Cornell. Closing his eyes, he conjured up an image of the voluptuous ash-blond woman with the engaging smile. If he wasn't mistaken, he had promised her a lunch date once he started working in New York.

"Hi, Phyllis," he said, wondering why he was disappointed that the caller was Phyllis and not someone else. He hadn't been expecting any calls; he didn't even know who it was he was hoping to hear from. All he knew was that, for some inexplicable reason, he didn't really want to be speaking to Phyllis Dunn right now. "What's up?" he asked with forced courtesy. "Are you in Seattle?"

"No. I'm home, on Long Island."

"Oh." He waited with uncharacteristic impatience for her to state her business. "So? What's up?" he asked brusquely when her silence extended beyond a few seconds.

"Well, I just thought I'd call and see how things were going for you."

How the hell did she think they were going? He was overburdened with chores still left to be accomplished before he left Seattle, and he was sneezing from the dust he'd raised by disturbing the items on the top shelf of the den closet. "Everything's going all right," he said, silently exhorting himself to remain polite. Surely Phyllis hadn't called all the way from Long Island to listen to him complain about the trials and tribulations of packing.

"I can't tell you how happy we all are that you're going to be living back east," Phyllis remarked in a bubbly tone.

Brad drummed his fingers against the edge of the night table and glanced at his alarm clock. "Yes, well...I guess it's nice to be moving somewhere where I already have a circle of friends in place."

"I thought you might be interested to know," Phyllis went on, "that Jim and I broke up."

"Jim? Who's Jim?"

"He was my Significant Other. You met him at Andrea's party, remember?"

Brad entertained a vague memory of a big, handsome hunk of a man hovering around Phyllis that evening. "Oh," he said lamely as another, clearer memory infused him, one of Daphne telling him that he was a home breaker.

He suppressed the urge to curse. Surely Phyllis hadn't ended her relationship with this Jim fellow because of something Brad might have inadvertently done. What had he done, anyway, other than tell her that perhaps they could meet for lunch someday?

Consider yourself forewarned.... He could hear Daphne's laughter-filled voice speaking the words from across a small, round table in an Italian restaurant. He could picture her, with her thick eyeglasses and her wild hair and that funny, lopsided smile of hers. That was the day she had told him about being invited to become a partner in her real-estate firm, and he'd taken her out for a fattening dinner to celebrate her professional coup.

His mind's eye focused on her hands folded before her on the tablecloth. He pictured the delicate amethyst ring adorning her right hand, and her smoothly filed fingernails. Three nights later, those fingernails would be running the length of his spine, digging into the muscled flesh of his shoulders, holding him deep inside her....

"What?" he blurted out, abruptly aware that he'd missed everything Phyllis had just said. He ignored the unnerving tension that gathered in his groin at the memory of the night he'd spent with Daphne. It had been a splendid experience, but it was over and done with and he had no intention of becoming obsessive about it.

"Well, I wanted you to know that I'm hoping we'll be able to renew our friendship when you get back. Jim was so possessive, but now that he's out of my life, I don't see why you and I can't get to be friends."

"We already are friends, Phyllis," Brad noted. Was that the right thing to say? Did he even care? "Look, Phyllis, I've really got to go. I'm really bogged down in work, and I'm kind of...in a hurry."

"Of course. Let me just give you my phone number, and you can give me a call once you're all settled in at your new house."

"Sure," he said, skimming the night table with his gaze in a halfhearted search for a pencil. Coming up empty, he shrugged. He figured he could always get Phyllis's number from Daphne when he arrived in Verona. He certainly wouldn't need the number before then.

"Well," she said after reciting a series of digits which he was unable to copy, "I'm looking forward to seeing you."

"Good talking to you, Phyllis," he mumbled. "Take care." Hanging up, he exhaled.

There had to be something wrong with him, something beyond his boredom over packing and his disgust with the unremitting rainfall to explain his lackluster reaction to Phyllis's telephone call. She had phoned him to announce her availability, and his response had bordered on rudeness. He ought to be jumping at the opportunity she offered. It wasn't every day that an attractive, well-educated, sophisticated woman telephoned from the other side of the continent just to let him know she was unattached and interested in him.

Yet he felt nothing, neither excitement nor revulsion. He had nothing against Phyllis Dunn—but he sensed, deep inside him, that he had nothing for her, either. If a fleeting memory of his carefully plotted one-night stand with Daphne Stoltz could do more to his libido than Phyllis's blatant innuendos about wanting to be "friends" with Brad, something was seriously out of kilter.

He'd been thinking a lot about Daphne since he'd returned to Seattle. Most of the time, when he thought about her it was in the context of their friendship—or of his new house. She had express-mailed a signed copy of the sales contract to him, and she'd phoned him a few times to keep him abreast of the progress being made on his mortgage application. Their calls were generally rushed, and they concentrated almost solely on business, but he couldn't blame Daphne for that. She was a busy woman.

He was always happy when she called, always delighted to hear her voice. After each call, he would often find himself daydreaming about living only a couple of miles from her, being able to call her at the spur of the moment and meet her for dinner somewhere, or drop in on her and shoot the breeze for an afternoon. Frequently, when he thought about his dream house, he thought not about the house itself but about its proximity to Daphne's modest L-shaped ranch house with its colorful, well-tended flower beds.

Usually, when he thought about Daphne, he tried not to think about the night they'd spent together. As fantastic as that had been, it had been planned essentially as a one-shot deal, arranged with a specific end in mind. They had accomplished what they'd set out to accomplish, and there was no sense in dwelling on it. Brad didn't love Daphne; he saw no reason to think of her as a lover. Eventually, he presumed, his body would accustom itself to that reality and he'd stop suffering from those unnerving jolts of arousal whenever he visualized Daphne's fingernails in his mind.

He trudged back to the den, determined to work his way through the remainder of the closet before calling it quits for the day. At the den doorway he halted to survey the cartons stacked along one wall, the bookshelf already emptied and the one still waiting for Brad to tackle its contents. His gaze came to rest on the photographs of Nancy scattered across the sofa bed.

Maybe she was the reason for his malaise.

They had broken up six months ago, and he hadn't seen her since. He had spoken to her only twice, when she'd contacted him to ask him what he wanted her to do with the toiletry items he had left in her bathroom. He had asked her to put them in a bag and drop them off at his office, but the day she'd stopped by with the bag he had been out for lunch with a client, so, through no deliberate design on his part, he had avoided coming face-to-face with her.

He wanted to resume his affair with Nancy about as little as he wanted to start something new with Phyllis Dunn on Long Island. Yet he felt as if he owed Nancy something. A goodbye, at least. As far as he knew, she wasn't even aware that he was leaving Seattle.

Hoping that tying up a few more loose ends would restore his equanimity, Brad returned to his bedroom and dialed Nancy's number. She answered almost at once.

"Nancy? It's Brad," he identified himself. "Are you busy right now?"

"You mean, this minute?"

That had been an irritating trait of hers, he remembered—she always demanded precision, even in the most innocuous of conversations. But Brad didn't respond with one of his sarcastic retorts. Instead, he said mildly, "How about in a half hour? I thought maybe we could meet somewhere for a drink."

"Why?"

"Because I want to tell you something."

"In person?"

"Obviously, in person," he snapped, having exhausted his supply of patience during his chat with Phyllis.

Nancy meditated for a minute. "All right," she said with exaggerated reluctance. "Where do you want to meet?"

Thirty minutes later, Brad was seated in a cocktail lounge, stirring the ice cubes in his glass of cola and lime. He had considered ordering something harder, then decided against it. When he'd taken a sip of the nonalcoholic beverage, he'd fleetingly thought of Daphne, the only person he'd ever known intimately who avoided liquor.

One cola and lime did not a teetotaler make. Just because Brad had ordered what Daphne might have ordered in a similar situation didn't mean he was emulating her.

He kept his gaze riveted to the doorway, watching for Nancy and wondering what great insight, if any, he would have when he finally saw her. When she swept through the door, fifteen minutes late, he experienced nothing beyond a twinge of regret.

She was as beautiful as he remembered, far more beautiful than she appeared in the photographs. Her hair was longer than it had been when they were a couple, but just as lustrous with red highlights. Her figure was still in perfect proportion. She was wearing a clingy blouse that displayed her bosom, and a swirling skirt of a slinky material that did equal justice to her hips and legs. As soon as she spotted Brad, she brushed off the hostess's assistance and strode regally through the lounge to his table.

Brad stood as she neared him. "Thank you for coming," he said, then kissed the cheek she offered him. He hadn't expected her to angle her face toward his lips that way, but he sensed subliminally that if he hadn't kissed her she'd have pivoted on her high heel and marched back out of the lounge. She glided to a chair and waited for him to pull it out for her. Once he did, she sat.

"Well," she said, setting her envelope purse on the table and pressing her hands together, fingertips to fingertips and palm to palm. "What do you want?"

Her brusqueness didn't faze Brad. "Would you like to order a drink?"

"I'll have what you're having," she said, eyeing his glass and then twisting in her chair in search of a waitress.

Brad doubted that she'd be satisfied with straight soda. He flagged down a waitress and ordered Nancy a rum and Coke. "You're looking well," he said once the waitress was gone.

"I know," Nancy concurred without fanfare. "I hope you didn't make me drop everything and come running here on a rainy evening just to tell me that."

She didn't sound arrogant as much as supremely self-confident. Brad forgave her. "No, I've got something else to tell you." He waited until the waitress delivered Nancy's drink before saying, "I'm leaving."

Nancy's densely lashed eyes lingered dubiously on him as she sipped through her straw. "Pardon me if I'm missing something here, Brad, but as I understand it, you left a long time ago."

"I mean Seattle. I'm leaving Seattle," he told her.

Her eyebrows rode high on her brow. "Oh?"

"I've accepted a transfer to New York."

"So? What do you want me to do about it?" she asked archly.

Throughout a leisurely drink of soda, he studied Nancy closely. She was so pretty, so unnervingly marvelous to look at. Her hands, too, had performed feats of sensual magic on him at one time, yet he could look at them and recall their dexterity without suffering any pangs of excitement. Her lips shaped a rounded valentine around the tip of her straw, yet for all the times she'd kissed him, for all the seductiveness of her kisses, he felt only a nostalgia for what had been, not a desire for what could be.

"I don't want you to do anything about it," he explained. "I just thought you ought to know."

"You don't have to keep me apprised of your plans anymore, Brad," she said.

"I know I don't," he granted, once again endeavoring to stifle his impatience. "I just thought it would be nice for you to hear the news from me instead of someone else. We had a long, intense relationship, Nancy. I don't want you thinking I skipped town in the dead of night."

"Fair enough." She took another dainty sip of her drink. "You're right—I probably would have gotten suspicious if you hadn't told me yourself that you were leaving. But you don't have to worry about me. I'll be fine."

"I don't doubt it."

"I guess..." She grinned meekly. "I guess now is as good a time as any to tell you I've been seeing someone else."

Brad found her announcement strangely gratifying. "Who?" he asked.

"I don't think you know him. His name is Larry Steele. He's a friend of Mac MacKenzie's."

Brad nodded.

"He's a good man," Nancy went on. "Reputable background, excellent schooling, solid career and all that. We have a lot in common."

Just like you and me, Brad mused privately. "Do you fight all the time with him?" he asked aloud.

Nancy's eyes met Brad's, and she laughed. "Not as much as we did," she conceded. "Just enough to keep the sparks flying." She leaned back in her chair. "How about you, Brad? Any women waiting for you in New York?"

A picture of Daphne flashed across Brad's brain. "I know a few women there," he admitted. "I've already got a date lined up with an old college acquaintance named Phyllis Dunn." Hearing him mention Phyllis's name momentarily took him aback. He must have thought of her because he'd spoken to her so recently. And yet, it had been Daphne he'd pictured in response to Nancy's question. "I've got friends there, too," he added, hoping his confusion wasn't evident.

"That's nice," she said. "You'll be happy living back east. That's always been your real home."

Brad nodded. He was glad he'd arranged to meet Nancy, glad that she was taking his departure in stride.

But the peculiar thing was, once he'd bade Nancy a final farewell, walked her to her car and headed for his own car at the far end of the parking lot, he felt at odds with himself. He didn't want to go back with Nancy, to figure out why they hadn't been able to make their romance work and to try to correct their mistakes. He had no urge to repair the damage of their past, or to build a friendship with her. Whatever had existed between them was over, finished, and he was content to leave it at that.

He wanted no future with her—that was why. You didn't go back and fix the past with someone unless you were planning for a future with her, he surmised.

And what future did he want with Daphne? A future in which they were neighbors, friends, pals?

"Damn." He grunted the oath out loud, startling himself. "Damn, damn, damn." Then he switched on his windshield wipers and decided that the incessant rain was what had driven him to start swearing.

Chapter Eleven

Daphne followed the receptionist down the hall to the conference room at the rear of the single-story stucco building that housed the offices of Kreitz, Ferragamo & Leeds, Attorneys at Law. She did a substantial amount of legal work with Jay Kreitz, and when Brad had empowered her to find him a competent real-estate lawyer for the closing, she'd arranged for Jay to handle it.

She knew she was going to be the sole woman present at the closing; both the seller and the buyer were bachelors, the seller's lawyer was also a man and Daphne was the only realtor involved in the sale. Ordinarily, being the lone female at a business meeting didn't bother her. Today, though, it did. She wanted to be as inconspicuous as possible. She was edgy and keyed up, and she was afraid the state of her nerves might lead her to make a fool of herself.

Unrequited love was a wretched condition, she pondered as she arranged a brave smile on her face, whispered her thanks to the receptionist and stepped into the conference room. She and Phyllis may have established that Daphne's best tactic was to fall out of love with Brad, but turning off one's emotions wasn't quite as simple as turning off a lamp. The light Brad had unknowingly lit inside her was still burning bright, and she hadn't yet figured out a way to switch it off.

The men all stood as she entered the room, and Jay greeted her by name: "Daphne! Come on in, we're just about to start." He waved her over to a vacant chair beside him at the far end of the table. "You know everyone here, don't you?" he asked, then proceeded to introduce her even though she did, indeed, know everyone. She dutifully shook hands with the seller's lawyer, exchanged a few pleasantries with the seller, and took a deep breath before turning to acknowledge Brad.

He was positioned diagonally across the long mahogany table from her, dressed in what she'd come to think of as his house-hunting uniform: a cotton oxford shirt, a sport jacket and corduroy slacks. He offered her an enigmatic smile, and her own smile lost what little strength it had. The silent pep talk she'd given herself before leaving her office twenty minutes ago—that she would have to be immune to Brad's dazzling looks, that the night they had spent together was as much history to him as was the night they'd left the fraternity party together eight years ago, that he considered her his friend and his realtor and nothing more—none of it had prepared her adequately for the visceral shock she suffered at seeing him. She disguised her nervousness by taking a seat and burying her nose in her briefcase, pretending to search for her folder of documents pertaining to the sale.

The closing was routine—a review of the documents, confirmation that each party to the sale had identical copies, a discussion of terms to make certain that none of the details was open to misinterpretation. Once the review was over, Daphne knew that checks were going to be written, including one made out to Horizon Realty to cover her commission. Until then, she had little to occupy her attention.

That was unfortunate. She honestly didn't want the freedom to contemplate the man seated across the table from her. Seeing his dark, silky hair as he bowed his head to peruse one of the documents made her think of how soft and thick the black tresses had felt between her fingers when she'd held his head to hers for a kiss. Watching the rolling motion of his shoulders as he shrugged in answer to a question forced her, against her will, to remember the tiny lines she'd scratched into his back with her fingernails. His open collar button revealed just enough skin to remind her of how much she had enjoyed kissing him there, how irresistibly sexy she found his neck.

A few times he raised his head and caught her staring at him. His shimmering sky-blue eyes filled with a gentle warmth, matched by the kindly emotion in his dimpled smile. Fondness—that was what she read in his expression. He was fond of Daphne. He'd settled the score between them back in May. Now, nearly two months later, he was content to view her as a pal.

Daphne ought to have been content, as well. She and Brad had achieved exactly what they'd set out to do— find him a house to buy and perform minor plastic surgery on an eight-year-old scar. She ought to be satisfied—and she ought to learn to live with the fact that the surgery on the old scar had left her with new scar tissue. If she wasn't satisfied, well, she had only herself to blame.

The closing took about a half hour. When it was over, the assembled participants engaged in a dizzying round of handshaking and congratulating. As Daphne packed up her briefcase, Jay Kreitz asked her whether she'd made any vacation plans for the summer, and she in turn asked the seller how he liked his new home in Boston. Daphne had participated in sales in which the negotiations had been so rancorous that, by the time of the closing, the buyer and seller were no longer speaking to each other. But no matter how bitter the negotiations, the conclusion of the sale was always an occasion for ritual politeness—more handshaking than most politicians had to endure during an election campaign, accompanied by the requisite charming chitchat.

After fifteen minutes, Daphne finally made her escape. She got as far as the parking lot beside the stucco building before Brad caught up with her. "Hey, Daff— where are you running off to?" he asked, jogging across the gravel lot to her car. He was carrying an oversize manila envelope filled with documents and lashed shut with a string. A warm breeze ruffled through his hair as he ran.

She could lie and tell him she had another appointment that afternoon, but that would be cowardly. Instead, she revived her brave smile and ignored his question altogether. "Welcome to Verona, Brad. I guess you're an official Jerseyite, now."

He drew to a halt less than a foot from her. In her high-heeled sandals, she stood just a couple of inches shorter than he, and it took only the slightest adjustment of her head to meet his gaze. She chastised herself for having failed to exchange her eyeglasses for sunglasses when she had left the air-conditioned office building for the bright late-June afternoon. Not only was the sun's glare magnified by the lenses of her eyeglasses, but their transparency gave Brad an unobstructed view of her face. She wondered if he could see the anguish in her eyes, the self-disgust and disappointment.

"How've you been?" he asked.

He had asked her that same question, with the same phrasing, every time he'd spoken to her in the past month. The last time they'd conversed had been eight days ago, when Daphne had told him the closing had been scheduled and Brad had informed her that he'd be starting his cross-country drive the following day. They had discussed his approximate date of arrival, the schedules he'd drawn up with the movers, his plan to spend a night or two at a nearby Holiday Inn until the closing, and Daphne's willingness to contact the telephone company and the gas company to arrange to have the house hooked up as soon as Brad moved in. When Daphne was ready to conclude the call, Brad had said, "So how've you been?"

She had responded, "Fine, Brad." A good, noncommittal answer—she decided to use it again. "Fine, Brad. How was your trip east?"

"Exhausting," he told her, laying his envelope on the roof of her car and sliding off his blazer. He unbuttoned his shirt cuffs and rolled up his sleeves, then unfastened the second button below his collar.

Objectively, Daphne knew his actions were an effort to remain cool in the summery afternoon heat. But she couldn't stifle an irrational voice inside her, complaining that Brad had opened his buttons merely to aggravate her with tantalizing glimpses of his body. Her gaze riveted itself to the strong column of his neck and she swallowed.

"When did you get in?" she asked, eager to keep the conversation alive so she wouldn't have a chance to think about how attractive she found him.

"Yesterday. I would have called you, but I got to the motel late, and by the time I grabbed a bite to eat and all..." He drifted off, evidently aware of how feeble an excuse that was. "Anyway, I knew I'd be seeing you today." His gaze ran the length of her, pausing at her ankles. Then he raised his eyes, shrugged and grinned apologetically.

It was a surprisingly eloquent gesture. He seemed to be saying, *I know, Daff, we fouled up again and I'm sorry.* Daphne wanted to assure him that she was sorry, too, sorry she hadn't been able to take their night of passion in stride, as they'd both intended to, sorry she was allowing her emotions to foul up their friendship. But given the way she felt, she suspected that it would require at least eight more years before she'd be able to engage in another heartfelt dialogue with Brad about their stupidity in sleeping together.

"How are your finances?" he asked. He seemed aware that his question might be misconstrued, because he hastened to clarify himself. "Have you figured out a way to pay for your share of the partnership yet?"

"I took a loan," she told him, wishing she didn't sound so despondent. The excitement of becoming a partner in her company had disappeared the day she'd signed the bank papers. A few good years of commissions and she'd be out of the red, but in the meantime she'd have to live her life so frugally that her greatest luxury would be her monthly twelve-dollar salads with Andrea and Phyllis in New York City.

"Well, that's great," Brad said with artificial enthusiasm. "I'm glad you were able to pull it off."

"I haven't pulled anything off," she retorted. "I'm over my head in debt at the moment, Brad. I don't consider it great at all."

"Look, Daffy..." Perhaps he could sense her discomfort; perhaps he even shared it. "You know, I—when you walked into the room before, and you—I mean, I—" He faltered, glanced over his shoulder at the building behind him, and then turned back to Daphne. His smile had lessened, and it was shadowed with a poignancy Daphne was unable to interpret. "You're looking well," he said.

The only honest way to compliment a woman who never looked pretty was to tell her she looked well. Health, after all, was supposed to be more important than beauty. "Thanks," she mumbled.

"I mean it," he swore. "It's a nice dress."

The dress she was wearing wasn't worth commenting on, she thought with an almost spiteful peevishness. In fact, it wasn't a dress at all. It was a straight below-the-knees skirt of lime green cotton knit, and a padded-shoulder jersey of the same fabric, and when Daphne had put it on that morning she'd thought it made her look a little like a toy soldier. However, she kept her opinion to herself and said, "Thank you."

"Are you busy?" he asked, his voice underlined with a strange urgency.

"Now?"

"This evening," he said. He seemed to be on the verge of taking her hand, but he switched directions in mid-move and grabbed his envelope from the roof of her car, instead. "I was thinking, maybe we could . . ."

"Have dinner?" she completed his dangling sentence. Her pulse quickened slightly, but she admonished herself not to become too optimistic. Even if she had dinner with Brad, it wouldn't constitute a real date. It wouldn't be as if he were trying to win her heart.

"Have sex," he said quietly. He raised his eyes to the sky and laughed, as if he couldn't believe he'd said such a thing.

"Tonight?"

"Yes"

"No!"

His smile vanished as he absorbed her emphatic tone. "I'm sorry, Daff."

"Why?" she shot back heatedly. "Why are you sorry?"

"You seem...offended," he said, searching for the right word.

She let out a long, steadying sigh. "I'm not offended," she told him. There was no reason to be, after all. He hadn't said anything cruel to her, or put her down in any way.

"It's not..." Again, he seemed to struggle with his words, to falter and grope for the most precise phrasing—or, at least, a phrasing that wouldn't send Daphne into a fit of pique. "It's just that, when you walked into the conference room and I saw you for the first time in so long, I remembered how good it had been with us and I...got turned on." He presented her with a sheepish smile. "Am I being too blunt here, Daffy? I'm just trying to tell you—"

"I don't want to hear it," she snapped. What she wanted to hear was that Brad loved her, that he worshiped her, that he wanted her to be his beautiful wife and to bear his beautiful children. He wasn't going to say that, though. He wasn't even going to say that *she* turned him on. What had turned him on was a memory—a memory of something going a bit haywire one night and taking both her and Brad by surprise. When he reminisced about it he became aroused.

Big deal. So did she. It didn't mean she was going to indulge in a repeat performance.

"You're angry with me," he guessed, appearing slightly miffed. "How come? All I said was—"

"I know exactly what you said," Daphne muttered. Brad's irritation was justified, she admitted silently. He had done nothing to hurt her, either that night or this afternoon. If she was hurt, it was her own fault for misjudging her feelings and overestimating her ability to remain detached after making love with him.

Shaping a crooked smile, she focused on the whitewashed wall of the building behind him and explained, "I don't want you to think of me as some sort of—of outlet for you until you settle in and meet other women. I know it was good betweeen us, Brad. But that was one special night, and . . . I think we ought to leave it at that."

She believed she was being sound and reasonable, but something she'd said clearly struck a raw nerve in him. "Outlet?" he flared. "Is that the way you think I regard you, Daff?"

"You know what I mean," she said, unsure of why he'd reacted so negatively to that word.

He toyed with various responses. "My parents . . . no, never mind."

"How are your parents?" she asked, oddly relieved to latch on to something else to talk about with Brad.

"I have no idea. I didn't call them last night, either."

Daphne wondered what it meant for her to be lumped with Brad's parents in his mind. Was he as exasperated by her as by them? Did he worry as much about her?

"Never mind," he said cryptically, cutting her off before she could think of what to say. "Just understand, Daff, that I never, *never* thought of you that way. What happened between us wasn't just some casual search for an 'outlet,' and you know it."

"Well, it sure as hell wasn't love," she pointed out in a gruff voice. She was beginning to grow exasperated herself. Who the hell did Brad think he was to sweep into town and try for a quick roll in the hay with Daphne? Who did he think he was kidding? He had once differentiated between relief and ecstasy for her, but she knew that even the ecstasy they'd shared in bed was a far cry from love and commitment.

His silence, his stare, the mysterious light in his distressingly beautiful blue eyes irked her. "Well?" she goaded him. "It wasn't, was it?"

"No," he said slowly, frowning as he examined her face in the fierce afternoon sunshine. "I thought we were both clear about that."

She understood the subtle reproach in his words. He had probably figured out the source of her simmering rage, and he was reminding her that she had no right to be angry with him. He was correct, of course. They had been clear about the fact that they didn't love each other—except that Daphne's feelings had backfired on her.

She directed her rage toward herself and spared him with a crooked grin. "Um...I really..." She cleared the raspiness from her voice and tried again. "I really have to be going, Brad. We'll get together some other time—for dinner," she thought it worth stressing. "Now, you've got the key to your new house, right?"

He nodded, still scrutinizing her, still frowning.

"Do you remember how to get there?

"Yes."

"Then you're all set. I had the gas turned on this morning, and the electric service has been transferred into your name. The telephone company's coming in two days. I'm sorry I couldn't get them to come any sooner—"

"It's fine," he said in a strained voice. "I appreciate everything you've done, Daff."

She assumed that by "everything" he meant getting the utilities hooked up, and maybe selling him the house. Surely he didn't appreciate getting turned down for a night of rapturous lovemaking by a homely single lady who obviously didn't have anything better to do that evening, but who had stubbornly chosen solitude over his company.

"Well." She held his gaze for a beat longer, then awkwardly turned away and poked her key into the handle of her car door. As soon as the lock gave, Brad chivalrously opened the door for her.

"I'll call you once my phone is installed," he said.

Daphne nodded. It was the sort of thing a man told a woman, just as he told a woman she was beautiful after he'd made love to her. Much as she hated to admit it, Daphne sensed that Brad wouldn't call her, that the next time she'd see him, if ever, would be at some massive gathering organized by Andrea and Eric. Daphne and Brad would be back to where they'd been at the start— two satellites following separate orbits, never intersecting. They had neutralized their past and ended up no better off than they'd been when they'd first met each other.

Or, perhaps, Daphne had ended up worse off, in love with someone who didn't love her—who hadn't loved her even during the most intense moments of their ridiculously brief affair. As he'd said, he had been clear about that.

She was worse off, but only temporarily. She would get over this, too, in time. She'd made yet another mistake with Brad, but she would recover from it, eventually. Trying to go back had been futile, and she wouldn't go back anymore. From here on in, she vowed, she would go forward, and hopefully, the past would fade into oblivion.

Maybe, in eight years—or eighty—it would.

HE WATCHED HER STEER her car across the bumps of the the unpaved parking lot to the street. Then he slung his blazer over one shoulder, slid the envelope containing his deed and mortgage agreement under the other arm, and continued to stare in the direction of her vanished automobile. Gradually, the dust settled back onto the earth and a muggy gale of wind cleared away the lingering scent of her car's exhaust.

He shook his head, but his mind wasn't as easy to clear as the air had been.

He ought to have been in a celebratory mood. He was now the proud owner of an exorbitantly priced dream house. He was officially back east, ready to move in and establish a new home for himself, ready to start a challenging new job. The limbo in which he'd existed for the past few months was over; he was grounded, able to start living again like a normal human being. He had an address. He belonged somewhere.

Although Brad had been looking forward to this moment for weeks, he had also been suffering from some vaguely defined apprehension. It had hovered over him when he'd left Seattle a week ago, growing stronger with each mile he traveled until that afternoon, when he'd entered the lawyer's office in a state akin to sheer dread.

Then Daphne had appeared at the doorway to the conference room, and her presence seemed to have miraculously calmed him. Seeing her, being in the same room with a woman he considered a dear friend and soul mate, had rejuvenated him, instilling in him the profound understanding that everything was going to be all right, that he *was* where he belonged. He'd felt overcome with sheer joy.

Closing his eyes, he relived the rush of happiness he'd experienced when she had nodded to the receptionist and then stepped across the threshold into the conference room. The shape of her dress had downplayed her already underendowed curves, making her look almost skinny, but he'd liked the way the vivid shade of it picked up the color of her eyes. He'd liked the way she had pulled back her hair with two tortoiseshell combs in an effort to tame her wild blond curls—and the way her curls defeated that effort. He'd liked the way her high heels had given her an almost statuesque grandeur, and the way her pale lips had curved into a modest smile as all the men had scrambled to their feet. As she'd stalked down the far side of the elongated table to reach Jay Kreitz, Brad had felt a deep sense of well-being descend over him. He'd felt as if he were finally back home, safe and sound.

Then Daphne had looked at him, and he'd felt something else, something unexpected but not at all unwelcome: lust. Throughout the entire process of finalizing the sale, he had sat in his chair and fantasized about taking Daphne back to his room at the Holiday Inn in Fort Lee—or, better yet, to another room at another motel, one of those motels that specialized in romantic rendezvous. He'd imagined them bouncing around on a water bed, watching their reflections in an overhead mirror, calling up room service and ordering peanut-butter and strawberry-jam sandwiches and eating them in the nude.

He wanted Daphne. He wanted to enjoy all over again what they'd both enjoyed so much last time. What was so terribly wrong with that?

Something, obviously. Judging by Daphne's reaction, Brad had botched things royally with her again. And once more, he felt inundated with guilt.

The problem was obvious: she'd fallen in love with him.

He should have done something to reassure her, or said something that would at least have salvaged their friendship. He should have sworn to her that he loved her, too. It was the truth—even if his love was very different from the love he assumed that she was feeling for him. He loved her as a friend, and he loved her as a sexual partner. Telling her that might have been enough to cheer her up.

"Sure," he snorted caustically, his shoes crunching against the loose pebbles as he trudged across the lot to his car. The State of Washington license plate affixed to the bumper looked peculiar to him, surrounded as it was by the blue and yellow New Jersey plates attached to all the other cars in the lot. The road dirt of Interstates 90 and 80 still clung to the metallic-blue chassis, and the remains of a few dead bugs were smeared across his windshield. His car almost seemed to taunt him, indicating to him that, as much as he wanted to belong in Verona, the lovely New Jersey town would never be home for him if he'd lost Daphne's friendship.

Telling her he loved her as a friend wouldn't be enough, he conceded. Nor would telling her he loved her as a sexual partner. She was an unusual woman, but she *was* a woman, and women were difficult that way. A man couldn't simply seek sexual pleasure with them. They needed more—and they were hurt when a man was unable to provide them with all they needed.

Not only hurt—they sometimes got downright nasty. How could Daphne have implied that Brad thought of her only as an "outlet"? He wasn't like his parents, damn it. He wasn't so crass that he was willing to settle for a simple physical experience, utterly lacking in depth. The only time he'd ever thought of sex in such unemotional terms was one icy February night during his senior year in college . . .

With Daphne.

All right. So maybe he couldn't blame her for accusing him of using her as an outlet now. Given that one precedent, she was entitled to assume that that was all she meant to him. But what about the other precedent, the more recent one? Something very real existed between them, and if it wasn't true love, it was still valid. Brad honestly liked Daphne.

Bewildered by the degree of loneliness he felt in the wake of her chilly departure, he headed back to the motel in Fort Lee to pick up his suitcase and check out of his room there. It was after seven by the time he reached his new house. His momentary alarm at seeing a couple of lights on in the house abated when he recalled that Daphne had left a few lamps on timers scattered throughout the house so it wouldn't look abandoned.

He was touched by the thought that, even if she was furious with him, she had illuminated his house for him. She had made it homey and welcoming. Rationally, he knew the timers had lit the lamps, but he saw no harm in pretending that Daphne herself had come to the house, glided through its rooms and switched on the lights for him. He was also touched to see that she'd hooked a Sold sign to the bottom of the For Sale—Horizon Realty sign posted at the end of the driveway. He wanted to believe that she was with him in spirit as he planted his feet on what had just become his very own property.

Even with the lamps glowing, the house seemed barren when he let himself inside. Curtainless windows invited in the dusk light, and his footsteps echoed whenever he walked anywhere where there wasn't a carpet. The refrigerator was empty and unplugged, its doors propped open, and the sink basin was dry. A fresh wave of loneliness swept over Brad.

Shrugging it off, he marched up the stairs to the spacious bedroom that would become his. He could have waited until his furniture was delivered the following day before checking out of the motel. But he had spent the last seven nights in motels, and he was ready to sleep in a real house.

It would have been nicer to sleep at Daphne's house, he mused desolately. Much nicer. Or even for her to sleep with him here, on the floor, with the eaves descending around them like a solidly constructed tent.

But she would never do that, he knew. She would never sleep with him in a room that reminded her so strongly of the past.

If she ever slept with him at all, he thought, grimacing at the possibility—the likelihood—that he would live the rest of his life without ever again making love to Daphne. He might socialize in New York, meet new women, find an ideal mate for himself, someone pretty and cultured and perfect in every attribute, and they would marry and live happily ever after...but always, deep within him, he would nurse an abiding sense of loss, a comprehension that he had failed Daphne.

A comprehension that in doing so, he had failed himself as well.

Chapter Twelve

"Mr. Torrance?" Cindy's well-modulated Katie Gibbs voice reached Brad over the intercom phone. "Your parents are here to see you."

Leaning back in the swivel chair behind his broad desk, Brad gazed around his office. It was more spacious than the office he'd had in Seattle, as befitted his elevated position in the firm. The windows overlooked a side street, but the building across the street was only six stories high, so plenty of sunshine managed to make its way through the sealed panes of glass and into the office. The floor was covered with the same plush green carpeting as the reception area, and a sofa, two arm chairs and a coffee table stood in a cozy arrangement across the room from his desk.

The one thing he didn't like about the office was that he couldn't control the air-conditioning. It blasted from the vents in frigid gusts. As a result, Brad had to keep his necktie and jacket on at all times.

But the news that his parents were in the reception area warmed him—if he'd heard Cindy correctly. "Did you say *parent* or *parents*?" he asked, realizing as soon as he spoke that if only one of his parents had come, she would have announced the visitor as "your father" or "your mother."

In the week since he'd taken title to his house, he had spoken to each of his parents several times, but he hadn't had a chance to see either of them. He had been overwhelmed by the mechanics of setting up his house—overseeing the delivery of his furniture, arranging it to his satisfaction, waiting for the telephone lines to be connected, shopping for food, toilet paper, a shower curtain and other odds and ends he hadn't thought to bring with him from Seattle.

He'd spent his days fixing up his house and his nights feeling lonesome. His first night, his next-door neighbors appeared on his doorstep carrying a loaf of fresh rye bread and a small platter of cold cuts from a deli on Bloomfield Avenue. Another morning, the woman who lived across the street gave him some advice about what hours he'd be likely to encounter the shortest lines at the motor vehicle department, where he'd have to go to change his car's registration. One evening after work, Brad had called Eric and invited him out to the new house for a beer, but Eric hadn't been available. "Now that you're living in the area," Eric had said, "we're going to be able to see each other whenever we feel like it. So I'm not going to feel bad about having to take a rain check on the suds, Brad." Just that morning—Brad's first day at work—Phyllis Dunn had tracked down his office phone number and asked him when he'd like to meet her for lunch.

He shouldn't be lonesome. For a newcomer to the region, he was unusually well connected. Yet there was an absence in his life, a void, an empty place that Daphne was supposed to occupy. Without her friendship, his expanded cape didn't seem like the dream house he'd thought it was. It seemed like... just a roof and four walls, a structure filled with his belongings and costing him a bundle.

He had started to telephone Daphne several times, but each time he'd hung up before dialing the final number. He wasn't an imbecile. He knew that when a woman was in love with you, she wasn't going to settle for being your buddy.

He blamed himself for the situation. He had been the one to suggest that they make love. Up to then, their friendship had been reasonably solid; she hadn't been in love with him before that one night. He should have known that the experience would have a strong impact on her—but then, he hadn't known it was going to be so special, so magical. It had had a pretty strong impact on him, as well; he couldn't fault her for losing her bearings in the aftermath of all that crazy passion.

"Mr. Torrance?" Cindy broke into his ruminations.

"Oh. Right. My parents." He reflexively straightened the knot of his tie, then said, "Please send them in." He hung up the receiver of his console phone and stood to receive them.

Cindy ushered them into his office. Brad was immediately struck by how gleeful they appeared. His mother's hair was arranged in a buoyant new style, and her eyes twinkled. His father was positively beaming. They were both dressed casually, and they were holding hands.

Holding hands! Maybe his "dream house" was going to fall short of his dreams, after all, but *this* dream— Brad's dream that his parents would rediscover their love and forge a reconciliation—seemed to be coming true. Thrilled, he bounded from behind his desk and greeted them with outstretched arms. "Mom! Dad! It's so good to see you!"

Penelope Torrance accepted the first hug. "Such enthusiasm," she muttered skeptically, although she willingly returned Brad's embrace. "I've tried to get you to come to the city for dinner three times now, and you kept putting me off. If it's truly so good to see me, Brad, you might have come to see me sooner. How about you, Roger? Have you had any luck getting Brad into town?"

Roger took Brad's outstretched hand and engulfed it in a vigorous handshake. "None whatsoever," he reported. "I suggested that he meet me at the club, but he swore he was too busy."

"Too busy for his parents," Penelope said with a sniff.

"You'd think he actually had things worth doing in New Jersey," Roger snorted, as usual putting a derisive twist on the words *New Jersey*.

Brad refused to be insulted. He was too delighted by the vision of his parents together, standing side by side and agreeing with each other. "I do have things worth doing there," he insisted mildly. "I'm barely settled in— I'm still trying to learn my way around the neighborhood. But let's not talk about me," he added quickly, guiding his parents to the sofa. "Let's talk about you."

"That's exactly what we're here to do," Penelope informed him, examining the upholstery of the couch and then giving Brad a nod of approval—as if he'd had anything to do with selecting the office's decor.

Brad's father sat next to Penelope on the couch, exchanged a meaningful look with her and echoed her hesitant smile with one of his own. They were acting almost like newlyweds, Brad thought—sending coded messages to each other with their eyes, positioning themselves close together, refusing to separate their intertwined hands. Grinning, Brad settled onto one of the chairs and leaned forward expectantly. "Well?" he prompted them.

Penelope eyed her husband, and he yielded the floor to her with a slight nod. "Brad . . . we know this is going to be hard for you to understand—"

"Don't worry about me," he said. "Whether or not I understand is irrelevant."

"Thank you for being so understanding," Penelope remarked, causing all three of them to laugh.

The laughter ebbed, leaving in its wake the sibilant hum of the arctic air-conditioning. "We're getting a divorce," said Brad's father.

At first Brad was positive that he'd heard wrong. Weren't his parents laughing, grinning, behaving with a harmoniousness Brad hadn't seen between them in ages? Hadn't they waltzed into his office like two smitten adolescents? "What do you mean?" he asked warily.

"He means," Penelope interjected, "we're going to get a divorce. We've decided that there's no chance of putting our marriage back together again, so we're going to legalize what already exists and move on from there."

"Move on?" Brad echoed, bewildered. "Move on where?"

"Your mother doesn't mean that we're literally going to move," Roger explained. "I've agreed to let her keep the Park Avenue apartment on a permanent basis, given how satisfied I am with my digs at Sutton Place."

"His 'digs,'" Penelope repeated with a giggle. "Listen to him talk. He sounds like a beatnik." Roger chuckled.

Brad gaped at his parents. How could they be so lighthearted, so cheerful as they planned to take such a catastrophic step? "Perhaps you ought to think this thing through a little bit more," he advised.

"Oh, Brad, we *have* thought it through," Penelope asserted. "It's not as if we're doing anything precipitously. We've been living apart for over a year now. It's quite enough."

"That's right—it's quite enough," Brad argued. "One year apart is enough. It's time for you to put your marriage back together again."

Roger didn't bother to dignify his son's claim with a rebuttal. "I know you're disappointed," he said. "But your mother and I feel as if an enormous burden has been lifted from our shoulders. Now we'll be free to find more suitable partners for ourselves."

"You've already found suitable partners," Brad asserted. "Each other."

"No," Penelope said, reaching for Brad's hand and folding hers around it. "We're not right for each other. Perhaps we've never been. We've always bickered, always been unhappy to some extent."

"But—but you loved each other, didn't you?"

Brad's parents exchanged meditative looks. "I suppose we loved each other, yes," said his mother. "But it was at best a superficial sort of love—you know, the sort of love a woman feels when she gazes into the eyes of a rich, handsome stranger. It's fun for a while, but it doesn't endure."

"We've never been friends," Roger added. "We've never really felt comfortable with each other. I think it's fair to say we're closer to being friends now than we've ever been before—simply because we no longer have this dreadful marriage standing in our way."

"It's tiring trying to love someone simply because he's rich and handsome," Penelope noted. "The next time I get married, I hope it will be to someone who's poor and funny-looking. As long as he possesses certain necessary talents, of course."

"Of course," Roger concurred, sharing a private smile with her. "I would like to find an intellectual power-house, myself. All my life, I've always wanted to be married to an intellectual powerhouse."

"But, Dad—you're such a sexist," Brad protested. "You don't even think most women should have careers."

"I've always wished someone would give me a worthy debate on the subject," Roger remarked. "Someone other than my son, that is. I would love for some fire-brand woman to come along and prove me wrong. Now that I'll be a free man, perhaps I'll find her."

Stunned, Brad sank deep into the cushions of his chair and gaped at his parents as if they were aliens from another planet. His father with a firebrand feminist? His mother with a funny-looking, poverty-stricken lover? Impossible.

"You're upset," Penelope fretted, squeezing Brad's hand. "You don't understand."

"He doesn't have to," Roger reminded her. "We've already established that, haven't we?"

"But I'm your son, damn it!" Brad railed. "I'm much more objective than you are, and I'm telling you—you're an ideal couple. You'll never find yourselves better partners anywhere else. You're perfectly matched—"

"Brad." Penelope tugged at his arm lightly, urging him around in his chair to face her. "Maybe we're perfectly matched, but we aren't happy. So what good is perfection? Let us find flawed, utterly unsuitable partners for ourselves. If they make us happy, we'll accept them, imperfections and all. Wish us happiness, Brad."

"Of course I wish you happpiness," Brad mumbled. He meant it, too. It vexed him to think that his parents' happiness depended on their divorcing each other, but he did want them to be happy. He loved them.

"Good," Penelope said, bringing the visit to a decisive conclusion. She tossed Roger another brief look, and they both stood. "We shouldn't take up any more of your time, Brad. It's your first day on the job—you must be swamped with work. But once things are settled at your new house, perhaps you'll invite us out to see it."

Brad accompanied his parents to the door. He kissed his mother, shook his father's hand, and remained in the doorway, watching rigidly as they presented Cindy with smiles of farewell and disappeared through the outer door. As soon as they were out of sight, he stepped back into his office and slammed the door shut.

He knew he hadn't imagined the whole thing. They were actually going to take that final step, sign the papers and part ways forever. He was heartbroken.

His intercom buzzed, and he crossed the room to his desk and lifted the phone. "Mr Torrance," Cindy said, "I just wanted to remind you that you've got a two-o'clock appointment with Stuart Pace."

Brad glanced at his wristwatch. It read a quarter to two. "Is he here already?" he asked.

"Not yet," Cindy reported. "I just thought I ought to remind you."

Cindy was going to be a gem, Brad could tell. He was glad he'd participated in the selection of his secretary; if Cindy was sharp enough to have noticed his shell-shocked look, and considerate enough to realize he'd need to be warned about an imminent appointment for which he mustn't be shellshocked, she was going to prove an invaluable assistant. "Thank you, Cindy," he said before hanging up the phone and preparing for his upcoming meeting.

There would be time enough that evening to sort through his emotions concerning his parents' divorce. There would be time enough to think, time enough to grieve for his parents' moribund marriage. He would return to that empty, strangely barren house of his and wonder why perfection was so hard to attain, and why dreams so rarely came true.

DAPHNE WAS TWISTING OFF the top of a bottle of ginger ale when she heard the car engine outside. She had already finished a low-calorie supper of cottage cheese and canned pears, and she'd exchanged her work outfit for a pair of cotton shorts and a T-shirt.

Even given her light meal and her relative state of undress, she felt sticky. The only air conditioner she owned was the window unit pumping away in her closed-off bedroom. She had her kitchen and living room windows open, and despite the oppressive evening heat she didn't mind the lack of air-conditioning too much. She liked being able to hear the summer sounds through her open windows—chirping crickets, the distant voices of a group of kids playing stickball a few blocks away, the isolated caw of a crow or the rumble of a car cruising past.

This car hadn't cruised past, however. Judging from the sound, she figured it must have steered into her driveway. The engine idled for a moment and then died.

She wasn't expecting any visitors. The only person who might drive to her house without warning was Phyllis, and as far as Daphne knew, Phyllis wasn't in the midst of any crisis that would require an emergency visit to New Jersey. The last Daphne had heard, Jim had moved out of Phyllis's house without incident and she was eagerly working on a scheme to woo Brad.

The ginger ale began to spurt through the half-open cap, and Daphne raced from the table to the sink with the hissing bottle. Leaving it there to overflow, she dried her hands on a towel and tiptoed into the living room to spy on her uninvited visitor through the picture window.

She saw Brad strolling up the front walk. Although it was after seven o'clock, he had on a navy-blue business suit. His striped silk tie hung loose around his collar. Even in the waning light she could see that his shirt was wilted and his hair was limp, his eyes were downcast and his lips were set in a grim line.

She didn't need any light at all to recognize that, even in an apparently sour mood, he was gorgeous. She knew that, however much he was scowling, his eyes were breathtaking in their color and intensity, and that regardless of his weary posture, his shoulders were strong and sturdy.

She wondered what he was doing at her house. If there was a problem with his house, he could have contacted her at her office. He must have come for personal reasons—and those reasons had better not have anything to do with sex, she thought irately. She'd stated her position plainly on that issue the last time she'd spoken to him, right after the closing a week ago. She wasn't going to sleep with him again.

Before he could ring the doorbell, she had the front door open. She glowered at him through the storm-door screen, suffering a strange mixture of anger and bitterness and desire as she was seized by a memory of what had happened the last time he'd come to her house. Afraid that she'd say the wrong thing if she spoke, she kept her mouth shut.

"May I come in?" he asked.

A simple enough request. Daphne switched on the porch light to see him more clearly, and decided that he looked too pathetic to pose a threat to her. He certainly didn't look lustful, in any case. Sighing, she held the door open for him.

He stepped inside, scanned the unlit living room, and then started toward the kitchen. "Can I have something to drink?" he asked.

Daphne snorted. "Can you say hello, first, or is that asking too much?"

He spun around and grinned crookedly. "I'm sorry, Daff. I've just had one of the worst days of my life."

"And you figured you'd top it off with a visit to me. No, you can't have something to drink," she said crossly.

His smile faded, and he pulled her into his arms. He hugged her tightly, clinging to her as if his life depended on her, and rested his chin against the crown of her head. "My folks are getting a divorce," he said. "I'm really upset, Daff. Please don't give me a hard time."

Daphne took a minute to digest his announcement. "I'm sorry," she said, less for having given him a hard time than for the news about his parents. Brad had confided in her regarding his parents ever since he'd first come east. She could imagine how devastated he must be over the finality of their decision. Her own feelings went forgotten as she focused her concern on him and the sorrow he must be feeling. "What do you want to drink? I was just about to get myself some ginger ale."

"I'd love some," Brad said, releasing her and following her into the kitchen.

Only a little of the soda had leaked out of the bottle. Daphne rinsed the spill down the drain, then filled two glasses with soda and handed one to him. "I'm sorry it's so hot in here, but—"

"I like it," Brad swore as he removed his jacket and draped it over a chair. "I'm sick of air-conditioning."

"Let's sit on the back porch," Daphne suggested, leading him out the kitchen door. They took seats across the glass-topped table from each other, just as they had a couple of months ago—the last time they'd had a heart-to-heart talk.

Brad took a long draught of soda, then lowered his glass to the table and slumped in his seat. "They came to my office and made their announcement this afternoon," he related, resting his head in his hands and eyeing Daphne dolefully. "I left the office at five, got off the train in Montclair at six, got into my car and sat in traffic for a while, and finally realized that I didn't want to go home. I wanted to come here, Daphne. I wanted to be with you."

"Lucky for you, I didn't go out tonight," she remarked—as if Brad would have had any reason to doubt that she would be at home. Daphne didn't go on dates, after all. She didn't gad about on weeknights—or weekend nights, for that matter. She was always home, ready for some wonderful man who didn't love her to come and weep on her shoulder.

"It was the weirdest thing," he went on. "It was more than just wanting to come here, Daffy. It was this deep knowledge that I *had* to come here. There's no one else I can face this thing with, Daff, no one else I can trust to help me see it through."

He sounded perplexed, yet there was a certain serenity about him, a comprehension that by her side was where he needed to be. As angry as she was about what had gone wrong between them, about her idiocy in falling in love with Brad and his predictability in failing to fall in love with her, she was touched that he still trusted her, that he still relied on her to comfort him in his sadness.

"Tell me what happened," she coaxed him.

He did. He described his parents' unexpected visit to his office, their lively mood and their resolution in going through with the divorce. "I just don't get it," he moaned. "They're so perfect—"

"You always say that," Daphne interrupted him. "What makes you think they're perfect?"

"Well...they mesh so well together," he struggled to explain. "They're well matched. They complement each other. When you look at them, you get a sense that they belong together."

"But they don't love each other."

"They should."

Daphne laughed. "Why should they? Just because their son has some crackpot idea that when people are well matched they ought to be in love? Your parents apparently *don't* love each other. They've told you they don't. You've simply got to accept it, Brad."

He stared at her. His gaze seemed to pierce the thick lenses of her glasses, to reach for her and hold her. "But it doesn't make sense," he complained quietly.

"You've been in love before," Daphne said, not bothering to disguise her growing impatience. "You ought to know there's no law that says love has to make sense." If love made sense, she added silently, trying to smother a fresh surge of bitterness, she would never have fallen in love with Brad. She would have fallen in love with a nice, safe fellow, possibly someone a bit gangly and a bit awkward, with unmanageable hair and Coke-bottle eyeglasses like hers.

But love wasn't sensible, and she'd fallen in love with Brad, instead.

"I'm not sure I like my new house," Brad said abruptly.

Daphne took a moment to absorb his non sequitur. "What don't you like about it?' she asked.

"I don't know." Brad exhaled and took another long drink of soda. His eyes remained on Daphne, glowing steadily in the descending gloom. "Whenever I'm there, I keep wishing I were here instead."

"Here? In my house?" At his solemn nod, she chuckled. "What did you have in mind? A swap? I think I'd come out ahead. The assessment on your house—"

"Daff," he silenced her. "It's not the house. It's you. I miss you. I want to be with you."

"You want to sleep with me," she muttered, spitting out the words just to get them said. She might have been amused by the notion that Brad seemed to view her as some sort of irresistible sex partner, a femme fatale of untold amorous skills. But as long as all he wanted from her was sex, she wasn't inclined to be amused.

"I do want to make love with you," he admitted. He raked his fingers restlessly through his hair, then leaned back in his chair and laughed. "Damn," he said softly.

His unexpected laughter put her on the defensive. "What?"

"Something my father said today. He told me that, even though he and my mother were married, they had never really been friends."

"And?"

"And I love you." Brad seemed astonished by his epiphany, speaking it as if it were a revelation from above. "You're my friend, and we're great in bed, and I love you."

"No, you don't," Daphne refuted him sharply. Brad couldn't possibly love her. He could love his pretty almost-fiancée in Seattle, or Phyllis Dunn, or any other woman as good-looking and self-possessed as he himself was. He could love any woman who complemented him and made a good match for him. By no stretch of the imagination did Daphne fit into that category, so he couldn't possibly love her. "You think of me as a sister," she accused him.

"Oh, no, I don't," he swore, rising and circling the table to her. "That would be incestuous." Cupping his hands around her elbows, he pulled her to her feet. Then he kissed her, slowly and thoroughly. "I'm an only child, Daff, but as far as I know, brothers don't kiss sisters like that."

"Yes, well..." Daphne fought to catch her breath. Brad's shatteringly sensual kiss had been an unfair tactic, and she strove to keep her wits about her. "I think you're confusing love with lust."

"No, I'm not," he defended himself, his smile gaining in certainty. "I happen to be lusting for you right now, Daphne, but that's not why I love you. I love you because you're my friend. Because I can talk to you. Because, when I'm angry and in pain, you're the only person I want to be with, the only person I can trust to see me through it." He kissed her again, sliding his hands up her arms to meet at the center of her back. "Make love with me," he whispered, his breath running over her lips and chin, fanning the blaze he'd ignited deep inside her with his kiss.

"I don't know..." she mumbled. "I'm dressed like a slob, Brad, and I'm kind of sweaty, and—"

"And you're beautiful," he vowed, touching his lips to her brow.

"But it isn't—I mean, maybe it won't be such a success," she worried aloud. "We haven't done anything to make it romantic—"

"What romantic things are we supposed to do?" he asked, his eyes sparkling with humor. "Smash a jar? Break out in hives?" He gripped the fabric of her T-shirt and edged it upward. "At least we don't have to worry about stuck zippers this time," he pointed out, sliding his hands underneath her shirt to stroke her back.

She issued a throaty sigh, savoring his tender caresses. She could tell from her body's instantaneous response to him, from the heavy ache spreading through her hips and the tingling sensation in her breasts, that she and Brad didn't need any artificial attempts at romance for their lovemaking to be successful. She could tell, as Brad's hands ventured down to the waistband of her shorts and wedged inside, pressing into the soft flesh of her bottom, that she needed nothing but Brad—and she prayed that he would need nothing but her.

She eased out of his arms, then took his hand and escorted him inside. They stole quickly down the hall to her bedroom. As soon as she opened the door, a blast of icy air slammed into them.

"Turn it off," Brad commanded, hurrying across the room to the air conditioner to turn it off himself.

Daphne was surprised. The atmosphere in the rest of her house was so hot and muggy, she would have thought Brad would appreciate the cooler, drier air in her bedroom. She herself preferred it. But it seemed too trivial to fight about. "Okay," she said. "We can leave it off if you want."

He rotated to her, his eyes wide with amazement. "You would rather have it on, wouldn't you?'

"Well, yes, but I'm willing to compromise."

He smiled and shook his head. "I didn't know it was possible for lovers not to quibble over every little thing."

"The reason we're not quibbling is that I let you have your way," Daphne noted.

"And next time you'll have your way," Brad promised, unbuttoning his shirt. "I like not fighting with the woman I love."

He pulled off his shirt and tossed it onto Daphne's dresser. Then he crossed the room to her and slid her eyeglasses from her nose. He placed them carefully on the night table.

"You think I'm ugly when I'm wearing my eyeglasses," she guessed, one last attempt to prove to him—and to herself—that he didn't truly love her.

"I think you look better without them," he answered frankly. "Maybe you ought to give contact lenses another try, Daff. It's not as windy here as in Chicago, and I think they've come up with more comfortable plastics in the past few years." He kissed the tiny red marks her glasses had left on the bridge of her nose.

His honesty moved her in a way nothing else could have. He *did* love her. Only a man who loved her deeply would tell her the truth about her looks. "All right," she concurred, running her hands over his naked chest. "I'll try contacts again."

"But only if they feel good on you," Brad insisted. "I don't want you to wear them if they're going to hurt you."

"Speaking of feeling good..." Daphne felt for the buckle of his belt.

Groaning, Brad stripped off her shirt, then helped her with his trousers. Before long they were both naked, and she and Brad tumbled onto the bed, kissing, tasting, touching, relearning each other with their hands and lips and tongues. Daphne's last conscious thought before Brad fused his body to hers in a wildly powerful surge was that, while love was definitely not the same thing as lust, both emotions had a great deal going for them.

"WE'LL SELL YOUR HOUSE," Brad said, a long time later.

Daphne lay beside him, her skin damp with perspiration and her chest still heaving as she wrestled with her erratic breath. Brad held her snugly to himself with his arm, and she used his upper chest as a solid pillow. He was sweating, too, but she wasn't going to recommend turning the air conditioner back on. To do that would require breaking from the shelter of his body, and the last thing she wanted to do was to move away from him.

"What do you mean, we'll sell my house?" she mumbled.

"We're both agreed my house is nicer than yours."

"I never agreed to that!"

"You said before that if we swapped houses, you'd get the better end of the deal."

"I was speaking monetarily," Daphne explained. "Your house is appraised at a higher value than mine."

"Okay," Brad said agreeably. "Let's go with the more valuable house."

"But your house has stairs. Vacuuming stairs is a real pain. That's one of the reasons I bought a ranch."

"I'll vacuum," Brad offered. "You can be in charge of cooking—as long as you don't serve me clam sauce."

"Linguini and clam sauce is pretty much all I know how to cook."

"I've eaten your peanut-butter sandwiches," he reminded her. "They weren't so terrible."

"All right," Daphne said simply, nestling closer to him. "We'll sell my house."

"You'll marry me?" he asked hopefully.

She leaned away and twisted her head to look at him. "I thought we were talking about houses."

"Both," said Brad. "We're talking about both."

"Oh."

"Because I don't want to go back with you anymore, Daff. I want us to go forward. And that's what marriage is about, going forward. Isn't it?"

Daphne smiled and settled against him again. His description of marriage was infinitely more romantic than flowers, wine, Mozart or zippered silk caftans. "I guess it is."

"Then say yes."

"Would you still want to marry me if I didn't get contact lenses?" she tested him.

"Absolutely."

"Okay." She kissed his chest, then grinned and settled contentedly against him, savoring the possessive strength of his arm tightening around her again. Closing her eyes, she imagined the Multiple Listing Service write-up she'd give her house when she listed it for sale.

Beautiful ranch in exc. cond. on 1/4 acre. Three brs, two baths, encl. porch, attached two-car gar., mature plantings. Lucky lady found her Mr. Right here.

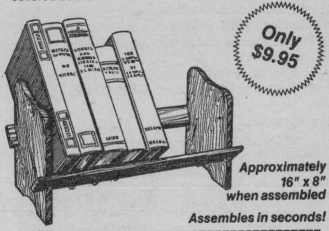

Lynda Ward's

LEAP THE MOON

... the continuing saga of *The Welles Family*

You've already met Elaine Welles, the oldest daughter of powerful tycoon Burton Welles, in Superromance #317, *Race the Sun*. You cheered her on as she threw off the shackles of her heritage and won the love of her life, Ruy de Areias.

Now it's her sister's turn. Jennie Welles is the drop-dead-gorgeous, most rebellious Welles sister, and she's determined to live life her way—and flaunt it in her father's face.

When she meets Griffin Stark, however, she learns there's more to life than glamour and independence. She learns about kindness, compassion and sharing. One nagging question remains: is she good enough for a man like Griffin? Her father certainly doesn't think so....

Leap the Moon ... a Harlequin Superromance coming to you in August. Don't miss it!

JOIN THE CELEBRATION!
THE FIFTH ANNIVERSARY
OF HARLEQUIN
AMERICAN ROMANCE

1988 is a banner year for Harlequin American Romance—it marks our fifth anniversary.

For five successful years we've been bringing you heartwarming, exciting romances, but we're not stopping there. In 1988 we've got an extraspecial treat for you. Join us next month when we feature four of American Romance's best—and four of your favorite—authors.

Judith Arnold, Rebecca Flanders, Beverly Sommers and Anne Stuart will enchant you with the stories of four women friends who lived in the same New York apartment building and whose lives, one by one, take an unexpected turn. Meet Abbie, Jaime, Suzanne and Marielle—the women of YORKTOWN TOWERS.

Look for . . .

#257 SEARCH THE HEAVENS by Rebecca Flanders

Jaime Faber didn't believe in bucking the system. Unlike her flamboyant mother, she lived conservatively, with no surprises. Until her social work took her to Victory House, in the ethnic heart of New Orleans. Jaime didn't know which threatened her more—the curse put on her by a voodoo queen, or the unpredictable, free-spirited Dr. Quaid Gerreau.

#258 REACH FOR THE SKY by Beverly Sommers

Suzanne Allman had read all about the depressing empty-nest syndrome, but now that her daughter, Mouse, was leaving for college, Suzanne felt nothing but happiness. She could finally quit her high-paying acting job and start living life for herself. But driving Mouse cross-country brings Suzanne more than just freedom. It brings her handsome young Wyoming cowboy Billy Blue. Now that she's finally on her own, is Suzanne ready for love?

#259 HARVEST THE SUN by Judith Arnold

For Abbie Jarvis, life in the big city was worth every sacrifice. But when prosecuting an emotional case leaves her needing R and R, she retreats to her small northern California hometown. In need of a friend, she walks straight into the arms of T.J. Hillyard, local hero. Like T.J., Abbie had tasted the glory she yearned for—but was it enough? Or had what she'd been looking for always been right in her own backyard?

#260 CRY FOR THE MOON by Anne Stuart

Marielle Brandt didn't have much choice after she was suddenly widowed and left alone to raise her two small children. The only legacy from her husband was Farnum's Castle, a run-down apartment house in Chicago. The building housed some eccentric inhabitants, including two psychics and a warlock—but it also was home to Simon Zebriskie, resident helper and late-night DJ. It seemed to Marielle a most unlikely place to fall in love, but how could she deny Simon's powerful sensuality?

Four believable American Romance heroines...four contemporary American women just like you...by four of your favorite American Romance authors.

Don't miss these special stories. Enjoy the fifth-anniversary celebration of Harlequin American Romance.

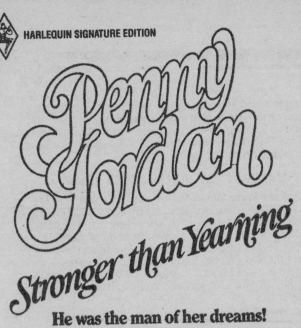

Penny Jordan

Stronger than Yearning

He was the man of her dreams!

The same dark hair, the same mocking eyes; it was as if the Regency rake of the portrait, the seducer of Jenna's dream, had come to life. Jenna, believing the last of the Deverils dead, was determined to buy the great old Yorkshire Hall—to claim it for her daughter, Lucy, and put to rest some of the painful memories of Lucy's birth. She had no way of knowing that a direct descendant of the black sheep Deveril even existed—or that James Allingham and his own powerful yearnings would disrupt her plan entirely.

Penny Jordan's first Harlequin Signature Edition *Love's Choices* was an outstanding success. Penny Jordan has written more than 40 best-selling titles—more than 4 million copies sold.

Now, be sure to buy her latest bestseller, *Stronger Than Yearning*. Available wherever paperbacks are sold—in June.